CRYPT SUZETTE

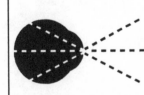

This Large Print Book carries the
Seal of Approval of N.A.V.H.

CRYPT SUZETTE

MAYA CORRIGAN

THORNDIKE PRESS
A part of Gale, a Cengage Company

Farmington Hills, Mich • San Francisco • New York • Waterville, Maine
Meriden, Conn • Mason, Ohio • Chicago

LIBRARY OF CONGRESS CIP DATA ON FILE.
CATALOGUING IN PUBLICATION FOR THIS BOOK
IS AVAILABLE FROM THE LIBRARY OF CONGRESS

ISBN-13: 978-1-4328-6927-4 (hardcover alk. paper)

Published in 2019 by arrangement with Kensington Books, an imprint of Kensington Publishing Corp.

Printed in Mexico
1 2 3 4 5 6 7 23 22 21 20 19

To my mother, Helen Roman, and my brother, Bill Roman, who were here when I started writing this book, but had passed on by the time I finished it. You live in my heart.

CHAPTER 1

Val Deniston smiled as she read the words painted on the store's display window — TITLE WAVE. The name suited a bookshop near the Chesapeake Bay's tidal waters. A sign on the entrance announced the shop's grand opening party would be a week from today. Good timing. The celebration would coincide with the Spooktacular, Bayport's annual festival held the weekend before Halloween.

Granddad had urged Val to offer her services as a caterer for the party. She looked forward to meeting Dorothy Muir, a retired teacher intrepid enough to open a bookshop when most people bought their reading matter online. The Title Wave had a good location on historic Main Street. Lots of foot traffic during the long tourist season on Maryland's Eastern Shore. The town's only bookshop had closed four years ago, so Val hoped the Title Wave would prosper.

With the late afternoon sun reflecting off the shop's windows, she pressed her nose to the glass and peered inside. Shelves lined the side walls from the floor to the ten-foot-high ceiling, tall bookcases sat at angles throughout the shop, and cardboard book boxes littered the floor. Only the shelves near the front had books on them. A staircase, with a bicycle propped against the railing, led to the second story.

Val knocked on the door. She'd never gone into the antique shop that used to occupy the building. The Victorian house she shared with Granddad already had plenty of antiques. She peered again in the shop window. No one stirred inside. Maybe Mrs. Muir had left the shop to run an errand. Val tried the handle.

The door opened. "Hello," she called out. No one responded.

She heard low voices coming from the rear of the shop. At five-foot-three, she couldn't see over the tall bookcases. She threaded her way around them. The shop smelled faintly of fresh paint. A woman's voice came from beyond a wide opening in the back wall. She spoke too quietly for Val to make out the words.

But a man's voice came through loud and clear. "I don't see why you want a caterer for the grand opening. It's a needless expense. You can buy snacks from the supermarket."

Val slowed down as she neared the back of the shop. According to Granddad, Dorothy's son had come from Silicon Valley to help her get the shop ready. Was he the guy complaining about hiring a caterer?

"I don't care about the expense," Dorothy said. "I've waited a long time to open a bookshop. I'm throwing a party to celebrate."

Val was standing close enough to the backroom that she could call out and be heard, but she didn't. Blessed with acute hearing, she'd frequently eavesdropped as a teenager, and now, in her early thirties, she felt no guilt about exercising her skill. Use it or lose it.

"I appreciate that, Mom." The man's voice had softened. "Have an opening bash, but do it in style. Get a full-service catering company from Annapolis, not someone who supplies dinner-party food as a sideline."

"She also runs a café at the athletic club. Cooking and serving food is what she does for a living."

"But catering isn't. Just because you knew her grandfather ages ago doesn't mean you have to hire her."

And just because Granddad knew Dorothy long ago didn't mean Val had to supply the food for the shop opening, but he'd be disappointed if she walked away without talking to the bookshop owner. He remembered Dorothy fondly from when he was in high school and she was the cute first-grader next door. Her family had moved away from Bayport five decades ago. Now she'd come back, determined to share her love of books in her hometown.

"You may know a lot about starting tech companies, Bram," Dorothy said, "but you don't know anything about doing business in small towns. It's all about community and relationships."

She should send her son packing before he chased away customers with his negative attitude. Val imagined what he looked like — scowling, tight-lipped, nose in the air. She hadn't particularly wanted to cater the shop's grand opening when Granddad suggested it, but now she'd do it gladly, if only to prove Dorothy right and her know-it-all son wrong.

"Mom, have you even checked this caterer's references?"

"I will deal with the caterer, Bram. Would you please go to the party store at the strip mall and pick up Halloween decorations?

Here's a list of what I want."

Uh-oh. If Bram left now, he'd catch Val lurking and listening. Better to announce her presence. Before she could do that, she saw movement out of the corner of her eye. Something brushed past her legs. She jumped back, startled. A black cat leaped onto a cardboard box and regarded her with mesmerizing copper-colored eyes. Val returned the cat's stare and heard a muffled sound from the backroom like a door closing.

A woman in jeans and a T-shirt bustled out of the backroom. She had a shapely figure with only a little thickening around the waist. "Hello! You must be Don Myer's granddaughter. I'm Dorothy Muir."

"Val Deniston." They shook hands. "Sorry for barging in. I knocked, and when no one came to the door, I tried the knob. I called out, but you must not have heard me."

"No problem." Dorothy studied Val with a gaze as intense as the cat's. Then smile lines appeared around her generous mouth. "I see the family resemblance. When your grandfather was a teenager, he had hair just like yours, curly and the same shade of reddish brown."

"He remembers you on your tricycle with pigtails flying behind you."

"Long gone." Dorothy fingered her chin-length silver hair. "Shall we get down to business? I'll show you the room where we'll serve refreshments at our grand opening party." She led Val through the opening wide enough for a double door, but it had no doors.

The backroom ran the width of the shop and was almost as deep. It was empty except for three folding chairs and a card table. Where was Dorothy's son? Val spotted an outside door in the far corner. He must have gone out that way.

"This will be the shop's coffee-and-tea area, the CAT Corner for short."

"Complete with cat," Val said as the black feline followed them.

"She's a stray that my son Bram took in. The cat was wandering in the cemetery. We call her Isis. She can't decide if she wants to be a bookshop cat or a graveyard cat."

The two back windows, framed by shelving, offered a view of a churchyard with the tombstones of long-dead Bayport residents. Isis sprang onto the windowsill and gazed out at the graves, setting the mood for Halloween without the decorations Dorothy had asked her son to buy.

Val looked up at the dark wood ceiling. "The ceiling is lower in this room than in the rest of the shop. This must be an addition."

"Yes, the original building was a shipbuilder's home in the nineteenth century. The family added this part in the early twentieth century." Dorothy gestured around the room. "I've ordered tables to be delivered Monday. For special events like book talks or signings, we'll put the tables against the walls and set up the chairs in rows. When book clubs meet here, we'll push the tables together to make discussion easier."

"My grandfather said you plan to start a lot of book clubs."

"I'll turn this into a gathering place for book lovers even if I have to lead each discussion myself. After forty years of teaching English I'm used to doing that. We'll shelve classics in here and random books that don't fall into any of the categories we feature in the shop." She pointed to a compact kitchen in the corner near the opening to the shop floor. "I hope the food prep area has all you'll need for the party."

Val glanced at the medium-size refrigerator, small cooktop, and large wall oven. Basic, but fairly new appliances. The commercial coffeemaker wasn't as fancy as the one she had in the Cool Down Café. You couldn't make a cappuccino or a latte here, but the machine would produce coffee aroma and a decent cup. A serving island about six feet long and a foot wide separated the prep area from the rest of the room.

"Looks fine," she said. "What type of food do you want for the party?"

"Halloween treats for children in the afternoon and for adults in the evening."

"A lot of Main Street shops will be giving out Halloween candy and cookies from the supermarket." And Bram had suggested his mother buy them. "If you want to do something special, the children could participate in making their own treats, decorating plain cookies. For a healthier snack, they can make boo-nanas."

Dorothy grinned. "Boo-nanas?"

"Cut bananas in half crosswise. Stand them on the flat end. The kids put mini chocolate chips on the tapered end to make ghost eyes and a big chip to make a round mouth. They can also draw jack-o-lantern faces on unpeeled tangerines. The longer they're busy here, the more time their parents will have to buy books."

"I like that idea. You'll supervise the children, Val?"

"No. I'm judging the pumpkin bake-off at the Spooktacular that afternoon. I can't cater until the evening." Val noticed Dorothy's face fall. "But a friend, Bethany O'Shay, might do it. She's a first-grade teacher and a certified food handler. She helps me with catering when I need an extra hand."

Dorothy's smile returned. "Wonderful. Please ask her if she'll come in the afternoon. What kind of treats do you suggest for the grown-ups?"

Val had been wracking her brain to come up with Halloween names for the desserts on her catering menu. "Mummy's apple pie, small rectangular hand pies with pastry strips on top. They'll look like wrapped mummies. Their raisin eyes will peek out from their wrappings." As Dorothy nodded her approval, Val thought of another treat she could give a spooky name, a favorite of Granddad's temporary boarder — Suzette Cripps. Val thought of her as cryptic Suzette because of her secretive ways. "Crypt Suzette is another option. If I serve a crêpe in an elongated paper container, it'll resemble a shrouded corpse in a crypt."

"Crêpes would be a hit, something the patrons would remember." Despite the positive words, Dorothy's face showed she had doubts. "Don't you have to ignite the liqueur when you make crêpes Suzette?"

"You can have the flavor without the

flame. I'll make the crêpes and the orange sauce ahead of time so I can just heat and serve them here. What time will the party start?"

"Six. You can take a break around seven when we hold the costume contest on the sales floor. The contestants will dress up as characters from books and talk about who they are."

"What fun!" Val hoped she'd get to watch the contest.

The cat jumped from the sill, went over to the door in the corner, and meowed.

Dorothy opened the door. Isis stood on the threshold and then ambled toward the cemetery.

Fifteen minutes later, Val left by the shop's front door, glad to have worked out the details of catering before Bram returned to raise objections.

She glanced up and down Main Street. The historic district was decked out in Halloween colors, pumpkins and chrysanthemums at shop entrances, autumn leaves clinging to the trees. Skeleton scarecrows mounted on the lampposts would greet visitors to the Spooktacular. If the usual autumn weather prevailed — sunny days and clear, crisp nights — the festival would attract visitors from Washington, D.C., and

Baltimore, as well as locals from the Eastern Shore.

Val drove to the supermarket in the mall between Bayport and the larger town of Treadwell and did her grocery shopping for the week. It was past seven and dark by the time she got back to Bayport. When she turned onto the street where she lived with her grandfather, she saw a crowd gathered in front of his house.

Her heart leaped into her throat. Had something happened to Granddad?

CHAPTER 2

A knot of people blocked the driveway where Val usually parked. She pulled in behind Granddad's Buick parked in front of the house and jumped from her car. A streetlamp dimly lit the crowd. She recognized no one. If anything had happened to Granddad, surely neighbors would be here, not a bunch of strangers. Who were these people and why had they gathered here? Val edged toward the group clustered around a woman.

"I've given you the history of this house with no mention of the *ghost.*" The woman emphasized her final word in a throaty stage whisper that could have been heard in the balcony. "This house is a unique stop on our walk. At all the other places, the ghosts have been around for decades and, in some cases, for centuries."

Val relaxed. The group was on a haunted house walk, and Granddad was fine. She glimpsed him creeping down the driveway, apparently to eavesdrop on the ghost tour. He and Val had heard from their neighbor, Harvey, that last weekend's ghost tourists had trampled his chrysanthemums and talked nonsense about haunted houses.

"A ghost would be right at home in a house like this," a woman on the tour said.

Val looked up at the gables and the turret on the Queen Anne Victorian. Less of an eyesore now than when she'd moved in a year and a half ago, but outlined against the night sky, the structure resembled a classic eerie house. Granddad was only now catching up on maintenance he hadn't done in the seven years since Grandma died. Despite the house's appearance, Val had yet to encounter a ghost, though she sensed Grandma's spirit in the kitchen, where they'd spent happy hours cooking.

"Who's haunting the place?" a teenage girl said.

"Someone only a little older than you." The tour leader pointed at the girl. "A year ago this month, she was *murdered* in the backyard."

Val's jaw clenched. That young woman's death had touched her and Granddad personally, and now someone was exploiting it.

A teenage boy nudged the girl who'd spoken up. "Maybe if we hang out in the backyard at night, we'll see the ghost."

Val was sure the young man had something in mind besides ghost hunting.

"Has anyone spotted this ghost?" an older man said, his tone skeptical.

The tour guide paused before saying, "Neighbors have noticed a shadowy figure and strange lights in the backyard."

Easy to explain. Granddad or his tenant, Suzette, might have taken out the trash at night and used a flashlight crossing the yard.

Granddad emerged from the dark driveway into the light cast by the streetlamp. He resembled a professor in a pullover sweater with patched elbows, wire-rimmed bifocals, and the beard he'd started growing for his Santa Claus role in December. "If you folks are looking for the ghost, you're wasting your time. It's gone. As a qualified ghost hunter, I got rid of it."

Val stifled a laugh. First a food guru, then a senior sleuth, and now a ghost hunter. It had bothered her when Granddad claimed cooking expertise to snag a job as the newspaper's recipe columnist. It had bothered her even more when he touted his skills as a detective after taking an online investigation course. But reinventing himself as a ghost hunter struck her as a fair response to the tour guide's invention of a ghost.

A man in the crowd laughed. "If there's no ghost, you'd better take this house off the tour."

A breeze ruffled the white curls over Granddad ears. "Yup. This is officially a ghost-free zone."

An older woman sidled up to the tour leader. "My neighbor says she has a ghost. Things keep disappearing from her house. You can substitute her place for this one."

Granddad waggled his finger back and forth. "Just 'cause stuff go missing doesn't mean you have a ghost. Ghosts have no use for material objects." He reached under his V-neck sweater, pulled business cards from his shirt pocket, and handed one to the woman. "I help people find missing things in my sleuth service. Tell your friend to call me. Anyone else want one?" He fanned out business cards in his hand.

"I'm not promoting this man's service," the tour leader said. "Let's move on to our next stop . . . the old graveyard."

Granddad's tactics made Val cringe, but she couldn't argue with success. He'd gotten rid of this group and possibly even kept his house from being on the next ghost tour.

A third of the people in the group took

Granddad's card before following their leader. The last to take a card was a young black woman. She stayed behind as the others disappeared in the direction of the historic district.

She squinted at Granddad's card under the streetlamp and approached him. "You're the same Don Myer who writes the Codger Cook column for the *Treadwell Gazette*?" At his nod, she introduced herself and added, "I have an internship as a reporter at the *Gazette.*"

Though Val didn't catch the young woman's name, the word *reporter* made her wary. Would Granddad's nonsense about ghost hunting make it into the newspaper? Val moved closer to him.

The would-be reporter glanced at her and then turned back to him. "My assignment is to write about Eastern Shore ghost walks. Can I ask you a few questions about your ghost-hunting experience?"

Val answered for him. "We haven't had dinner yet. Maybe some other time." She tried to nudge Granddad toward the house. Proclaiming himself a ghost hunter to get rid of gawkers wasn't bad, but making the same claim in print would open him up to ridicule.

"I'll answer your questions, young lady,

but only if you agree to my terms. You can't print anything about the death of the young woman the tour guide said haunted this place."

The reporter's brow knit. "Why not?"

"Every other person whose afterlife is part of a ghost walk died long ago. All the folks who knew those people are also dead. But the family and friends of the young woman killed in our backyard are still alive. They still grieve for her. They don't want to read that she's a stop on a Halloween ghost tour."

The reporter took a moment to respond. "I understand. If I leave the ghost out of my article, I can't write about how you got rid of the ghost here."

"I wouldn't tell you that anyway. Magicians don't reveal how they do tricks. They have a code of secrecy, and so do ghost hunters. They wouldn't want any ghosts to find out their methods, and you never know when one of them might be listening in."

Val forced herself to laugh. "My grandfather has a great sense of humor." She tugged on his arm.

The reporter's pen was poised over her small spiral notebook. "Where did you get your training, Mr. Myer? Did you intern or apprentice with an experienced ghost hunter?"

Val couldn't tell from the young woman's face if she really believed in spirits or was just humoring an old man. Would she write a tongue-in-cheek piece about ghosts and those who believed in them? Or would she use her column inches to expose charlatans who ran ghost tours or claimed to get rid of ghosts?

"I might be a self-taught ghost hunter, but I'm a trained investigator," Granddad said. "Believe me, ghosts are easier to identify and get rid of than your average criminal."

The reporter stopped jotting in her notebook. "Even though ghosts aren't always visible?"

"But you know where to find them. They don't move from town to town or even from house to house like the living do. Ghosts are tied to their locations."

The young woman nodded. "The place where they died."

"Yup. Ghosts return to earth in search of justice. Once you show them justice was done, they can rest easy."

"And stop haunting." The reporter put her notebook away.

"Nice talking to you, young lady. I'm looking forward to your article." He shook hands with her and walked back to the house.

Val pulled her car into the driveway, and Granddad helped her take the grocery bags to the kitchen.

They were surprised to see Suzette at the stove.

She was melting butter in a frying pan. "Sorry if I'm in your way. I thought you two had eaten already."

"You won't be in our way," Val said. "We have groceries to unload before starting dinner." By seven thirty on most evenings, she and Granddad had already eaten and cleared out of the kitchen. Only then did Suzette come down and use the stove. As often as not, she had no use for the kitchen, making do with the small fridge and the microwave in a niche near her room.

"I'm just making an omelet. I'll be out of here before long." Suzette poured beaten eggs into the pan.

With her long dark hair in a high ponytail, she resembled a high schooler from the 1960s. Val had seen Suzette's hair fixed in myriad ways — hanging straight, in a low bun, entwined in French braids, piled high in a topknot, cascading down in loose waves, held back by barrettes, and woven with ribbons, to name a few. Each styling made her look like a different person, at least from a distance. Val's hair also varied from day to day, not because she fixed it differently, but because it had a mind of its own. The shape of its curls depended on whim and weather, and its cinnamon color tended toward brown or red depending on the light. She envied Suzette's ability to impose her will on her hair.

Granddad took a beer out of the fridge. "Take your time cooking, Suzette. How did it go at the bookshop, Val?"

"Okay." Except for having to listen to Bram question her competence. "I'm going to cater the grand opening party in the evening. I think they'll have a good crowd, especially for the costume contest at seven. The winner will get a gift certificate to buy books."

Suzette looked up from the omelet pan. "I'd really like to win that."

Granddad exchanged a look with Val. They both knew how much the certificate would mean to Suzette. Working her way through community college, she had barely enough to make ends meet. Last month he'd heard through his church that a college student needed a place to stay close to the Harbor Inn, where she'd just gotten a job. After meeting Suzette, he'd offered her the small spare bedroom upstairs for nominal rent. In return for her room and kitchen privileges, Suzette typed the recipes for his Codger Cook newspaper columns, kept the house spotless, and made herself as invisible as possible.

Val wanted to make sure Suzette knew the costume contest details early, to give her time to prepare. "You have to go dressed as a fictional character and give a short speech as the character."

Granddad grinned. "That sounds like something Dorothy dreamed up. She's the bookshop owner," he said for Suzette's benefit. "She used to be a teacher and now she's turning a costume contest into a learning experience."

"What fun. Even if I don't win, I'll enjoy the show." Suzette plated her omelet, took the pan to the sink, and washed it. "I'll eat upstairs. I have a salad waiting there. You all have a good night."

She took the back staircase that led from the kitchen to the hall just outside her room.

As soon as the stairs stopped creaking, Granddad said in an undertone, "I'm worried about her. She spends hours in that tiny room."

"It's a cozy room with a good view of the backyard." Val had slept there whenever she stayed with her grandparents as a child and when she first came to live with Granddad.

After a few months, she'd moved into the larger front bedroom upstairs. With him in a bedroom on the main floor, and her and Suzette at opposite ends of the upper floor, everyone had private space.

"What's for dinner?" Granddad said.

"Pork and parsnips." She opened the refrigerator. "Could you chop the parsnips and a medium onion? I'll slice the pork tenderloin and make the salad."

Granddad set out his tools on the counter — a peeler, a knife, and the swimming goggles he always wore when he chopped onions, to keep his eyes from watering. "Suzette has been here six weeks and she hardly ever goes out except to jog in the morning. She never seems to party with friends like most young people do."

"She's on her feet at a hotel desk five days a week, taking classes the other two days, and studying when she can. That doesn't leave her much free time." Since she didn't own a car, she had a long bus ride to the college. Val took the pork and leftover rice pilaf from the fridge. "When Suzette worked as a nanny, she lived near the college, so she probably has friends there. And she occasionally goes out in the evening. I wouldn't worry about her being isolated."

"I wasn't, until yesterday." Granddad

peeled a parsnip. "When Harvey came over to complain about the ghost tour stopping here, he told me Suzette takes different routes when she walks here from the Harbor Inn after her shift. Sometimes she goes out of her way and comes from the direction of Main Street. Other times she slips through the backyards of houses, the ones across the street and the ones behind us."

Val shrugged. "I wouldn't pay much attention to Harvey. As you've said before, he has nothing to do since he retired but spy on his neighbors and let his imagination run wild."

"And grouch about ghost tourists."

Val kept herself from saying that Granddad was no slouch as a grouch either. She had to give him credit for grumbling less than he used to, now that he had outside interests like his newspaper column and his sleuthing service. "Maybe Suzette just likes variety on her walks."

"Or she's trying to dodge someone from the inn who's following her." As Granddad cut through the thick parsnip, his knife thumped against the cutting board. "Yesterday she asked me to teach her what I'd learned in my investigator course about finding information online about people. I showed her some databases that are either free or inexpensive to use. She zeroed in on the one listing people who have criminal warrants against them."

Surprised, Val looked up from slicing the meat. "Maybe she met someone she doesn't trust." That wasn't the only option. "Or she wants to find out if she's on that database."

"I checked. She doesn't have criminal charges against her. For a young person, she keeps a low profile online. She doesn't even have a Facebook page. I tell you, Val, something's wrong."

Val heated the oil in the skillet. She could explain away Suzette's roundabout routes to the house, but interest in criminal data and avoidance of social media suggested Granddad might have a reason for concern. Everyone Val knew in her own age group or younger was on two or three social sites. "You've roused my curiosity, Granddad. I'll try to talk to her. I can't knock on her door, demanding answers, but I'll waylay her when she's slipping in or out of the house."

"Good." Granddad donned his goggles and started peeling the onion. "She might be more willing to talk to you about a problem than to me."

"You spend time with her when she's typing your column. Has she ever said anything that suggests she's worried or scared?"

Granddad shook his head. "She doesn't talk about herself much. She told me she moved to the Eastern Shore three years ago and originally came from western Maryland, but she didn't say exactly where. When I asked about her family, she said she has contact only with a cousin. It's hard for young people not to have family around."

Val agreed. After working in New York City for ten years with no relatives nearby, she was thrilled to be in Bayport with Granddad. Her parents visited every few months from Florida, and her cousin, Monique, lived nearby. Val felt at home in Bayport because of family ties and the new friends she'd made here.

Wielding his knife like a pro, Granddad chopped the onions quickly. "I'm glad you got a chance to meet Dorothy today. How did you like her?"

"Very much. She was friendly and full of energy." And she didn't let her son talk her out of having the kind of grand opening she wanted. "Have you met her son, Bram?"

Granddad shook his head. "He was here for a weekend last month, when I went to Baltimore for the Orioles games. He came here to advise her on business practices and marketing. She said he'd been working seventy hours a week in a start-up company.

He just sold it, and now he's treating the bookshop as another start-up. She says he needs to relax."

Val would second that. "Does she have other children?"

"Nope."

The phone in the front hall rang. "I'll answer it." Val moved the skillet off the heat.

Though Granddad had a cell phone, he liked his landline too much to give it up, yet not enough to add extensions to it.

The woman calling asked to speak to him. When Val went back to the kitchen and told him, he dumped the onions he'd chopped into a bowl, took off his goggles, and washed his hands before going to take the call.

Val continued to cook and thought about what Granddad had said about Suzette. He might be right about her trying to dodge someone. Could her hairstyle changes have less to do with fashion than with fear?

By the time he returned to the kitchen, Val was ready to put dinner on the table. "That was a long call," she said as they sat down.

"Congratulate me. I have my first ghost-hunting gig."

Val winced. "Please tell me you're not going to take that woman's money for getting rid of ghosts."

"I'll only charge her if I locate what she's missing. I'm pretty good at finding things."

Yes, he'd traced lost cats, missing keys and eyeglasses, and even a purloined garden gnome. "What has this woman lost?"

"Jewelry, but I can't look for it right away. I promised Dorothy I'd help her get ready for the bookshop's grand opening, and I want to finish the Harry Potter books before Halloween. Ghost hunting's on hold for at least a week."

Good. Maybe the missing jewelry would turn up before then, and the woman wouldn't require ghost hunting.

A few days later, when the *Treadwell Gazette* article about local ghost tours came out, Granddad called Val at the café, pleased about the publicity it gave him.

He read her the section of the article that mentioned him. " 'One house on the Bayport Ghost Tour lacked a ghost, but it had a ghost hunter — the *Treadwell Gazette*'s Codger Cook, Don Myer. A woman taking the tour said her neighbor had a ghost who'd made things disappear from the house. Mr. Myer explained that ghosts have no use for tangible objects. Rather than assuming a house has ghosts, he suggested people contact him for assistance if they're plagued by mysterious disappearances.' "

And contact him they did. Instead of losing a client whose missing jewelry turned up, as Val had expected, he got two additional requests for his services.

CHAPTER 3

On Saturday Val arrived at the bookshop at four thirty, toting coolers with apple pastries and the crêpes she'd spent the afternoon making. She now had a stack of fifty crêpes and enough batter to make more if she ran out.

The Title Wave's grand opening had attracted customers of all ages. Some teens and children wore Halloween costumes. People with stacks of books lined up at the counter, where Dorothy stood at the cash register. In a floppy black witch hat, a green velvet robe, and an ornate brooch at her neck, she resembled Maggie Smith as Minerva McGonagall, the headmistress at Harry Potter's school.

Val waved to her and headed for the back of the shop, where her friend Bethany was closing the curtains over the entrance to the CAT Corner. The heavy curtains hadn't been there the last time Val visited the shop.

The fabric with its bookshelf pattern blended with the real shelves on either side and camouflaged the entrance to the back-room.

Bethany hung up a closed sign outside the CAT Corner. "Good timing, Val. The final bunch of kids left a minute ago." She pulled the curtains aside just enough so that the two of them could slip into the room.

Val put the coolers in the food prep area and surveyed the room. The shelves around the windows, bare when Val last saw them, held books and decorations like skulls and pumpkins. The long table where the children had sat was covered with an orange paper tablecloth and the remnants of cookie decorating. Isis the black cat added to the holiday atmosphere by sitting on the win-dowsill, apparently keeping watch over the graveyard.

"How do you like my costume?" Bethany twirled in an electric-blue dress decorated with foam stickers of stars, planets, and rocket ships. The outfit was similar to the kind of clothes she often wore — bright, bold, and appealing to the first-graders she taught.

Val wouldn't have even realized her friend was in costume if it weren't for the eight-inch stuffed lizard pinned to her shoulder

36

— a dead giveaway. "Ms. Frizzle from the Magic School Bus books. Your hair is perfect for the part." Aside from the bun on top, a concession to the character, Bethany's ginger ringlets cascaded down as usual.

Val shed her trench coat and hung it on a hook near the back door.

"I thought you would be in costume too," Bethany said.

"I am." Val wore a black jacket cinched at the waist, a matching A-line skirt, and a long scarf. She put one hand on her hip, bent forward from the waist, whipped a magnifying glass from her jacket pocket, and held it a foot away from her eye.

Bethany's eyes lit up with recognition. "Got it! Nancy Drew in silhouette."

"I thought it was appropriate. A sheriff's deputy once accused me of playing Nancy Drew. He meant it as an insult. For me it's a badge of honor."

"You've earned it after solving five murders."

"I can't take full credit for the last one. It was a group effort, and you were part of it." Val pointed to a glass drink dispenser with spider stickers on the outside and an amber liquid inside. "What's in there?"

"Spider cider. Bram comes in and replenishes the cider from gallon jugs."

Val unloaded a cooler. "I haven't met him yet. What does he look like?"

"Count Dracula."

"Not real attractive, huh?"

"I didn't say that." Bethany rolled up the paper tablecloth. "He might be good-looking when he gets rid of the black chalk circles around his eyes and the blood dripping from his mouth. He's a bit hyper, but charming."

"So was Count Dracula." Val had pictured Dorothy's son as fussy and condescending. Maybe he was scary too. "Don't fall for a vampire, no matter how charming."

"I won't. I'm involved with the baritone in my chorale." Bethany pointed at her. "*You* aren't involved with anyone because you're haunted by ghosts of boyfriends past. A fling with Bram might be just what you need to move on."

Val wasn't haunted by either of her exes, but by a fear of commitment after two mistakes. "If I wanted a fling, Bram wouldn't be high on my list."

"You haven't even met him."

"People choose costumes that mirror their personalities and their hidden desires. You identify with the vivacious teacher, Ms. Frizzle. I have an affinity for Nancy Drew. When a man dresses up as Dracula, that tells you something."

"It tells me that it's Halloween." Bethany unpinned the lizard from her shoulder.

Val stored her empty cooler under the sink. "Are you entering the costume contest?"

"It wouldn't be right for someone working at the shop to compete." Bethany peered at the pastries Val was arranging on a large platter. "The little mummies with raisin eyes are cute. Are you serving them on plates?"

Val shook her head. "In a pastry bag. Then people can hold them without getting their fingers greasy. I'm making crêpes Suzette. They'll go into paper food boats, like the ones we used for sandwiches at the festival last fall. The containers will look like coffins holding shrouded bodies in a crypt."

"Cool." Bethany frowned. "It's weird how we poke fun at corpses and crypts around Halloween and shudder at them the rest of the year."

Dorothy held the curtains aside and stepped into the room. After greeting Val, she gushed over Bethany. "You make a terrific Ms. Frizzle. I sold out of the Magic School Bus books and took orders for more."

Val tucked the empty cooler under the sink. "Maybe the costume contestants this evening will boost sales of the books their characters appear in."

Dorothy crossed her fingers. "Bram said the same thing. If you need anything, let him know. He'll be roaming around the shop. Thank you again, Bethany." Her tall, pointed hat fell off as she slipped through the curtained entrance. She stooped to pick it up. "I don't know how Minerva could stand to wear such a ridiculous hat."

As Bethany was about to leave, she pointed to a poster advertising the Bayport haunted house with an image of a creepy mansion and bats flying around it. "Don't forget that we're going to the haunted house on Halloween, Val."

Judging by Bethany's reaction to the haunted corn maze last year, Val expected her friend to run shrieking from the house before getting far into it.

Val brewed regular and decaf in the dual-carafe coffeemaker while Bethany cleaned up the evidence of cookie decorating on the chairs and the floor — orange sprinkles, mini chocolate chips, and blobs of icing. Then she left to meet her baritone for dinner. At six o'clock Val pulled back the curtains covering the entrance to the room and removed the sign that said the CAT Corner was closed. As she warmed the orange sauce and crêpes, customers began trickling in.

She'd just served mummy's apple pies to a middle-aged couple when Count Dracula arrived. He had a high forehead, short black hair, and a pronounced widow's peak. As Bethany had said, it was hard to tell what he really looked like beneath the pasty face makeup, black-rimmed eyes, and dribbles of fake blood.

He grinned, showing enlarged vampire teeth with fangs. "Hello. I came in for a bite." His words sounded slurred, possibly because of the fangs.

Val forced herself to smile at the vampire pun. She thrust out her hand to shake his. "Hi. I'm Val."

His dark brown eyes warmed up like a puppy's. He held her hand a bit longer than necessary. "Hello, there. I'm Nick."

Nick? So Bram wasn't the only bookshop vampire tonight. How many more were there? "Would you like a bite of mummy's apple pie? Or, as a vampire, you might prefer the crypt Suzette."

"The crypt appeals to me." He snapped off the false teeth that had turned his canines into fangs.

"Help yourself to coffee or spider cider." She pointed to the carafes and drink dispenser. "Have a seat, and I'll bring the crypt to your table."

He poured a coffee and ignored her suggestion to sit, standing instead near the serving counter. After she gave him a crêpe and a plastic fork, a pair of teenagers came in for treats, followed a minute later by a family of four. Val didn't introduce herself or shake hands with any of them, as she had with Nick. He must have taken her warmer welcome for him as a come-on.

Nick lingered long after he'd finished his crêpe. Any moment she wasn't busy, he peppered her with questions. Was working at the bookshop her full-time job? No, she ran a café at a fitness club. Are you from around here originally? I didn't grow up in Bayport. How long have you lived here? Almost two years. She continued to give curt answers to his personal questions. Finally, he took the hint and left the CAT Corner for the front of the shop.

Ten minutes later, another vampire arrived. He was taller than Nick and had medium brown wavy hair. He wore a stiff-collared jacket and a black cape covering his broad shoulders. The sides of the cape, attached to the cuffs of his white shirt, fanned out into batwings when he moved his arms.

He marched up to her and stuck out his hand. "Bram Muir."

His handshake was firm and his manner businesslike for a man with fluttering batwings.

At least he didn't have fangs.

Val had planned to be friendly, despite overhearing him diss her. She changed her mind, took her cue from his terse, unsmiling manner, and said, "Val Deniston."

"Everything going okay in here?"

She glanced at the drink dispenser Bethany had said he would refill. "We have enough cider and snacks to last the rest of the evening."

"In half an hour we'll cut off the snacks, close the curtains, and have the contestants gather here."

"How many contestants are you expecting?"

"A dozen people signed up. I told them to come in the back way." He crossed the room and unlocked the door to the outside.

"You want me to stay here while the contest is going on?"

"That's up to you. The contestants will go out one by one from behind the curtain to the sales floor, talk about their character, and walk down the center aisle so everyone can see their costumes. Once I announce the winner, we'll open this room again for snacks. I'd like you back here by then. You're staying until we close the bookshop, aren't you?"

Yes, Lord Dracula. Was that the correct form of address for a Romanian count? "I contracted with your mother to stay until nine. Will the audience vote on the best costume?"

"No. They might favor their friends. I'm going to judge the contest. I don't know anyone here, so I can't be biased."

Not true. He'd been biased against Val without having met her. She noticed him eyeing the snacks. "Care to sample a mummy's apple pie or a crypt Suzette?"

He shook his head. "No time." He rushed out of the CAT Corner. As Bethany had said, he was hyper. She'd also said he was charming, but he hadn't been to Val. She kept her eye on her watch to make sure she stopped serving snacks when he'd told her to. She didn't want to give him an excuse to complain.

She'd just pulled the curtains closed when Suzette came in the back door, wearing a green plastic poncho. Her hair, parted in the middle, hung down loose. Another woman arrived at the same time. Her black cloak reached to her ankles and its hood overwhelmed her small, pale face. She looked to be a few years older than Suzette and three inches shorter, about Val's height.

"Hi, Suzette." Val pointed to the poncho. "Is that your costume?"

"No. The weather forecast said there was a chance of rain. I came prepared. I'll take the poncho off for the contest." She held up a plastic trash bag. "The rest of my costume's in here."

The black-cloaked woman said, "She won't tell me what character she's going to be. So I won't say who my character is either."

"But I'll tell Val who you really are. This is Morgan Roux," Suzette said. "We're in a creative writing group together, the Fictionistas. Morgan, this is Val. She runs the café at an athletic club and made the snacks for tonight."

"Nice to meet you, Morgan. Would you two like anything to eat before the contest?"

Morgan took a mummy's apple pie, but Suzette said she was too nervous to eat. The two women sat at a table near the serving counter. The next arrival, a lanky man with thinning sandy hair, joined them at the table. He had a head like an upside-down pear, a broad high forehead tapering to a narrow mouth and chin. Like the vampires

Val had met this evening, the man wore a black cape, but his was shorter, hanging from his narrow shoulders and ending at his hips. Under the cape he wore a maroon brocade vest, a dress shirt, and a bow tie.

Morgan looked askance at him. "Casper! I was convinced you'd cover yourself in a sheet and play Casper the Friendly Ghost. Who are you supposed to be?"

He chose to show instead of tell. He took a rigid white plastic mask from the canvas bag and put it on. It hid most of his forehead and angled down his face, covering one eye, half his nose, and none of his mouth.

Suzette clapped. "The Phantom of the Opera."

A man who'd just come into the room approached them. He wore a huge tattered and blood-stained white shirt. He must have bought it in the big-and-tall department, and he was neither.

He eyed Casper. "Half of your face looks good, the part covered by the mask." He took the fourth seat at the table.

Casper glared at him. Morgan laughed.

Val watched the foursome from behind the counter.

Morgan surveyed the newcomer. "No part of *you* looks any good, Wilson."

Val disagreed. The shirt was hideous, but

46

the thirtyish man wearing it was handsome. He had blond curls, full lips, and straight, gleaming teeth that belonged in an orthodontist's ad.

Wilson pointed to his grungy shirt. "You think this is bad? Wait till you see the rest of my costume." He extracted a pliable mask from a pocket in his tunic and held it in front of his face. The eyes were sunken like empty sockets, the lips black, and the cheeks bloody and half eaten away.

Casper flicked his wrist. "You shouldn't have bothered with the mask. It's not much different from your real mug. You're supposed to be a character in a book, not a horror movie." He shrugged. "Not that you know much about books."

"I'm from a book you haven't read, dude." Wilson poked his index finger at Casper. "You come from a musical."

"Knock it off," Suzette said. "You're behaving like schoolboys."

And vying for her favor, Val suspected. If they were trying to impress Suzette, they were failing at it.

Casper took his mask off and held it up like a piece of evidence. "For your information, Wilson, *The Phantom of the Opera* was a book before it was a musical."

Morgan nodded. "By Gaston Leroux."

Suzette beckoned Val and introduced the two men, Casper Crane and Wilson McWilliams, as fellow Fictionistas.

Granddad had been wrong about Suzette not knowing people in the area. She'd spread the news about the costume contest to her writing buddies.

"None of us has published fiction yet," she said. "We're all trying our hand at writing novels."

"How many in your group?" Val said as a scarecrow and a pirate came in the door.

Wilson said, "The four of us and my aunt Ruth, who'll be here soon. She was putting the finishing touches on her costume when I left."

Morgan glared at him. "You should have waited for her instead of using two cars. She'll drive here in her gas guzzler. While we're on the subject" — she turned to Casper — "I saw you parking your old clunker. It's time you replaced it with a car that pollutes less."

"It's time you stopped preaching," Wilson muttered.

Casper nodded. "Yeah, and not everyone likes to get off the road to recharge."

Good thing Morgan didn't know how old Val's car was. Morgan hadn't done the environment any good by scolding Wilson and Casper, but she'd turned the two men who'd insulted each other a minute ago into allies against her.

"To get back to Val's question about our group," Suzette said, "we also have a group leader, Gillian Holroyd. She's published a lot of books. We took a fiction-writing class with her in the summer and bribed her to mentor us and —" She broke off and smiled broadly. "Wow, it's Professor Dumbledore!" She pointed to the curtained entrance.

Val turned to see Granddad in a round velour hat with a gold tassel and a long gray bathrobe, a gift he'd received last Christmas from her cousin, Monique. He'd never worn it until now, but after his recent obsession with Harry Potter books, he'd found a use for it. Now he looked the part of the white-bearded headmaster of Harry Potter's school.

Granddad grinned. "I'm glad you recognized me. Some teenager from the costume police gave me a hard time because my hair's short and my beard's not as thick as Dumbledore's."

Val was surprised to see him dressed for Halloween. He hadn't done it last year. "I didn't know you were going to be in the costume contest."

"I'm helping out, not competing." He

49

cleared his throat and addressed the contestants assembled in the room. "I'll be standing by the curtain and telling each of you when it's your turn to come out and say your piece. Can anyone guess why I got the job of doorman?" When no one answered, he said, "Because I'm Dumble*door.*"

His pun produced a few chuckles and a lot of groans in the room. Suzette called him over to the table and introduced her fellow writers to him.

Val chatted with some of the other competitors. Two of her regular customers at the athletic club café were competing, one dressed like the scarecrow from Oz, the other like Captain Hook. The owner of the vintage clothing shop wore a flapper dress as Daisy Buchanan from *The Great Gatsby.* Isis came in, inspected each contestant, and then curled up on the windowsill.

The last contestant to show up was Wilson's aunt Ruth McWilliams. She swept into the room in a long red brocade dress with gold braid trim and an elaborate headdress. Val didn't get a chance to talk to her because Granddad announced the order in which the dozen contestants would go out. As they lined up behind the curtain, Val sank into a chair near the serving counter. She needed a minute off her feet.

When she stood up, the costume contest was underway. The curtain separating the CAT Corner from the sales floor served as a stage curtain. The only way she could watch the contestants perform was to go out the back door and walk around to the front of the shop.

As Val left, she noticed that Suzette still hadn't removed her poncho. As the last contestant on Granddad's list, she had time to get ready before her turn came.

Val joined the crowd in the bookshop just in time to catch the tail end of Ruth's performance as Lady Macbeth.

She rubbed her hands and cried, " 'Out, damn'd spot! out, I say! . . . Yet who would have thought the old man to have had so much blood in him?' " She then held up a bloody hand.

The audience applauded this Halloween gesture, though someone muttered that Lady Macbeth only imagines blood on her hands in Shakespeare's play. Tough crowd.

A pirate emerged from behind the curtain, brandished his hooked hand, and vowed revenge on Peter Pan. Then Casper came out as a deformed conjurer hopelessly in love with a beautiful opera singer.

Wilson was next. He apologized for his appearance, saying he wasn't always a zombie. He took off his mask, reached for the hem of his knee-length tunic, and pulled it up over his head, revealing a formal jacket with tails, a high-collared white shirt, and snug breeches. "A zombie attack transformed me from one of the most eligible bachelors in the county into a wretch who preys on others in *Pride and Prejudice and Zombies.*"

The audience laughed and clapped.

Morgan came out from behind the curtain, her face largely hidden under the hood of her cloak. She traced the history of Morgan le Fay, a powerful healer in some legends and a spiteful sorceress in others. She plots revenge against her brother, King Arthur, while pretending devotion to him. In recent books, Morgan appears as a librarian-mentor to children in the Magic Tree House series.

The presentation, basically a lecture, ended as Morgan proclaimed her namesake the ultimate shape-shifter. While Val enjoyed Morgan's talk, it lasted twice as long as anyone else's and made the audience restless. The applause was lukewarm.

When Bram announced the final contestant, a moan came from the CAT Corner. No one emerged from behind the curtains. Then there was an even louder and longer moan. The audience murmured. Val started to move toward the entrance to the CAT Corner, afraid Suzette or Granddad needed help.

The curtains parted. If Val hadn't known who was scheduled last, she'd have had trouble recognizing the contestant. Suzette had gathered her hair into two ponytails sticking out sideways behind her ears. She had red spots on her face and wore thick dark-framed glasses. A toilet seat encircled her neck, her head in the seat's "doughnut hole."

She whimpered.

"It's Moaning Myrtle!" a boy in the audience called out.

"Yes," Suzette sobbed. "I haunt the girls' bathroom at Harry Potter's school. I was a student of witchcraft there in the 1940s. I was bullied and then killed. Now I live in the toilet. And I cry a lot."

She took a handkerchief-sized rag from a pocket, dabbed her eyes, and wrung it. Droplets of water fell to the floor. The audience laughed.

"You're not in a school uniform," a teenage girl said.

The costume police again. Val hadn't even noticed Suzette's gray tunic with large pockets.

Suzette moaned again. "That's true. I'm wearing a maid's uniform for a good reason. Outside my school, the people whose heads are in toilets are maids. They're poorly paid and invisible like ghosts to the people they work for. They have every right to moan."

A moment of stunned silence followed, and then Bram started clapping. The audience joined in. Dorothy moved forward and thanked everyone for coming to the grand opening, led a round of applause for the contestants, and turned the floor over to Bram. He announced the contest winner. Moaning Myrtle would receive the gift certificate.

Happy for Suzette, Val returned to the CAT Corner with a slightly better opinion of Bram Muir than she'd previously had. Later, when the contestants gathered the belongings they'd left in the CAT Corner, Granddad congratulated Suzette.

She was the happiest Val had ever seen her. "Thank you, Mr. Myer. I hope you don't mind that I borrowed the toilet seat from my bathroom for the costume. I'll reinstall it."

Granddad waved off her concerns. "No hurry. Go out and celebrate your win first."

"Okay." Suzette turned to Val. "Would you take the toilet seat back and put it outside my room? I'll attach it when I get home."

Val agreed and went back to serving customers. When the bookshop closed, Granddad invited Dorothy and Bram to the house for champagne to cap off opening day. Dorothy thanked them profusely for helping, but asked for a rain check on the champagne, saying she was too tired to enjoy it.

Val left behind the few remaining crêpes and apple pastries for Dorothy and Bram.

At seven thirty Sunday morning, Val went downstairs to the foyer, glanced through the sidelight near the front door, and saw a Bayport Police car pulling up to the curb. Chief Earl Yardley, a barrel-chested man in his fifties, climbed from the car and came up the walk to the house.

A longtime friend of Granddad, the chief visited the house now and then, but never this early in the morning. Puzzled, she opened the door for him.

The grim expression on his ruddy face made it obvious that this wasn't a social visit. "Good morning, Val. Your granddaddy up yet?"

She looked down the hall toward Granddad's bedroom door, which was closed, and picked up the sound of rhythmic snoring.

"He's still sleeping. Should I wake him?"

The chief shook his head. "I'd like to talk to the woman he's renting a room to."

A prickle of anxiety like a tiny electric shock passed through Val. What had Suzette done to bring the police to the door? "I'll go get her."

To Val's surprise, the chief followed her up the stairs.

She knocked on Suzette's door and called her name. No answer. Val tried the knob, found the door unlocked, and peered inside. The room was empty. "Suzette's shift at the Harbor Inn starts at eight. She should be coming back now from her morning jog." Val noticed the chief's eyes flicker at the word *jog*.

"What does she look like?" After Val described Suzette, the chief said, "Does she have any relatives in this area?"

"She never mentioned any." Val had suppressed her curiosity as long as she could. "Why are you asking about her?"

"I'm trying to identify a woman found on the side of the peninsula road this morning. Looks like a car hit her. Your description matches her, but that's not a definitive identification."

Val looked around the room and spotted a slim wallet near a pile of books on the night table. She unzipped the wallet. "Here's a photo of her." She showed the chief Suzette's non-driver's ID card.

The chief peered at it. "That's our victim. I'm sorry to tell you this, Val, but she's dead."

CHAPTER 4

Val sank down on the bed. A lump formed in her throat and she blinked back tears. Could the chief have made a mistake? A woman hit by a car might have injuries that would make her hard to identify with certainty. "Are you sure that Suzette is the woman who was hit?"

"Sure as I can be without scientific proof, but I should have that soon. I'll send a team here to dust for fingerprints. We'll compare them with the prints of the accident victim. I expect to find a match." He pointed to a heart on Suzette's ID card. "This shows she's a donor. Some tissue donation may be possible with the medical examiner's approval. I'll take the card with me." He tucked it into his breast pocket.

Val sighed. Poor Suzette. And poor Granddad. He'd grown fond of her, and he'd worried about her, convinced she was evading someone. Could he have been right?

58

The chief's words echoed in Val's mind: *Looks like a car hit her.* Why wouldn't he know definitely that a car hit her? Val could think of only one reason. "It was a hit-and-run?" When he nodded, she took a deep breath and said, "You just called Suzette an accident victim. Are you sure it was an accident?"

Chief Yardley folded his arms. "I don't know anything for sure."

Val stood up, anxious to leave the room. "Let's talk about it in the kitchen. I haven't had any coffee yet."

"I haven't either."

They went down the back staircase. The outside door Suzette had always used was straight ahead at the landing, which opened to the kitchen on one side.

Val started the coffeemaker.

The chief stood next to the kitchen island. "Tell me what you know about Suzette. Where did she live before she moved in here?"

"Until a few months ago, she worked as a live-in nanny for a professor at Chesapeake College and took classes there. She had that job for two or three years. When the youngest child started school, the family no longer needed a full-time nanny and Suzette left."

59

"You ever talk to the professor?"

"Granddad did. She recommended Suzette highly."

"Did they talk in person or by phone?"

"Phone." Val understood the point of his question. Anyone could be at the other end of the line, giving a glowing recommendation. "You'll have to ask Granddad whether he called a number Suzette gave him for the professor or contacted her through the school."

Val handed the chief a mug of coffee, poured one for herself, and took a plate of muffins to the small breakfast table where she and Granddad ate most of their meals.

The chief sat across from her at the table. "How did the girl wind up in Bayport?"

"She hoped to transfer to a four-year school after next semester and was saving up money to pay the higher tuition. She couldn't find any work near the college that paid as well as the desk clerk job at the Bayport Harbor Inn. Without a car, she needed to live nearby."

"She could walk there from here." The chief sipped his coffee. "She have any boyfriends?"

Val shrugged. "Last night at the bookshop I met the young men in her creative writing group. I think they were both attracted to her. I didn't get the impression she felt the same way about them. She might have a boyfriend in the community college, though. She took classes there on her days off."

"Did she jog every morning?"

"She went for a quick jog on days when she worked and a longer one on Tuesdays and Thursdays before she took the bus to the college."

The chief sipped his coffee. "What time did she usually leave to go running?"

"Before seven. As the days got shorter, she was leaving while it was still dark. She could warm up with a brisk five-minute walk and reach the peninsula road when it starts to get light this time of year. She'd come back thirty minutes before she was due at work to fit in a shower and walk to the inn." Val cradled her mug in her hands. "Do you have any idea what happened?"

"We won't know for sure until we get reports from the accident scene investigators and the medical examiner, but it appears the side of the car hit her. She was knocked off her feet and hit the ground headfirst, resulting in traumatic brain injury."

Val winced. "Why didn't the driver stop and report what happened?"

The chief drank more coffee. "The driver

might not have seen her. It was foggy, not in town, but on the peninsula road where it runs along the Chesapeake. She was on the road in low light before sunrise, wearing dark clothes, and jogging in the same direction as the traffic. Running against the traffic is safer."

"When the car hit her, the driver must have heard a thud and seen something. You tend to look in the direction where the noise is coming from. And after the impact, wouldn't you check the rearview mirror if you heard something hit the car?"

"She would have landed behind the car and to the side of its path. With low visibility, the driver could have missed her." The chief bit into his muffin and took a moment to chew it. "We're gonna request anyone who was on that road around that time get in touch with us."

"And if the person who drove into her doesn't come forward, will you question your assumption that it was an accident?"

"Do you have reason to believe it wasn't?"

"I have suspicions." Val told him about Suzette's roundabout routes from work to home and her interest in researching criminals online. "I tried to sound her out last week. When I thought we had some rapport, I asked if she had any concerns or worries. She took a moment to answer. Then she said everything was fine and changed the subject. I think she was tempted to tell me something. And I thought, maybe the next time we talk, I'll get it out of her." But there wouldn't be a next time. "She acted as if she was afraid of or avoiding someone. Maybe that person caught up with her and killed her."

The chief shook his head. "A car isn't a reliable murder weapon. You can't guarantee the person you hit will die. If you succeed, you've used a weapon traceable by the damage to it."

"Not if it's a stolen vehicle." Something had been nagging at Val, a discrepancy in what the chief had said. "You'd never seen Suzette. The woman on the road had no ID. What made you think she could be Suzette?"

"She was found by a bicyclist. He spotted her on the side of the road and called 911. He told me she resembled a woman named Suzette he'd seen in costume last night. That rang a bell because your granddaddy had told me his tenant's name. When I came here, I wasn't sure if Suzette was the victim or a family member who looked like the victim." He downed his coffee. "I have to locate your tenant's relatives, her next of kin. You think your granddaddy has that information?"

"I don't know. The Harbor Inn must have emergency contacts for their employees." Val went over to the counter for the coffeepot and refilled the chief's mug, pondering what he'd said about the bicyclist. She remembered the bike she'd seen on her first visit to the bookshop. She had an idea about the bicyclist's identity. "Is the man who reported the accident Bram Muir?"

The chief stared round-eyed at her. "How did you figure that out?"

"He has a bike. Last night he saw Suzette in costume. She had big glasses and ponytails behind her ears, not how she looks when running. I understand how he could notice a resemblance, but not realize he was seeing same person. Suzette could fix her hair in a dozen ways and make herself look really different."

Val heard the squeaking hinges of the heavy front door and the muffled sound of its closing. "That's Granddad going out to the front porch to check the weather. He does that every morning. I dread telling him about Suzette. He felt protective of her, and he's going to be upset."

"Leave that to me. I'll head him off. I've had a lot of experience delivering bad news." The chief stood up. "Don't give out the victim's name until we make it public."

With that, he left the kitchen.

Val cleared the table and made fresh coffee for Granddad. Usually, she set cereal in front of him for breakfast, but today he might need something sweet for comfort. She put two muffins on a plate and poured him orange juice. Would he be as skeptical as she was about the chief's conclusion that Suzette was hit by accident?

When he came into the kitchen and sat down, he barely glanced at the muffins. He took a few sips of coffee and said, "I feel terrible about Suzette. If I hadn't offered her a room here, she wouldn't have gotten hit by a car this morning."

Val joined him at the table. "You can't know that. She'd have rented a room from someone else in Bayport and kept to the same schedule."

"But if she came from a different location, she wouldn't have been at that spot on the road at the same time as the car that hit her." He stared morosely into his mug.

Val saw no point in discussing a hypothetical. "Were you able to give the chief contacts for Suzette's family?"

Granddad shook his head. "I told him I'd look for the phone numbers of her two references, but they weren't family." He lapsed into silence.

"What's on your schedule today besides church?"

"I have an appointment with Mrs. Hill, one of the women who called me about ghost hunting, but I may back out of it."

"Why? I thought you were looking forward to it."

"I was gung-ho at first. I don't really feel like bothering now. It seems kinda silly."

Val wanted to head off his possible slide into depression. If he had nothing on his schedule, he might go to church and spend the rest of the day in his easy chair, watching old movies. Better for him to get out of the house and talk to people. She'd never expected to be grateful for his ghost-hunting gig, but she was. "Mrs. Hill is counting on you to find what she's lost, ease her mind about ghosts, or at least listen to her troubles. It wouldn't be fair to let her down after you promised to help her."

"Okay. I'll talk to her. It shouldn't take long."

Then he'd go back to moping. Val had another idea for keeping him busy and his mind engaged. "Do you think the driver might have plowed into Suzette deliberately?"

Granddad shrugged. "Earl said it was an accident. He knows what he's talking about."

"He may have second thoughts once he gets the autopsy results or delves into Suzette's background." Val took a bite of a muffin, giving Granddad time for her words to sink in. "You thought she was trying to dodge someone following her. If that's true and a killer targeted her, it wouldn't matter whether she was living here or somewhere else."

"Because whoever wanted to hurt her would have found a way to do it, no matter where she was." He picked up his mug. "She was trying to investigate someone. Maybe she discovered a crime."

"Exactly." Val now had a way to keep him occupied and feel as if he was doing something positive. "We couldn't have prevented what happened to Suzette, but we can help now. You and I can dig up some information in case it turns out not to be an accident. Then we can pass on what we've learned to the chief so he can catch the culprit sooner."

"I can try to find out where Suzette went after she left the bookshop last night. She said she was going out to celebrate. Did anybody see her? Did she meet someone? I can ask at the restaurants and bars that were open last night, but I need a photo of her." Granddad reached for a muffin. "People took pictures of her last night."

"We need a photo of the real Suzette, not the one in costume. By the time she left the bookshop, she'd shed the toilet seat, the glasses, and the bands holding her hair in place. The chief took her picture ID with him. It showed her stiff and unsmiling. Maybe I can find another photo of her in her room." Val crossed the kitchen and took the back staircase to Suzette's room.

Suzette's computer might be a good place to look for photos. It was an older laptop, probably bought secondhand. It would suffice for basic tasks like writing college papers, checking email, and surfing the Web, until it died of old age. She pressed the power button and jiggled the mouse. Darn. The laptop was password protected. The police could probably crack the password, but Val didn't want to waste time trying.

She opened the closet to look for albums or photo boxes, but didn't find any. The shelf above the clothing rod held a couple of winter hats and scarves. The clothes Suzette wore to work — a navy blue blazer with a hotel logo, navy pants, and white tops — were hanging on the rod, along with her rain poncho, a parka, and the gray tunic she'd worn last night, possibly a maid's uniform. The rest of Suzette's small wardrobe consisted mostly of jeans, T-shirts, and sweatshirts.

Val closed the closet door and looked under the bed. She found two empty suitcases and switched her attention to the drawers. No photos in the nightstand drawer. The dresser drawers weren't nearly as full as when Val had used them for her clothes. Suzette had six folded T-shirts, four long-sleeve tops, and two sweatshirts. Val felt underneath them for a folder or envelope that might have pictures in it. Nothing there. When she got to the bottom drawer, she found a file folder under Suzette's jeans and shorts.

The folder contained papers rather than the photos Val had hoped for. She flipped through Suzette's college transcripts, bank statements, pay stubs, and income tax forms without reading them. Then she came to a couple of stapled pages. The words on the cover sheet sent a chill down Val's spine: The Last Will and Testament of Suzette Cripps.

CHAPTER 5

Val was ten years older than Suzette and didn't have a last will and testament. Why would a woman in her early twenties make a will? Either she had valuables to dispose of or she expected to die soon . . . or both. Val had skipped over the academic and financial records in Suzette's folder, but the will was just too tempting to ignore. She flipped the cover sheet over.

The document contained the usual terminology about being of sound mind. Suzette named her second cousin, Sandy Sechrest, as her executor and the person who would inherit all of her possessions. Ms. Sechrest would handle the arrangements for a cremation to be paid from Suzette's funds. Any money left over after that would be split between her cousin and the children's literacy charity named in the will. Under no circumstances were any of her assets to go to her mother, Wanda Cripps of Cumberland, Maryland.

Val was pretty sure Suzette didn't have a lot of money. A glance at the financial records confirmed that she'd had a rather modest balance in her accounts and paid little income tax. She could, of course, have funds squirreled away somewhere.

Val called the chief, told him about the will, and gave him the mother's name. "Did the hotel already give you that information?"

"No, the emergency contact on file was the cousin, Sandy Sechrest. No mention of the mother, but legally she is the next of kin, and I have to get in touch with her. She's the right person to identify her daughter."

Even though the daughter had wanted nothing to do with her. "Will the mother have to come here to identify Suzette?"

"Cumberland's in western Maryland, about three hours from here. She can make the trip if she wants. Or we'll arrange for her to go to a police station near her home and identify her daughter from a photo. The body won't be released, of course, until after the medical examiner has done his job."

"Once you've talked to Suzette's mother and have the legal identification, would you let me know? I'd like to contact her cousin

71

about picking up Suzette's things."

The chief agreed.

Val then went back to searching for a photo. She found one in a box of costume jewelry on the closet shelf. Suzette's hair was shorter and curled under. She stood by a slightly older young woman.

Val took the picture and the will to the study to scan and photocopy them. She'd just finished when Granddad came into the study. She showed him the will.

He read the short document. "Funny how people are about their wills. Most folks want to be fair and divide things up evenly. Some of them favor whoever's been good to them. And a few write grudge wills to settle scores." He handed the will back to Val. "No lawyer had anything to do with this will, or it would have been ten or fifteen pages longer."

"It's signed, witnessed, and notarized with a raised seal. I'm going to ask Althea if the will is legal." Val's friend and tennis teammate practiced family law. "I don't want to get in the middle of any controversy if Suzette's mother shows up here to claim her things."

"Once you know the will is valid, get the cousin here fast to pick up the stuff. Then it's her headache. Did you find a picture of

Suzette?"

Val took the photo off the scanner bed and showed it to him. "Even though it was taken a few years ago, it looks like her."

"To us it does, because we've seen a lot of her. But someone who saw her once probably wouldn't recognize her from this picture."

Val snapped her fingers as a solution to that problem occurred to her. "We'll consult the family photo doctor." Her cousin Monique, a professional photographer, had aged the headshots of young men when Val had needed them for an informal photo lineup. "I'll ask Monique to make Suzette look older in the picture, change her hairstyle, and cut out the other woman."

"I hope she can do it fast. I'd like to show folks a photo before their memories of last night fade and —" He broke off. "I just thought of something. Ask Monique to age the other woman in the photo too."

"Why?"

"Maybe Suzette went out to celebrate with her after the costume contest." Granddad pointed to the woman next to Suzette in the photo. "She could be the cousin who *inherits everything*. Follow the money."

Everything probably amounted to very little in this case, but Val didn't bother saying that. Better that Granddad try to solve a puzzle than sit around despondent. She checked her watch. Already ten fifteen. "I've got to get to the café. I'll e-mail Monique the photo before I leave."

At ten thirty Val parked at the Bayport Racket and Fitness Club and headed into the Cool Down Café alcove. Half the tables had customers sitting at them.

"Thanks for covering for me here this morning," she said to Tanisha Johnson, who'd opened the café and served the early customers. A college student home for the weekend, Tanisha was the daughter of Val's lawyer friend, Althea.

"No problem. We had a lot of coffee drinkers and bagel eaters between nine and ten, but it's been calm since then. I put the casseroles in the oven around ten fifteen."

"Good. They'll be ready when the brunch crowd comes in." Val expected business to pick up then. "When are you going back to Swarthmore?"

"My ride leaves at five from the outlet mall in Queenstown. Mom and I are going out to lunch and then we'll do some shopping there before I leave. She's picking me up here at eleven."

"Oh, good. I have a quick question for

74

her." Val had brought a copy of Suzette's will with her, hoping to see Althea.

"The guy sitting alone at the corner table is waiting to talk to you about catering."

Val glanced at the broad-shouldered man with his head in a book. "Thanks." She reached into the drawer behind the counter for a copy of her catering menu and crossed the café to the table where he was sitting.

Before she could introduce herself, the man looked up, a lock of brown hair falling over his forehead. "Hi, Val."

If he'd gotten her name from a previous client or her business card, he'd have probably introduced himself. She must have met him, but he didn't have a memorable face. It was pleasant enough, though, and slightly familiar. "Hi. My assistant said you asked about catering. Just so we're on the same page, my business is catering small in-home dinner parties. I don't do large events like weddings."

"I'm not planning a wedding." He looked intently at her. "You don't know who I am, do you?"

She did now . . . by his voice rather than his face, which looked far better than it had last night. "Of course, I do." But she'd never expected him to hire her as a caterer. She sat down across from him at the bistro table.

"How's your day been going, Bram?" Would he say he'd had a fine day and pretend he hadn't run across a dead woman?

"Not well. But it's looking up now." He flashed her a friendly smile. "My mother and I enjoyed the crêpes you left. We could taste the butter."

She could taste it now as he buttered her up. He wanted something from her, and she wanted something from him too — a detailed account of what he'd seen this morning on the peninsula road. If she came right out and asked for that, she'd have to explain how she knew he'd been there. She couldn't do that without revealing the identity of the victim, which the chief had told her to keep to herself.

Val could, however, take a roundabout route to the subject of Suzette. "I was surprised you chose Moaning Myrtle as the costume prizewinner last night."

He folded his arms and sat back in the chair. "Who would you have chosen?"

Apparently, he preferred talking about the costume contest to focusing on the woman who resembled the one he'd found dead. "Morgan le Fay told a fascinating story about how the character evolved through the centuries."

"But she exceeded her time by a lot, so I

eliminated her. And her costume wasn't much anyway."

Val agreed. Morgan could have worn the black cloak as a wrap for a party or evening event. "The zombie had a really unique costume."

"Once he stripped off his outer layer. He spent a lot of money on that fop outfit he wore underneath it."

Val glanced at Bram's plaid sport shirt and black jeans. Definitely not a fop. "Why did you choose Moaning Myrtle as the winner?"

"She was creative. She didn't buy her costume, she put it together with drugstore props and household items. And it had a meaning for her. Her explanation for wearing a maid's uniform tied the costume to a real social problem."

Val approved of his reasons for giving Moaning Myrtle the prize. He hadn't bestowed a gift certificate on a guy with money to throw away on a costume. Instead, Bram gave it to a woman he figured had less cash to spare. He didn't know she also had a voracious appetite for books and wanted desperately to win that certificate. Val's eyes welled with tears.

Bram stared at her. "Are you okay?"

She blinked rapidly. "Just something in my eye."

"What hours do you work here?"

A question out of the blue. "From eight to two weekdays, shorter hours on weekends."

"So your evenings are free."

Coming from any other man, those words might precede a suggestion to spend time together. She didn't expect to hear that from Bram. "Not all evenings."

"Because you cater dinner parties too. Do you ever create meals built around a theme?"

"Uh-huh. I've done a colonial dinner, a last dinner on the *Titanic,* and a French meal for a book club reading a mystery set in Paris."

Bram's hazel eyes lit up as if he'd just looked into his Halloween treat bag and found it full of his favorite candy. "Super. My mother's setting up lots of book clubs. She's got people who want dinners related to the books they're discussing. One group reads books set in foreign countries and would like food from whatever country they're reading about. Another club wants what people ate in the historical period their books cover. It sounds as if you don't mind doing the research to cater meals like that."

"I enjoy researching food, but custom meals require more of my time."

"It's a great opportunity for you. The clubs meet once a month. You'll have regular clients instead of looking for and working with new ones."

"Most of my clients choose food from my catering menu." She passed a menu across the table at him. "You're asking me to come up with unique menus and test different recipes all the time. So the prices would be higher than what you see on my standard menu."

He waved away her concerns. "We'll also have groups that are happy with dishes from your regular menu, as long as you vary what you serve each time. Since you'll be catering at the bookshop a number of times each month, I hope you'll give my mother a discount."

Though Val enjoyed the challenge of themed dinners, she wouldn't sell herself short. "I set prices that are fair to my clients and allow me to make a small profit. Your goal is to increase book sales. You can tack whatever percentage you want onto my prices." And good luck finding another caterer who'd make custom dinners for small groups.

He folded her menu and tucked it into his shirt pocket. "You drive a hard bargain. I'll talk it over with my mother and get back to you."

"Your mother told me you're visiting from California. How long are you planning to stay in Bayport?"

"Not sure yet. I just sold the company I started in Silicon Valley. I'll probably head back there when I come across a promising idea for another start-up. For the time being, I'm living on the second floor of the Title Wave."

"You and Isis?"

"Yes. The cat prefers the bookshop to my mother's place and so do I. Mom moved to Bayport two months ago, but most of her stuff is still in boxes on the floor. She's been too busy setting up the shop to unpack. Isis likes a little more room to roam." He stood up. "While I'm here, I'm going to check out a short-term membership in the club here. It's the only exercise facility around."

Finally, an opening to the subject Val wanted to bring up. She walked him to the club's reception area. "Doesn't biking give you enough exercise?" She anticipated his answer. He hadn't developed his shoulder muscles and biceps riding a bike.

He looked puzzled for a moment. "Ah, you noticed the bicycle at the Title Wave. I like to bike, but it isn't a full workout."

"When do you find the time to bike with all the work at the bookshop?"

He hesitated. "I usually go out early in the morning, before the shop opens. Good seeing you, Val. We'll talk again." He turned to the manager behind the reception desk.

Having stumbled on a few bodies herself, Val couldn't blame Bram for not mentioning what must have been a disturbing bike ride this morning. She hadn't heard what she'd hoped from him, but the prospect of catering regularly at the bookshop intrigued her.

She went back into the café alcove. Tanisha had set the ingredients for smoothies on the counter, ready to go into the blender if anyone ordered them. Val checked that the breakfast casseroles were done and took them out of the oven.

Tanisha's mother strolled into the café at exactly eleven. The slender African-American woman resembled her namesake, tennis champion Althea Gibson.

Val took her aside. "I want to show you a one-page will, which I think was written without help from a lawyer. I'd like to know if there's any question about its legality. Should I make an appointment to consult with you on it?"

"Don't be silly. I won't charge you for

looking at a page. I owe you more than that after the way you helped my nephew when he was wrongly accused."

Althea skimmed the photocopy Val gave her. "Assuming the original has an embossed notary seal, the signatures check out, and a more recent will doesn't turn up, it's a valid legal document. The mother could contest the will if she has proof that the heir exerted undue influence on the daughter to draw up this will. Are we talking about a fortune here?"

"I doubt it." Though anything was possible. The occasional millionaire chose to live frugally.

Althea said nothing for a moment, possibly waiting for more details about the source of the will. Then she said, "If you have other questions, don't hesitate to contact me. I'll keep it confidential."

"Thank you."

As Val served brunch, she thought about Bram. Though he'd tried to negotiate low prices for her services, she'd warmed to him this morning, and not just because he was better looking than she'd expected. She liked his reasons for awarding Suzette the gift certificate. He'd also led the applause after Suzette's remarks last night about the hard life of maids.

What was the story behind those remarks? Perhaps Suzette had once worked as a maid or befriended one at the Harbor Inn, someone who'd lent her the tunic. Suzette's sympathy for a friend who worked hard and was underpaid could explain her comments during the costume contest. A visit to the Harbor Inn might solve the mystery of the gray tunic. But Val couldn't just walk up to the reception desk and ask to talk to a maid or two. She'd need a cover story to get her past the lobby and onto a floor where the maids would be working.

By closing time at the café, she had a plan. She'd need Bethany's help to execute it.

CHAPTER 6

Val called Bethany and told her about the hit-and-run. "Granddad thinks Suzette was evading someone following her home from the Harbor Inn. She might have made friends with a maid there and confided in her. I'd like to talk to that maid. Would you go to the inn with me and pretend to look for a wedding reception venue?" She then explained the cover story the two of them would use at the Harbor Inn.

Bethany hesitated. "I'll go along with it, but I don't want to be the one planning a wedding. Why not you?"

"Because I need to slip out of the bridal suite while you're looking at it and find someone cleaning a room. The only other way I can get near the maids is to pay for a room, and I don't want to throw away my money."

"Can't you just act like you're a guest and walk around until you find a maid?"

Val had already discarded that idea. "In lots of hotels you need a room keycard to use the elevator or the stairs to a guest floor. I could hang around the elevator until a guest comes along with a keycard, but if someone on the staff notices me and I can't prove I'm registered, a security guard will perp-walk me to the exit."

"How about we say a friend just got engaged, and we're scouting out places for her wedding reception?"

"That'll work. You can take photos to show our engaged friend while I roam around. But we need to get there before the maids quit for the day. I'm leaving the club now, and I want to stop by the house before going to the inn."

"You want me to pick you up there?"

Val could easily walk to the inn from the house, but arriving with Bethany fit their story better. "Okay. See you in half an hour."

Val hung up and drove home. Granddad wasn't there. Just as well. She didn't want to take the time to explain where she was going and why. She went up to Suzette's room for the gray tunic. She folded it and put it in a clear plastic bag. Then she made room for it in her shoulder bag by removing her hairbrush, a notebook, and the wad of gasoline and supermarket receipts she'd accumulated.

Bethany picked Val up and drove to the inn, which sat on land that jutted into the river. They parked in the lot between the wings of the V-shaped four-story building.

"Looks like both wings have rooms facing the waterfront. Not a great view from the rooms on this side." Bethany pointed at the windows overlooking the parking lot.

"I'm sure they charge less for them."

They walked under the awning at the juncture of the two wings. The modest lobby had two groupings of sofas and easy chairs surrounded by large potted plants. The long line of people standing in front of the reception desk destroyed any illusion of a gracious living room.

Val and Bethany went to the end of the line. A fortyish man in a suit stood near the reception desk and apologized to those in line. "We're shorthanded at the desk today. If you're not checking in or out, you don't need to wait. I'm the assistant manager, and I'd be happy to answer any questions and help you with any issues."

A woman approached him and asked how to use the hotel Wi-Fi. He gave her simple instructions and repeated them. If she had any trouble connecting, she should bring her device to the lobby. He'd personally assist her.

When the woman left, Bethany signaled to him. "We'd like to talk to someone about holding a wedding reception here."

"Certainly. I'll be glad to —" He broke off, looking taken aback. "Val?"

Val hesitated. "Uh, hi." For the second time today, she couldn't place a man who called her by name. Had the facial recognition wires in her brain suddenly snapped? So embarrassing. She studied his features, all of them angular except for a rounded chin. He had a beak nose, inverted-V eyebrows, and raven hair with a widow's peak. The hairline was the dead giveaway. He was the first vampire she'd met last night. His name popped into her head. "How are you, Nick? I didn't know you worked here."

"I didn't know you'd come here to set up a wedding. Good seeing you again." He locked eyes with her. "Are you the bride?"

"No. We're helping a friend." A friend who could no longer help herself. "She couldn't make it here today." Val gave herself a mental pat on the back. She hadn't lied, strictly speaking.

"You should come back with the bride and talk to our events manager. She's the wedding expert, but this is her day off. If you call ahead for an appointment with her, you'll get her undivided attention."

Bethany frowned. "You mean there's absolutely no one here today who can help us?"

"Now that we're here, Nick," Val said, "we'd like to look at the banquet facilities and the bridal suite."

"We have a new office assistant who can help you with that. I'd show you around except it's crazy in reception today. One of our desk clerks couldn't make it to work today, and her backup is sick." He turned to Bethany. "Sorry. I should have introduced myself sooner. I'm Nick Hyde."

"Hi. I'm Bethany."

"What is the bride's name?"

Bethany pretended she hadn't heard the question and dug out her phone, leaving it to Val to give the bride a name.

An image of Isis on the bookshop's windowsill popped into Val's mind. "The bride's name is Kitty Black."

"Kitty Black. Easy name to remember. I'll get my assistant, Ursula, to show you around. I won't even try to pronounce *her* last name. It's a tongue twister."

Val learned he was right about that when the tall, blond Ursula introduced herself.

She looked to be in her twenties and spoke formal English with an Eastern European accent. "I will give you information about the Harbor Inn. We have seventy-four guest rooms or suites. We also have a marina with fifty slips. Guests who arrive by water can reserve a spot for their boats here."

She showed them the restaurant and banquet room. Both had floor-to-ceiling windows facing the marina and sliding doors that opened to decks for outdoor eating and lounging. Even with a brisk breeze and temperatures barely sixty today, a dozen people sunned themselves on the decks. Bethany took photos of the banquet room.

"Would you please show us the bridal suite," Val said.

"The inn has VIP suites. These are the bridal suites when we have weddings here. I will show you one that is not occupied today." Ursula took them back through the lobby to the elevators. They went up to the top floor.

On the way to the suite, they passed a service cart parked outside a room with an open door. Val glanced inside, but couldn't see anyone.

When they went into the living area of the two-room suite, Ursula flicked a switch that made the logs glow in the fake fireplace.

She then slid aside frosted glass doors to reveal a two-person whirlpool tub. "When you are in the bathtub, you enjoy the fireplace and also the view of the harbor. Very romantic." She crossed the room to the balcony doors and pulled the drapes aside. "The balcony is completely private. You can go there from the living room or the bedroom."

Bethany snapped pictures of the tub, the fireplace, and the view. When Ursula led her into the bedroom, Val slipped out of the suite and went down the corridor toward the service cart.

She poked her head into the room with the open door. The woman making the bed looked to be in her forties, shorter than Val, and sturdy. She had no trouble lifting the end of an eighteen-inch-deep mattress. She wore black pants and a gray tunic like the one Suzette had used for her Moaning Myrtle costume.

Val went into the room. "Excuse me."

The maid looked up from tucking in the sheet. "Hello. This your room?"

The maid's tag identified her as Juana. The name and her accent suggested she was Hispanic.

Val hadn't spoken Spanish lately, but she'd learned it well enough years ago to carry on a simple conversation. "No, it's not my room. I would like to ask you a question." She hoped she'd understand the answer. "I am a friend of Suzette. Do you know her?"

The maid studied the carpet. "No, señora."

"She works in reception from eight to four most days. I think she has a friend here who cleans the rooms."

The woman shrugged. *"No sé nada."* She went back to making the bed.

I know nothing, she'd said in Spanish. She'd avoided eye contact, but that didn't mean she was lying. She might be shy, or maybe the maids had instructions not to chat with guests.

Val left the room and hurried past the elevators to the inn's other wing. She saw a young, slim woman in a gray tunic, taking towels from a service cart in the hall.

When Val asked her about Suzette, the maid didn't respond at first, but after a moment, she said, "You wait here."

She took the towels into the room she was servicing.

From the hall Val could hear the maid's muffled voice. She'd apparently called someone.

She came to the door of the room, but

91

not into the hall. "Meet Maria. Three o'clock. On the street outside the parking lot." She turned away. "Go now."

Val retraced her steps to the VIP suite, noticing the surveillance cameras in the hallway.

Bethany looked up from her phone as Val went back to the suite. "I was about to call you. We were beginning to wonder if you'd gotten lost."

"Where did you go?" Ursula said.

Val had an answer ready, a half-truth. "I wanted to see where people stay who aren't lucky enough to be in a suite. I peeked at a couple of rooms that were being cleaned."

Ursula frowned. "I will be happy to show you rooms already clean."

"That's not necessary. I think we've seen enough."

Bethany nodded. "You've been very helpful, Ursula."

They thanked her for showing them around and made a quick escape from the inn.

Once they were in the parking lot, Bethany said, "That was more fun than I expected. Did you come across anything suspicious when you poked around on your own?"

"No. I'm glad we got out of there without

having to talk to Nick again about the wedding."

"You didn't tell me about Nick. When did you meet him?"

"Last night. He was dressed as Dracula, which is why I didn't recognize him at first. He came into the CAT Corner for a snack, hung around longer than anyone else, and asked me a bunch of personal questions."

"He's interested in you." Bethany aimed her fob at her Hyundai. "And he's not bad looking."

"He's okay." But Val had more important things on her mind than Nick. "A maid I talked to called a friend of Suzette's. I'm supposed to meet the woman here in fifteen minutes."

"If you don't need me, I'll take off now. I've got to go to the supermarket, buy food for the week, and cook it. I'm going on a soup diet. Since I don't have time to make soup on weekdays, I have to do it today."

"The cabbage soup diet again?" It hadn't lasted long the first time Bethany tried it, but none of her fad diets did.

"No, that was awful. I still can't smell cabbage cooking without my stomach turning. On my new diet, I have a cup of broth with vegetables before lunch and dinner. The idea is that you eat less if you start with soup."

At least the diet didn't involve periods of unhealthy fasting as some of Bethany's diets had. "That theory makes sense." But giving up billowy clothes in bright, clashing colors would make Bethany look instantly slimmer. "Thanks for helping out."

"See you Thursday at the haunted house." Bethany climbed into her car and drove away.

Rather than loiter near the parking lot, Val walked around the block, taking deep breaths of the crisp air and enjoying the fall foliage. When she returned, a dark-haired woman about the same height and age as Suzette stood outside the inn's parking lot entrance, peering around. She wore jeans, a gray sweat jacket, and a red bandanna holding back her long hair.

Val approached her. "Maria?"

"Yes. You are Suzette's friend?" She spoke English with a slight accent.

Val nodded, relieved not to be having this conversation in Spanish. She introduced herself and explained how she knew Suzette.

"Suzette told me about you and your grandfather. We meet, she and I, two times a week to practice English and Spanish. Half an hour for each language. It's good to

—" Maria broke off. "Why didn't she come to work today? Is she sick?"

Val took a deep breath. "I'm sorry to tell you this. She was hit by a car this morning."

Maria's hand flew to her mouth. "Oh no. Poor Suzette. Is she hurt bad?"

As far as Val knew, the chief hadn't confirmed the victim's identity. She didn't want to say Suzette was dead or give Maria false hope. "She's badly injured."

"I am so sad," Maria said. "I like her very much."

"I thought she might have a special friend here. Maybe you?"

"We are friends. Yes."

"Last night Suzette dressed up for Halloween and wore a maid's uniform. I came to return it. Did she borrow it from you?"

When the maid nodded, Val took the tunic from her tote bag and gave it to her.

Maria clutched it. *"Gracias."* Her eyes filled with tears.

Val had no words of comfort, but she had questions about Suzette's workplace, based on her circuitous and varied routes home from the inn. "Did Suzette have problems at work? Any trouble?"

Maria gave her a long look. "She talked to you about that?"

95

Val wished she could say yes. "No, but I had a feeling something was wrong." Val reminded herself to use the present tense. "Is Suzette friendly with others who work here besides you?"

"I don't think so, but I have little to do with the office and reception workers."

"Is there anyone at the inn who has a reason to dislike her?"

Maria bit her lip. "Wherever you work, some do not like others. It is best not to ask such questions of people you do not know. I must leave now."

Nothing stirred Val's curiosity more than being warned not to ask questions. She fished a business card from her tote bag and gave it to Maria. "Please call me if you want to talk more about your friend. We can do it half in English and half in Spanish if you like. I could use the practice."

Maria thanked her for the offer and hurried away, as if brushing off a street vendor. Why had she warned Val off? Could Grand-dad have been right that Suzette didn't want someone from the inn finding out where she lived? Maybe she'd asked him about investigating people online in order to check the criminal background of a coworker.

Thinking about Suzette's avoidance of the direct way home, Val took a zigzag route away from the inn. When she was halfway to the house, her phone chimed. She pulled it from her bag and read the caller ID. Chief Yardley. He might have an update about the hit-and-run.

CHAPTER 7

The chief told Val that Wanda Cripps had identified her daughter from a photo. "She hadn't seen Suzette in six or seven years."

"Suzette was still a teenager. Why would she leave home and never go back?"

"Her momma didn't volunteer that. Neither of them reached out to each other during those years. She didn't seem broken up about the death of her child."

Val groaned. "Something awful must have happened between them. Did she mention other family members?"

"When I asked about notifying Mr. Cripps, she said there wasn't one. Wanda Cripps raised her daughter, her only child, alone. She asked where the girl had been living so she could clear out her belongings. I didn't want to give out your granddaddy's address or phone number. I told her someone would be in touch about that."

"You didn't mention the will?"

"The executor should contact the mother and tell her the terms of the will. It's not a police matter or anything your granddaddy needs to deal with."

"I'll call the cousin. Her phone number is in Suzette's will." Val had kept walking while on the phone. She turned onto Grace Street. Home was now a block ahead. "Have you heard from drivers or joggers who were on the peninsula road when Suzette was?"

"I put out a bulletin for anyone who was there around seven this morning to contact the police. So far no one has responded, but the bulletin's only been online and on the radio. I'll release Suzette's name to the media tomorrow but not her address. The news of the accident will be on local TV and in the newspaper. We may hear from someone after that."

Possibly a witness, but probably not the driver, who wouldn't want to admit to having killed someone. "I'll let Granddad know where things stand. Thanks for keeping us up-to-date, Chief."

Approaching the house, Val saw that Granddad's Buick wasn't parked in front of the house. Once inside, she called Suzette's cousin, Sandy Sechrest, and reached her voice mail. Val wouldn't want to hear about the death of a relative on voice mail. She left a message saying who she was and asking Sandy to call back for important information about Suzette.

Suzette's mother might have already notified Sandy and other family members. But who would tell Suzette's writing group before the news was announced locally? The easiest person to locate might be the published author mentoring the Fictionistas. She was sure to have an online presence. Val hadn't recognized the woman's name when she heard it last night, but she remembered it.

She sat down at the computer in the study, entered *Gillian Holroyd writer* into a search box, and clicked on the author's website. It listed almost a dozen books by Ms. Holroyd, including suspense, paranormal romances, and historical fiction. The contact information on the site included the writer's e-mail address.

Val wrote a message similar to the voice mail she'd left for Suzette's cousin. She also explained that she'd learned Gillian's name while talking to the writing group. After sending the message, Val noticed an e-mail from Monique. Attached to it was a doctored photo of Suzette and her cousin. Monique had made both young women look a few years older. Granddad came into the house while Val was printing copies of the picture.

She called him into the study and told him what the chief had said about Suzette's mother. "I left a voice mail for Suzette's cousin. I hope she'll tell Wanda Cripps the terms of the will, so we don't have to deal with her."

"I'm glad Suzette's name won't be released until tomorrow. If I can find the number of her previous employer, Mrs. Patel, I'll call her. It's better she hears what happened to Suzette from me than from the TV or the newspaper."

"Same for the people in Suzette's writing group. I e-mailed the leader, assuming she'd have contact information for them." Val showed him the touched-up photo of Suzette. "Not a perfect likeness, but closer than the picture of her as a teen."

Granddad studied the photo. "It'll do. This evening I'll go to bars and restaurants near the bookshop and show it to the folks who were working Saturday night. Maybe one of them saw her last night with her cousin or someone else."

A long shot. If she'd met a person who had a car, they didn't necessarily stay in Bayport. "Where have you been this afternoon, Granddad?"

"Talking to Mrs. Jackson, the widow who blamed a ghost for swiping things from the house. She lives on the other side of Easton. Took me a while to drive there and back with the weekend traffic." He turned to leave the study. "I'm going to the kitchen for a snack. Come with me, and I'll tell you about her problem."

They trooped from the study through the sitting room, the dining room, and the butler's pantry to the kitchen.

Val put the kettle on. "Would you like some tea?"

"No, I want a beer." He opened the fridge. "Mrs. Jackson didn't have the problem I expected — misplaced keys or glasses. Some of her sterling silver is missing. She had a service for twelve, but now she has only five or six of each piece."

Val sat down at the small breakfast table. "Could Mrs. Jackson be wrong? Maybe she only ever had a service for eight. It's easy for knives, forks, and spoons to go astray. You know how careful Grandma was with her silver, and she lost a few pieces over the years."

"Mrs. Jackson said she used to have ten people at family dinners and they had enough silver to go around. All her serving pieces are gone too." Granddad filled a bowl with pretzels. "She doesn't use the silver much anymore. It could have disappeared months ago without her knowing."

"Hard to catch a thief when you don't know when the theft occurred. Who else has access to her house?"

"You're asking all the same questions I did." Granddad brought his beer and the pretzels to the table. "Mrs. Jackson's hired a few repairmen to fix things in the last six months. A cleaning team comes every other week. Once a month she invites neighbors for happy hour."

"The repair guys or the housecleaners could have stolen those things when she was in another room. Did you convince her she had a thief, or did she cling to the ghost as the culprit?"

"She gave up the ghost." He chuckled. "But she won't report the theft to the police. I told her she'd have to do that in order to file a claim with her insurance company. She cares more about keeping the theft secret than collecting on her insurance."

"Why?"

"The newspaper lists the crimes reported each week. She's afraid her neighbors will read about the theft and mention it to her daughter, who's been pressuring her to give up living on her own. The daughter will be even more insistent if someone broke into the house."

Val stood up to take the whistling kettle off the burner. "Could the daughter have swiped the silver?"

"Sure. She visits for a couple of days every other month." Granddad reached for a pretzel. "She might have financial problems and need quick cash. I didn't say that to Mrs. Jackson, of course."

Val poured hot water into her cup. "Your ghost hunting did some good. She wasn't comfortable telling the police, her daughter, or the neighbors about the stolen items. You gave her a sympathetic ear."

"I'm doing more than that. I arranged for Ned to change her door locks in case the thief swiped a key along with the silver." Granddad munched on his pretzel.

He'd previously asked his best friend, a retired locksmith, to dust off his skills, but this time, at least, Granddad wasn't trying to coax Ned into doing something illegal. "Did you also suggest she change her cleaning service?"

"Yup, but she didn't want to. Her last cleaning crew wasn't up to the job, and she's happy with this bunch. I talked her into getting a safety deposit box for her valuables."

Val brought her tea to the table. "Are you going to make more ghost calls this week?"

"Not until Tuesday. Tomorrow I gotta work on the recipes for my column."

Val's phone chimed. She checked the caller ID — Gillian Holroyd. "I've got to take this, Granddad. It's the woman who leads Suzette's creative writing group."

She left the kitchen so Granddad wouldn't have to listen to her rehash the grim details of Suzette's death. "Thank you for getting back to me, Ms. Holroyd."

"Call me Gillian. What's going on with Suzette?" She sounded wary.

As Val walked through the sitting room to the study, she told Gillian about the fatal hit-and-run.

Gillian's sigh was loud enough to come through the phone line. "How sad. She was a hard worker and a talented writer. She'd have made something of —" Her low-pitched voice broke. A moment later she said, "Where did it happen? Was she crossing the street?"

Val sat on the sofa in the study and recited all the details she knew about the hit-and-run.

"She must have heard the car coming," Gillian said. "Did the car go off the road and hit her?"

"I'm not sure. Everything I told you comes secondhand, from the chief of police who was at the scene. He said it appeared the car sideswiped her."

"I don't understand how a sideswipe could kill her," Gillian said in a barely audible voice, as if talking to herself.

"The police chief said the impact lifted Suzette off her feet. Her head hit the ground, and she died of brain trauma."

Gillian gasped. "Her head was smashed. Good lord."

Val couldn't guess what was behind that weird remark, so she let it go. "The police aren't going to reveal Suzette's name until tomorrow. I'm telling you so you can pass the news about her death to her writing group, but please don't mention it to anyone else."

"I'll talk to them. How did you happen to meet them?"

"I catered the bookshop's opening party. They were all there to compete in the costume contest." Val had answered every question she'd been asked and hoped Gillian would now return the favor. "Did you get the impression Suzette was concerned about her own safety?"

Gillian took a moment to respond. "You

wouldn't ask that unless you thought she was."

Val curled up on the sofa and said nothing. She wouldn't give out more information until some came her way.

Gillian broke the silence. "Are you still there, Val?"

"I'm here. I was waiting for your take on Suzette's state of mind."

"She didn't act afraid. But after talking to you, I wonder if I could have missed signs that she was."

Had all the Fictionistas missed those signs? "Would Suzette have confided in anyone in the group if she'd feared for her safety?"

"All I can say is that she didn't confide in me." Gillian sounded regretful. "I looked you up online before returning your call. You've sniffed out the truth about some deaths that weren't what they first seemed. Based on your history and the questions you've asked, I assume you suspect the hit-and-run wasn't an accident. I'm beginning to think you may be right."

Val uncurled herself and sat up straight. "Why?"

"Because of what she wrote. Suzette was working on a historical murder mystery. In her latest chapter, which we were going to discuss at our meeting this week, a young woman died in a way eerily similar to how Suzette herself died. It's as if she had a premonition."

CHAPTER 8

Val needed a moment to get over her surprise. The idea that Suzette had foreseen her own death struck her as implausible. Gillian Holroyd, author of paranormal romances, must have a vivid imagination. How could a character in a historical novel have died the same way Suzette did? An image flashed through Val's mind of a woman in a hoop skirt and bonnet trotting along a dirt road. More fantasy than historical reality.

"Suzette wrote about a woman who's run over while jogging?" Val said.

Gillian laughed. "Don't take me so literally. The woman in Suzette's book was found at the side of the road with her head smashed. It appeared she'd stumbled while walking in the dark and hit her head on a boulder. But remember, Suzette was writing a mystery. So her character didn't die by accident. She was murdered."

But that didn't mean Suzette had been murdered. "Aside from the head wound and the outdoor location, are there other similarities between what Suzette wrote and what happened to her?"

"Yes, but it's complicated. I can't take the time to explain it now. I have an appointment with the bookseller at Title Wave to arrange a signing. If you can meet me there at four thirty, we'll talk more about it."

"Okay. I'm looking forward to it."

Val didn't expect Gillian to convince her that Suzette had foreseen her own death, but an experienced teacher like Gillian might have gained insights into Suzette's mind from her writing.

While Val had been on the phone, Granddad had switched from sitting at the kitchen table to reclining on his lounger in the sitting room. With today's ghost hunting behind him, he was napping peacefully.

When Val went into the Title Wave, Dorothy smiled as if an old friend had just walked in. "I'm so happy. Bram told me you agreed to cater for our book clubs."

Val glanced at Bram behind the counter. He gave her a quick wave and bagged a customer's books. She turned back to Dorothy. "Tentatively. We still have to iron out the details."

"Details, where the devil lies, but we'll work them out. People have been signing up for the book clubs. I think we'll have half a dozen starting next month and more after the holidays. Not all of them will want a meal, of course, but your services are in demand. I got a call half an hour ago from a man who'd talked to you last night about your catering business. I wouldn't give him your phone number, but I took his name and number." Dorothy joined Bram behind the checkout counter. "Did you see a sticky note here, Bram?"

"I put it in my pocket." He took the note out and handed it to Val. "Your fame has spread, after you've catered only one event here."

Implying that working here would bring her more business and therefore she should lower her prices? *Good luck with that, Bram.*

Val glanced at the name. Nick Hyde. "Yes, I talked to him last night." And this afternoon. Did the Harbor Inn's assistant manager really want to hire her as a caterer or had he called in order to get her phone number? She stuffed the sticky note into her shoulder bag and craned her neck to see if any of the women browsing for books could be Gillian Holroyd. If the headshot on her website could be believed, she was dark-haired and middle-aged.

"Are you looking for Gillian?" Dorothy said. "She told me she was waiting for you. She's doing a book signing here in December. She may be interested in having you cater."

Wishful thinking by Dorothy, or had Gillian actually said that? Val spotted a woman who might be the author browsing the shelves at the back of the shop. "Is she the one with the colorful poncho?"

Dorothy nodded. "It's a work of art. I'll bet it came from Mexico. Go talk to her about catering."

"Okay." Val headed for the back of the shop.

Viewed from the side, Gillian's hair looked as it did in her online photo except for strands of gray in her dark hair. It fell straight down to her shoulders. The red and turquoise poncho made a dramatic contrast to the black skinny pants on her long legs.

Val approached her, introduced herself, and shook hands with Gillian. "Where would you like to talk? There's a wine bar next door and —"

"I'm driving, and I'd rather not drink wine before getting behind the wheel. Let's talk in there." Gillian pointed to the CAT

Corner. "I checked a few minutes ago, and it was almost empty."

Only one table was occupied when they went into the CAT Corner. A teenage girl sat on a stool behind the counter, a book in her hand and the black cat in her lap. Isis jumped to the floor as the girl stood up and took their orders, Gillian's for coffee and Val's for iced tea. Gillian paid for both.

Val set her drink down on the table farthest from the counter.

Gillian pointed to Isis, who'd followed Val across the room. "You have a friend."

"She remembers me from last night." Val sat down. "This is the room where Suzette introduced me to the other Fictionistas. She said they'd all taken your fiction class before forming the group."

"All except Wilson." Gillian blew on her steaming coffee. "During the class I divided the participants into discussion groups to critique each other's writing. Suzette, Casper, Morgan, and Ruth approached me after the class. They'd found the critiques helpful and wanted to continue to exchange their writings with one other. They asked what I would charge to facilitate their first five meetings. I gave them a price, and they split the cost."

Isis jumped into Val's lap and curled up.

"How did Wilson get into the group?"

"Everyone takes a turn hosting. Ruth held our first meeting at her house on the bay. She's a widow, and Wilson's her nephew by marriage. Halfway through our discussion, he poked his head into the dining room, took one look at Suzette, and pulled up a chair next to her. At the end of the meeting, he said he'd like to join the Fictionistas."

Val stroked Isis. "The others were okay with that?"

"Not all of them. Casper objected that the group would become too large, but Suzette and Morgan liked sharing the cost. Ruth encouraged Wilson to spend his time studying for the bar exam. He said he'd write a legal thriller and do research, which would help him on the exam. She relented." Gillian raised her cup of coffee. "The little writing Wilson's done so far shows no evidence of research."

Val steered the conversation back to Suzette. "How did Suzette get to Ruth's house without a car?"

"Casper gave her a ride. He lives in Easton. She took the bus there from the college. He brought her to the meeting, and when it was over, he drove her home. At first I thought Casper and Morgan might get together, but if he had any interest in her, he lost it after Suzette hitched a ride with him. He apparently expected to be her chauffeur from then on, but she had other ideas. Our second meeting was at Morgan's house. Suzette turned down Casper's offer of a ride and left with Wilson."

To avoid imposing on Casper again, to discourage any romantic ideas he might have had, or to encourage those ideas in Wilson? "Based on what I saw last night, Casper must have been annoyed when Wilson drove her."

Gillian nodded. "So you noticed the rivalry between those two. Our third meeting was at Casper's apartment. Wilson assumed he'd take her home, but she refused to get into his car. She said he'd drunk too much wine at the meeting, and she didn't ride with anyone who drank. She asked Morgan for a lift."

"What happened at the next meeting?"

"That's scheduled for two days from now. Suzette was hosting it. She arranged for our group to meet here."

Val stirred her iced tea with a straw. "They could have come to our house. My grandfather told Suzette she could invite friends. I don't think he'd have minded your group using our dining room." But he'd have grumbled if they'd stayed long.

"Our meetings last around ninety minutes," Gillian said, as if reading Val's mind. "We start at five thirty and usually finish by seven. I suspect our meeting will go longer on Tuesday. We'll talk about Suzette, not just everyone's writings. The host usually provides only drinks and snacks like pretzels or cookies. But this week I want to mark Suzette's passing with more than that, to give her a send-off, and I'd like you to cater it."

Val didn't usually agree to cater on such a short lead time, but last spring she'd pulled off a ten-course dinner for eight with less than a week to prepare, and this would be easier. And she had a personal reason to take this job. "I don't usually cater on two days' notice, but I'll do it for Suzette. What kind of food do you have in mind?"

"The Fictionistas make notes during the meeting, so finger food would work better than a meal that needs forks and knives." Gillian sipped her coffee. "The only restriction is no meat. Suzette will be with us in spirit, and she was a vegetarian. I want to respect that. For dessert we could have little tarts, cupcakes, or cookies."

"So it will be like a cocktail buffet for five people, but sitting down?"

"For six. I want you at the table, not busy

with food, when we talk about Suzette's latest chapter."

Unusual for the caterer to take part in the meal, but Val couldn't pass up the chance to get to know the Fictionistas. They'd interacted with Suzette at meetings, read what she'd written, and probably knew her better than anyone she'd met since moving to Bayport. "Okay, I can prepare platters ahead of time." Val had drunk most of her iced tea and not yet heard about the subject they'd met to discuss, but now she sensed an opening. "About Suzette's writing . . . you were going to explain the connection between what she wrote and what happened to her."

Gillian put her cup on the table with an air of finality. "I've changed my mind about that."

Val was taken aback. "So there's no connection?"

"You can decide that for yourself. I'll e-mail you a copy of everything Suzette wrote since the group started up. It's only around forty pages, so you should be able to read it before Tuesday evening."

Huh? Besides catering on short notice, Val now had a homework assignment. "Won't the writing group see me as an interloper?"

"I'll tell them you're Suzette's housemate

and say you have a right to be there. You'll be listening, not contributing for most of the meeting. Our routine is that everyone e-mails ten or so pages to the others three days before the meeting. They read and comment on each other's work. During the meeting we focus on smaller segments. I select a couple of pages for each of them to read aloud. Then we talk about what works and what doesn't in those pages. I don't have permission to e-mail you what the others wrote for this week, but you'll get the flavor when they read aloud."

Val had finished her tea while Gillian was talking. "Are you planning to read some of Suzette's pages aloud?"

Gillian nodded like a teacher pleased that a pupil had caught on. "Exactly, and I'm going to lead a discussion that might spark controversy and give you clues about what happened to Suzette."

As Val stroked Isis, she realized for the first time what the author wanted from her. Gillian doubted Suzette's death had been accidental. Her plan for Tuesday night suggested she suspected involvement by a Fictionista in that death. Gillian wanted her suspicions validated. She didn't trust her own instincts enough to go to the police, but with Val's support, she might.

Dorothy poked her head into the CAT Corner. "I'm sorry to make you hurry, but Title Wave is going to close in ten minutes." She left the room.

Gillian looked at her watch. "My mother lives in the retirement village outside Bayport and is expecting me. I always visit her around this time on Sunday. I'll send you Suzette's writings when I get home tonight."

"And I'll e-mail you a proposed menu. Once you approve it, I'll tell Dorothy and she'll draw up a contract. Your agreement will be with the bookshop and they'll subcontract for my services."

"Should I talk to her before I go?"

Definitely not. Val wanted to tell Dorothy and Bram about Suzette's death, not have them hear it from Gillian. "You don't have to wait around until the shop closes. I'll let Dorothy know what we discussed." She set the cat gently on the floor. "Sorry, Isis, you'll have to find another lap."

With the customers all gone and no laps available, Isis perched on the windowsill, where she could watch over the churchyard.

Val walked with Gillian across the selling floor, said goodbye to her at the door, and then peered around the shop. No sign of Dorothy. Bram was at the counter. Val approached it and spoke to him after he

119

finished with the last customer in line. "I need to talk to you and Dorothy in private. If it's okay with you, I'll wait in the CAT Corner until you've closed up." She scooted away before he could object.

Sitting again in the CAT Corner, she dug her phone from her shoulder bag to check if she might have missed a call from Suzette's cousin.

No, Sandy Sechrest hadn't called back. As Val put her phone away, Bram came into the room and sat down across the square table from her. Isis leaped from the window-sill and chose the lap she preferred — his.

His mother joined them, and Val explained that Gillian wanted her to cater for a small group on Tuesday evening.

"Uh-oh," Dorothy said. "A woman called last week about holding a writing group meeting in the CAT Corner at that time. I told her she could. We might not be able to fit two groups at the same time. I was so busy getting ready for the opening that I didn't write down her name or how many people were involved."

"There's only one group, Dorothy." Val steeled herself to reveal Suzette's death. "Gillian took over planning the meeting because the woman who called you last week died suddenly."

Dorothy's mouth turned down. "I'm sorry to hear that. She sounded young and full of life on the phone. How did she die?"

Val watched Bram as she answered Dorothy's question. "She was hit by a car this morning on the peninsula road."

His brows shot up. "The woman I found when I was biking?"

Val nodded. "Her name was Suzette Cripps."

Dorothy leaned toward Bram. "That's the girl who won the costume contest. You didn't recognize her this morning?"

Bram returned his mother's steady gaze. "I thought the woman on the road resembled Moaning Myrtle from last night, but I wasn't sure she was the same person. At least I remembered Myrtle's real name was Suzette."

He sounded like a student angling for partial credit on an exam question he'd blown.

Dorothy turned from him to Val. "He's better with names than faces."

"The name helped the police identify her sooner," Val said. "The police chief is a family friend and knew my grandfather was renting a room to a young woman named Suzette."

Dorothy's jaw dropped. "Don told me he

121

had a student staying in his place. How sad for you and your grandfather."

Bram's eyes bore into Val's. "Did you know who she was when we talked in the café today?"

Val resented his accusatory tone. "Yes, but I couldn't tell you because her relatives hadn't yet been notified. The news won't be public until tomorrow. The only reason I'm telling you now is so you'll understand the context of Gillian's meeting here on Tuesday."

He looked puzzled.

His mother said, "I get it. The meeting is like a memorial for that poor girl. We'll close the CAT Corner while that group is here, Bram, so her friends can grieve in private."

Val had hoped for that. "Thank you for being so thoughtful, Dorothy."

"The poor girl was on my mind today. When I gave her the prize last night, she said she'd come here after work today and pick out books to buy with her gift certificate."

Val flashed back to the scene in the kitchen when she told Suzette about the contest. "She had her heart set on winning the certificate." Val's eyes welled with tears. She tried blinking them away, but they kept coming. She wiped them away. "Sorry. I

122

planned to talk business, and here I am blubbering."

Dorothy patted her on the shoulder. "Take your time. Any death is stressful, but it's worse when it's sudden."

And when it's violent. The last few times Val had dealt with violent death, she hadn't known the victim more than a few days, if at all. Suzette was also younger than the other victims, which somehow made her death sadder.

Bram set a glass of water in front of her. "I can get you something stronger, if you like."

Val held up her hand. "This is fine." She gulped down some water. "I'll price what Gillian wants for Tuesday's meeting and e-mail you my contract for the catering. Then you can draw up a separate contract for her with your pricing on it."

"I'll take care of the contract, Mom." Bram pulled out a business card from his shirt pocket and gave it to Val. "Here's my e-mail."

Granddad was on the hall phone when Val went into the house. She waved to him and headed for the study. Scraps of paper were strewn on the computer desk. Folders lay open on the sofa, their contents spilling out.

She sighed. Granddad must have been trying to find something he'd misplaced. When he got off the phone, she asked what he'd been searching for.

"The phone number of the woman Suzette worked for as a nanny. Mrs. Patel. I found it, but it took a lot of digging." He surveyed the study. "This room is a mess. We'd better close the door on it. I was just on the phone with Earl. He's on his way here. I asked him to stop by. Based on what Mrs. Patel told me, I think Suzette mighta been run down deliberately. So it's murder, not an accident."

CHAPTER 9

Val, Granddad, and Chief Yardley sat around the large mahogany table in the dining room, not in the sitting room where Granddad usually talked to the chief. Obviously, this wasn't a social call, though Val thought the chief might be on his way to one. She'd caught a whiff of his aftershave and noticed that his casual clothes looked less rumpled than usual.

Granddad, in his seat at the head of the table, had a yellow legal pad in front of him. "I made notes as soon as I got off the phone with Mrs. Patel. She was really upset about the hit-and-run. Once she got over the shock, she talked about how much her two sons missed Suzette. Their new nanny couldn't compare with her."

Val held up her hand. "Wait a minute. Didn't Suzette say she left her job because the children no longer needed a nanny?"

"Yup, but Mrs. Patel said Suzette quit."

Val wondered which of them had lied. "I could understand Suzette not wanting to say she'd been fired, but why wouldn't she tell the truth if she quit?"

"If you let me finish the story, Val, you'll find out." Granddad cleared his throat. "I'll cut to the chase. Mrs. Patel said Suzette was good-hearted. She had a strong sense of fairness. If she saw something that wasn't right, she tried to make it right. And because of that she made enemies."

The chief took a small spiral notebook and pen from his pocket, accessories he apparently never left home without. "Where do the Patels live?"

"Near Chesapeake College."

"Did she tell you who the enemies were?"

"Not by name, but it wouldn't be hard to figure that out. One of the neighbors broke the leash laws. Suzette asked the neighbor not to let the dog roam in the Patels' yard because the children played there and might be exposed to dog feces. The neighbor ignored her. So Suzette collected feces in a plastic bag and put them in an envelope with a note that said *Your dog left this behind.* She stuck the envelope in the neighbor's mail slot."

Val winced. "That probably didn't go over well."

"The neighbor went to the Patels in a rage. Her dog was innocent. Suzette had done a disgusting thing. The neighbor would report her to the police and the health department. Suzette then produced a photo of the dog doing what she claimed he'd done in the Patels' yard. She welcomed the chance to show it to the police and the health department."

The chief rolled his eyes. "Glad I wasn't the officer called to the scene of that crime."

Granddad chuckled. "The neighbor didn't call the police, and the dog didn't visit the Patels' yard again."

"A crude but effective solution," Val said.

"Suzette's next try at improving the world didn't go as well." Granddad checked his notes. "She scolded a boy who was tormenting smaller kids in the playground. She told him that no one liked him because he was a bully and that he'd never have any friends if he didn't change."

The chief jotted in his notebook. "I can guess what happened next. The bully's parents complained to the Patels."

"Even worse," Granddad said. "The kid's mother went to the playground the next day. She berated Suzette for yelling at him and keeping the other boys from playing with him. Then the mother told her son he should be nice to all the kids except the two Patel boys. They didn't belong in the playground because they weren't real Americans."

Val groaned. "She punished the children for what Suzette did. Did the Patels hear about it from the boys or Suzette?"

"Suzette told them. Though Mrs. Patel didn't say this, I got the impression she thought Suzette had made a bad situation worse. And it went downhill from there. A day later, a dead squirrel appeared on the doorstep. Road kill. Suzette disposed of it." Granddad peered at the legal pad. "A few days after that, the Patels' older son saw a paper sticking out from under the door mat. He's in second grade. He was proud of himself for being able to read it. It said something like *You'll pay for what you did.*"

The chief made a note. "Did they report it to the police?"

"Suzette wanted to, but the Patels didn't. They were convinced that the woman with the dog or the bully's mother had written that note. Getting the police involved would make it harder to mend fences with their neighbors." Granddad flipped over his first page of notes. "When a dead possum showed up, Suzette quit. She told the Patels the harassment was aimed at her. The next dead animal could be rabid, and she didn't want to put the children in danger."

"That experience affected her even after she moved here," Val said. "She must have been afraid that whoever harassed her at the Patels would find out where she lived and go after her again. That would explain why she changed her hairstyle every day and never took a direct route to this house." But it didn't prove that anyone really was after her.

The chief looked up from his notebook. "Were there any incidents at the Patel house after Suzette left?"

Granddad shook his head. "That proves Suzette was right about being the target."

"Any sign of harassment here?" the chief said. "Notes or dead animals left for her?"

"No, but just because Val and I didn't see them doesn't mean they weren't there. Suzette used the door that opens to the staircase by the kitchen, and we almost never do." Granddad turned from the chief to Val. "I don't think she wanted us to know what happened at the Patels. That's why she didn't tell me she quit her last job. I'd have asked why she left. She was afraid I wouldn't let her stay here because she'd bring trouble with her."

Val thought of another explanation for

Suzette neglecting to say she'd quit. "Don't rule out that Mrs. Patel may have said she didn't need a nanny so she'd have an excuse to get rid of Suzette."

The chief tapped his pen on the notebook. "Anything else?"

"One more thing," Granddad said. "Mrs. Patel asked if the hit-and-run driver could have run over Suzette on purpose."

Val felt as if Granddad had zapped her with an electric current. He'd left the most important information for last. The number of people doubting the accident theory was growing.

Across the table from her, the chief also looked jolted. "How did you answer her?"

"I told her the hit-and-run was under investigation. Then I asked if she had a reason to think someone might try to hurt Suzette. The note left in the door bothered her because it said Suzette would pay for something she'd done." Granddad looked up from his legal pad. "I'll give you Mrs. Patel's phone number, Earl, so you can find out about those neighbors of hers."

The chief jotted down the number Granddad gave him. "The Patels live half an hour from here. It would have taken a lot of persistence for their neighbor to drive here regularly for two months, keep tabs on

130

Suzette, and wait for the perfect moment to run her down."

Val shared the chief's skepticism about the Patels' neighbors as suspects in a fatal hit-and-run. "The neighbors were rid of her when she moved. They had no motive to go after her."

Granddad frowned. "Mrs. Patel knows her neighbors. She must have had them in mind when she asked me whether someone could have hit Suzette on purpose."

"Not necessarily, Granddad. Mrs. Patel used the neighbors to illustrate what she'd said about Suzette's sense of justice and fairness. Suzette never looked the other way when she saw a problem. She attacked it head-on, with a *sledge hammer.*"

"And made enemies because of it," Granddad said.

Val nodded. "And she could have made enemies since she moved to Bayport." Possibly in her workplace or writing group. Val noticed the chief checking his watch. They wouldn't have his ear much longer. "Mrs. Patel is the second person today who raised the possibility that Suzette didn't die by accident, Chief."

"I know. *You* mentioned it this morning."

"I wasn't counting myself. The other woman who raised the issue leads the writing group Suzette belonged to. I'll tell you more about Gillian Holroyd when you're not so pressed for time." Val held up her three middle fingers. "Including me, three people who didn't know one another questioned whether the hit-and-run was an accident. Unless the medical examiner has strong proof that it was —"

"If he doesn't, I'll look into the alternative." The chief stood up. "I've got to get on my way."

Granddad walked him to the door and then joined Val in the kitchen. "Let's have something quick for dinner. I want to show Suzette's photo at the bars and restaurants near the bookshop. The sooner I do that, the better the chance that someone might remember her and who she was with last night."

Pasta was Granddad's comfort food, and he could use some comfort today. "How about pasta primavera?"

"You can't go wrong with noodles. I'll make the salad."

While he did that, Val chopped and sautéed the vegetables, surprised that he hadn't complained about a meatless meal.

His mind was on something other than his dinner, though he didn't speak up until dinner was almost ready. "Based on how

Earl reacted to what I learned from Mrs. Patel, I wasted my time talking to her."

"He was preoccupied with his plans for the evening, and you didn't waste your time." Val drained the pasta. "Before you talked to Mrs. Patel, we suspected Suzette was nervous about someone following her, but we had no idea why anyone would want to hurt her. Mrs. Patel suggested a reason. We found out how Suzette reacted to bad behavior by a playground bully and by a scofflaw dog owner. Suppose she tried her heavy-handed tactics against a major law-breaker?"

Granddad set the table. "That could explain why she asked me how to search criminal databases. She mighta gotten wind of a crime and tried to stop it herself when she should have gone to the police."

"Maybe she got only a whiff of something wrong and didn't realize she was dealing with a dangerous person." As Val stirred the pasta with the vegetables, she told him about her visit to the Harbor Inn and Maria warning her not to ask questions about Suzette there.

"That smells like a whiff of something wrong," Granddad said, echoing her words. "You'd better stay away from that place."

"Unlike Suzette, I wouldn't try to right a

wrong on my own. I'd go to the police."

As they sat down to pasta studded with green asparagus and red pepper, Granddad said, "What's the deal with the woman you mentioned to Earl, the leader of Suzette's writing group? Why does she think the hit-and-run wasn't an accident?"

Between bites, Val told him about her telephone conversation with Gillian.

His eyes popped out when he heard what Gillian had said about Suzette's possible premonition of her own death. "Suzette wrote about a woman who died the same way she did?"

"The character in Suzette's book was found dead on a roadside from an apparent accident. Gillian's going to e-mail me what Suzette wrote. I might see other parallels between what she wrote and her real life."

"She didn't tell us much about her life."

"Her fellow writers might know her better." Val described the plans for Tuesday's meeting. "I'll be there when they discuss what Suzette wrote. Gillian hinted that someone in the group had a grudge against Suzette."

Granddad stood up. "Writers work out their grudges on paper. They don't take action." He took his empty plate to the sink. "I'll eat dessert later. Hope you don't mind cleaning up tonight."

"I don't mind. I know you're anxious to canvass with Suzette's photo."

When Val finished cleaning up the kitchen, she went into the study to work on the menu for the Fictionistas' meeting. She then e-mailed her suggested menu to Gillian. The response came back quickly. Gillian accepted Val's recommendation and attached a document with all the chapters Suzette had submitted to the Fictionistas. Val saved the file to read later. She finalized the catering contract, e-mailed it to Bram, and then started reading Suzette's chapters.

Val discovered on the first few pages that her image of the victim running on a dirt road in a hoop skirt and bonnet had been wrong. Suzette's story took place in 1920s Maryland, where cars ran on paved roads and women wore sensible clothes. It was set at a millionaire's country estate, like *Downton Abbey* transported across the pond but surrounded by woods rather than farms. The upstairs characters were a ruthless businessman, his social-climbing wife, their almost-thirty playboy son, a grandniece from England who was their ward, and her prim governess, about the same age as the son.

The story was told from the point of view

of the thirteen-year-old niece, who roamed the house, spying and eavesdropping. She was a favorite of the housekeeper, the head butler, and the chauffeur, if not of her relatives and governess. She also made friends with a vivacious lady's maid.

The attraction between the playboy son and the maid came up often in conversations the niece overheard upstairs and downstairs. The playboy's mother fretted about his habit of seducing servants and told him to stay away from the maid. He declared his love for the girl. His mother had no intention of firing the maid, who knew how to fix hair exquisitely and how to apply makeup to give her mistress the bloom of youth.

Val took a break from scrolling through the document. Did Suzette have maids on the brain? They seemed to pop up everywhere, in her talk at the costume contest, in the book she was writing, and at her workplace. Val wished she knew more about that workplace. Apart from the tight-lipped maid Maria, she had another possible source at the Harbor Inn — the assistant manager. And Nick wanted to talk to her, trying to reach her through the bookshop. She would call him later, after she finished Suzette's story.

The front door creaked, announcing Granddad's return.

He joined her in the study. "That was a bust. I stopped at half the eating and drinking places in town. No one recognized Suzette or her cousin. Some people who worked last night had tonight off, so tomorrow I'll have to go back to the same spots and also hit the ones I didn't get to."

"Aren't you and Ned going for pizza tomorrow?" Every Monday evening, after Granddad submitted his weekly recipe column, he met his friend at Giovanni's restaurant in a strip mall outside town.

"Ned won't mind a change of pace. We'll have a bite here and there, at places I didn't visit tonight."

Val had encouraged him to show Suzette's photo around town to give him something to do besides sitting at home. Now she felt guilty about sending him on what would probably prove a useless errand. "Don't get hung up on finding where Suzette went last night and who was with her. If the person she met had a car, they didn't necessarily stay in Bayport. She also could have gone to someone's house."

"Yup, and whatever she said or did last night mighta had nothing to do with the hit-and-run, but I gotta give it a try."

Granddad peered over her shoulder at the computer screen. "What's that?"

"The mystery Suzette was writing."

"Did you get to the premonition yet?" When Val shook her head, he stopped squinting at the screen. "Any of those mummy apple pies left over from yesterday?"

"I kept a few ugly mummies for us, the ones where the filling oozed out of the pastry. Help yourself."

Granddad left for the kitchen.

Val went back to reading Suzette's chapters. The romance between the son and the lady's maid caused discord among the staff. The housekeeper warned the maid she'd lose her job if her liaison with the son came out. The saucy maid declared that he loved her and that one day she'd be mistress of the house. She'd previously encouraged the chauffeur's advances until the businessman's son showed interest in her. After she switched her affections, the chauffeur spied on the son and the maid, seething with jealousy. The governess, who'd hoped to attract the son, was infuriated that he might prefer an uneducated maid to her.

Early one morning the lady's maid was found dead at the edge of the woods along the road leading to the house. Her bashed head rested on a rock. Members of the household considered how she might have died. Had she stumbled on a root and fallen on the rock? Had someone hit her with the rock and then placed it under her head? The niece with sleuthing instincts considered another possibility — that a car ran into the maid and she landed on the rock.

On the last page Suzette had written, members of the household awaited the arrival of the police.

Val leaned back in the desk chair. Suzette's plot was more country house murder than *Downton Abbey.*

Granddad came into the study. "What's the verdict? Did she have a premonition?"

"I'm too down-to-earth to believe that." A different interpretation occurred to Val. "Something more ominous could explain the similarity between Suzette's death and the one in her story. She sent what she wrote to five people. Maybe the fictional crime wasn't a premonition by the writer but an inspiration to a reader."

139

CHAPTER 10

Granddad sat down on the sofa in the study and listened to Val's summary of the first chapters of Suzette's book.

He stroked his chin. "I don't buy that Suzette's story inspired a member of her writing group to copycat the crime in the book. The killer would have been stupid. That would narrow the suspects to people who read her story."

Val couldn't argue with his logic, but he'd assumed the killer was also logical, not always the case. "I mentioned inspiration because it makes more sense than premonition, but coincidence is also a possibility. The chief told me the hit-and-run driver couldn't have predicted Suzette would suffer a fatal head injury. Her story doesn't say for sure that the maid was hit by a car."

Granddad stroked his chin. "Maybe Suzette wrote more of the story and shared it with one person in the group. It could be on her computer."

"Which is password protected. The police have ways to crack passwords. They'd scour her laptop for leads if they thought she was hit deliberately."

"I did my best to convince 'em, but I didn't succeed." He yawned. "Been a long day. I'm ready to turn in."

Val popped up and kissed him. "Goodnight, Granddad."

After he left, she rummaged in her shoulder bag, located the note with Nick's phone number on it, and called him. He was delighted to hear from her. As she'd anticipated, he had no questions for her about catering. Instead, he asked if she'd meet him for a drink tomorrow night. She suggested the wine bar next to the bookshop at five thirty. The place served only nibbles, so drinks wouldn't evolve into dinner.

After hanging up, she gave Suzette's cousin another call and once again reached only her voice mail.

She then went upstairs to try some obvious passwords on Suzette's computer. Val remembered reading that nearly twenty percent of passwords are a series of numbers starting with one. She tried sequences of different lengths and then reversed the numbers. Almost as common as numbers in sequence was the word *password* used as the password. Val tried it with various upper and lowercase combinations without success. She also tried shortened forms of Suzette's name and repetitions of her initials. Then she did what she should have done before depending on guesswork. She dug out the folder in which she'd found Suzette's bank statements and her will to look for a password list. No list.

Val shut down the computer and went to bed. In her dreams passwords floated by her too fast for her to read.

The next day Val was taking the lunch quiches out of the café oven when Suzette's cousin called her.

Sandy Sechrest apologized for not returning Val's call. "Suzette's mother got in touch with me yesterday. I assumed you called to give me the same sad news. I delayed getting back to you because I couldn't face talking about what happened."

"I understand. My grandfather and I are sorry for your loss."

"Thank you. I'm grateful to him for giving Suzette a place to stay. She told me how kind both of you were."

"I'll pass that on to my grandfather. We didn't know who should get the news about

Suzette, so we looked in her room for contact information. Your name and number were in the will she'd written." The silence that followed suggested Sandy was surprised.

"She made a will? Her mother didn't tell me that."

"I doubt she knew. Suzette named you her executor and primary beneficiary." Val heard a gasp on the other end of the line. "I'll scan and e-mail you a copy. You can pick up the notarized version when you come to collect Suzette's belongings."

"She never had many belongings. Her mother told me she was going to collect whatever Suzette left —"

"Suzette didn't want that," Val interrupted. "She put a clause in her will that said — this isn't an exact quote but it's close — *under no circumstances should my mother, Wanda Cripps, inherit anything I own.*"

"Wanda's not going to believe me unless I show it to her. Can you send me a copy right away?" Sandy recited her e-mail address.

Val made a note of it. "I'm at work now. I'll send it later from home."

"I just hope you don't find Wanda on your doorstep when you get there."

Good thing the chief hadn't given Granddad's name, address, and phone number to Suzette's mother. "She doesn't know where the doorstep is."

"Yes, she does. I told her your address. Suzette had given it to me."

Yipes! Val would have to warn Granddad. "I'm sorry. I have to get off the phone in a minute. When do you think you might be able to come for Suzette's belongings?"

Sandy took a minute to check her calendar. "I have time at the end of the week. Let's say Thursday afternoon."

That would work for Val too. "My condolences again on your loss."

While Val was on the phone, half a dozen customers had arrived. She put off calling Granddad, took their orders, and made their lunches. Then more people came into the café. One of them left behind a copy of the *Treadwell Gazette.* Val spotted the headline BAYPORT HIT-AND-RUN VICTIM IDENTIFIED. Citing a Bayport Police Department news release as the source, the reporter gave the time and location of Sunday morning's fatal accident, identified Suzette by name and age, and mentioned she'd recently moved to Bayport. The article ended with a request that anyone with information contact the police.

Val had just finished reading it when her

phone rang. She glanced at the caller ID. "Hi, Granddad. Did you see the article on the hit-and-run in today's paper?"

"Yup. Bare bones. I'm glad our address wasn't in the paper, but Suzette's mother knows it. She's on her way here. Can you come home early? She might be a handful."

An understatement, Val suspected. "Suzette's cousin gave her our address. Mrs. Cripps must have looked up the phone number. She didn't give you much notice."

"She phoned this morning. She wanted to see where her daughter had spent her final days and asked if I'd be home today. I told her to come at two thirty when you'd be back from work. She just called again to say she's made great time and will arrive at one thirty. Can you get Jeremy to relieve you early?"

Val's afternoon assistant was usually willing to earn extra money. "I'll try to reach him. See you as soon as I can."

When Val arrived home at one thirty, a Ford Taurus occupied her spot in the driveway. It looked as old as her Saturn, but in worse shape with dents and rust. *Must be Wanda Cripps's car.* Val parked in front of a neighbor's house, walked up the driveway, and went in by the side door.

With the vestibule door cracked open, she heard a woman's voice coming from the sitting room.

"Suz always liked older men, but I didn't expect someone as, um, mature as you."

"Glad you called me mature, not ancient," Granddad said.

Mrs. Cripps laughed. "Were you her sugar daddy?"

The silence suggested her question had left Granddad speechless.

Val decided it was time to make her entrance. She waltzed into the sitting room and introduced herself to the middle-aged woman on the sofa. "You must be Suzette's mother."

The black-clad woman nodded. "Wanda Cripps."

She was younger than Val had expected, early forties at most. Her chin-length hair, dark-rooted and bleached to platinum blond, framed a pale face with more makeup on it than Val used in a year. Black eyeliner, lashes thick with mascara, and maroon lipstick gave Wanda a look closer to Goth than glamour.

Val expressed her condolences and sat down in the chair near the fireplace, facing Suzette's mother.

"Mrs. Cripps just told me that Suzette

liked older men." Granddad turned to his guest. "Did she have an older boyfriend when she was living at home?"

"She didn't have one of her own. She made a play for my boyfriend. I guess she was jealous of me."

And vice versa, Val suspected. "Is he still your boyfriend?"

"Not after what Suzette did. One night when I was working, she talked him into taking her drinking. Then she crashed his car. Someone older was supposed to be with her because she only had a learner's permit. She said he was drunk, and that's why she had to drive."

"Was she tested for alcohol?"

"Yeah, and don't ask me how she passed. She probably flirted with the cop who tested her." Mrs. Cripps shrugged. "I can't hold that against her. I'd have done the same thing to avoid a ticket. My boyfriend wanted nothing to do with us after that mess. He was a good man, my best chance of happiness ruined."

"What's his name?" Granddad said.

Suzette's mother stared at him. Then her eyes narrowed with suspicion. "Lloyd Leerman. Did he show up here?"

Val was about to say they hadn't seen Suzette with any men, but Granddad got the first word in. "What's he look like?"

"Tall. Blond. Beefy. Scar on his forehead."

Granddad looked at the ceiling for a moment, as if searching for a memory up there, and said, "Nope, never saw him. Was Suzette involved with other men?"

"If she was, she didn't tell me. The police chief said she was jogging when she got hit. I always told her she was crazy to do that. If she needed exercise, she shoulda done what I did and got paid for it."

"What did you do?" Granddad said.

"Worked two jobs. First thing in the morning, I made up the rooms at a motel. You lift up those thick mattresses, you don't need barbells." Wanda Cripps raised an arm like Rosie the Riveter showing her bicep.

Val wondered if Suzette's concern for the plight of maids stemmed from her mother's work. "What was your other job?"

"Waitress. On my feet the whole time. You don't need to jog when you wait tables. That's what I told Suzette. But reading, writing, and running — that's all she ever wanted to do. Work didn't interest her."

"She was a hard worker as long as we knew her." Granddad hit the chair arm with his fist like a judge cutting off idle talk with a gavel. "Have you told Mr. Cripps about Suzette?"

"If I knew where he was I might tell him . . . or I might not. He checked out when Suzette was a baby. I tracked him down a few times over the years to get him to pay child support. He'd do it for a while, and then he'd move on to somewhere else, so I'd have trouble finding him." Mrs. Cripps stood up. "I've got a three-hour ride back. I'd better get a look at what Suzette left to see if anything's worth keeping and hauling back home. Would you show me her room?"

Granddad looked pointedly at Val, expecting her to deliver the bad news.

She briefly explained the terms of Suzette's will, leaving out what it said about her mother. To forestall any objections Mrs. Cripps might have, Val added, "I showed the will to a lawyer, who said it was valid. It's up to Sandy Sechrest to dispose of Suzette's property. We have no say in it." *And neither do you, Mrs. Cripps.*

Mrs. Cripps put her hands on her hips. "Why didn't Sandy tell me that before I drove here?"

"She only found out an hour ago," Val said.

"Did she ever come here to visit Suzette?" Mrs. Cripps looked first at Val and then at Granddad for an answer. They both shook their heads. She smiled briefly. "Since I've come all this way, you can at least point me to her room. I'd like to say goodbye to Suzette in the place where she spent her last days."

Granddad raised an eyebrow at this hint of sentimentality, but he probably wasn't fooled by it. "Will you please show her Suzette's room, Val? Holler if you need my help."

She took the hint that she was supposed to stay with Suzette's mother and make sure nothing disappeared. She led the woman up the front staircase and through the hall to the back bedroom.

Val stood in the doorway as Mrs. Cripps walked around the small room, looked into the closet, and peered at the computer. She jiggled the mouse. Its blank screen lit up and displayed the password prompt. Her next stop was the dresser. She moved the items on it around — a couple of books, the prop eyeglasses Suzette had worn as part of her costume, a hairbrush, and a comb. Mrs. Cripps leaned toward the mirror over the dresser, picked up the comb, and ran it through her hair. She probably had her own comb in the faux leather satchel she carried, but by using the one on the dresser, she seemed to make a claim on her daughter's property.

She put the comb down and picked up the brown teddy bear that sat on the dresser propped against the wall. The golden brown bear was about a foot tall. Its fur looked mangy in spots, and one of its button eyes was missing. "I gave this to Suzette when she was really small. I didn't know she kept it all those years."

Wanda's sigh sounded heartfelt to Val, the first sign of any emotional attachment to her daughter.

She clutched the stuffed animal and sat down on the bed. "I need a few minutes to think about my little girl. You don't have to wait."

"That's okay. I don't mind." Val would have left her alone to grieve, but felt obliged to follow Suzette's wishes and keep her property out of her mother's hands. Mrs. Cripps couldn't be trusted to pay attention to Suzette's final request.

Val noticed Suzette's gift certificate from the Title Wave on the dresser. Mrs. Cripps must have uncovered it when shifting things around. It had probably been under the books. Val took one of them and put it on top of the certificate.

Wanda Cripps stood up within two minutes. "I'd like a little something to remember

Suzette by. Once I pick out what I want, you and your grandfather could do the same. Sandy would never know." She ran her fingers over the marble-topped night table. "I could fit this in my trunk. It's a nice piece."

Val forced herself to smile. "It was one of my grandmother's favorites. Suzette rented the room furnished. If you want anything of hers, you'll have to talk to Sandy."

Mrs. Cripps glared at her. "I want something to remember my daughter by." She grabbed the teddy bear she'd dropped on the bed, stomped out of the room, and went down the stairs. She slammed the front door behind her.

Good riddance.

Granddad was no longer in the sitting room, but Val knew where to find him. On Mondays, when his Codger Cook column was due, he spent most of his time testing recipes in the kitchen. Val went into the study, ignoring the mess Granddad had made the day before in his search for the Patels' phone number. She scanned a copy of Suzette's will, e-mailed it to Sandy Sechrest, and then joined him at the kitchen island.

He looked up from studying a recipe card. "Is that woman still here?"

Val shook her head. "She absconded with a stuffed bear, but I saved everything else from her clutches."

"I now know why Suzette left home as soon as she could. Her mother harangued her about the car crash."

"The crash explains why Suzette didn't want a driver's license and wouldn't drink alcohol. It must have traumatized her." Val remembered her own anxiety about driving after a car accident, and she'd had years of experience behind the wheel, unlike Suzette, who was just learning. "Do you believe what Mrs. Cripps said about Suzette trying to steal her boyfriend?"

"Nope. I think the boyfriend made a play for her. Either way, he had a grudge against her for wrecking his car."

"Years ago."

Granddad opened the refrigerator. "Revenge is a dish best served cold."

"It was smart of you to ask Mrs. Cripps his name. You can do research on Lloyd Leerman and see if he lives around here." Val sniffed the aroma of mint. It came from some sprigs Granddad had put in water on the windowsill. He must have just picked the mint. "What are you making?"

"Orzo salad with lemon, artichokes, feta, and mint. The recipe is in pretty good shape, but I want to make sure it's perfect."

When he first snagged the job of recipe columnist, he'd used Val's recipes and cut out a few ingredients without bothering to test the results. He still used her recipes. At least now, he took the time to try out variations.

Val filled a glass with water. "I was surprised by what Mrs. Cripps said about Suzette and older men."

"She might've been attracted to older men because she grew up without a father in the house. She was looking for a daddy substitute." He drained the can of artichoke hearts. "Before she came here, she lived and worked in a house where there was a daddy."

"Mr. Patel." Val understood what he was implying. "It wouldn't be the first time a man became involved with the family babysitter or nanny. Do you have any reason to think that's what happened at the Patels'?"

"Not yet. I want to visit them and get them talking about Suzette. Their body language might tell me if there was anything going on between her and Mr. Patel." Granddad sliced an artichoke heart in half. "I also want to know more about the note that was left on their doorstep, but I need an excuse to drop in on them."

Val thought of a pretext for his visit. "Take

the Patel boys a book. Tell them Suzette was going to buy it for them with the gift certificate she'd won." She didn't get the enthusiastic reaction she expected from Granddad to her suggestion, so she added icing to the cake — an excuse for him to chat with his favorite bookseller. "Dorothy can help you pick out a book for the kids."

Granddad looked up from the cutting board, suddenly more interested. "Good idea. If I bake cookies for the Patels, they won't just say thank you for the book and slam the door in my face. I'll make some cookies for Dorothy too. She told me she doesn't do much cooking or baking."

Val smiled. He'd previously tried to capture the heart of an attractive widow by touting his cooking skills. Now he actually had a few skills. Val wished him better luck this time. She much preferred Dorothy over his previous attempted conquest. "Have you finalized the other recipes for this week's column?"

He nodded. "Still have to type 'em up. Then Ned and I will canvass places Suzette might have gone Saturday night. You want to come with us?"

"Suzette's boss, Nick, invited me for a drink." But she didn't plan on spending the evening with him. "I'll call you when I'm done and join you."

"Is Nick an older man?"

"Not to me, but to Suzette. He looks to be in his late thirties. Don't get hung up on what Mrs. Cripps said about her daughter and older men. Since Suzette was in her early twenties, just about any man is an older man."

"And not all older men are bad." Granddad turned on the burner under a pot of water. "If you're having fun with Nick the hotel manager, stay and have dinner with him, not just a drink."

"You've got the wrong idea." *Nick probably did too.* "I'm meeting him to find out what he knows about Suzette. She spent more time at the inn than here. If she had trouble with her coworkers as she did with the neighbors at her last job, he'd have noticed."

"But would he tell you about it?"

"I'll find out."

Val wondered which Nick would show up at the wine bar — the coolly efficient hotel manager or the prying vampire who'd come on to her at the bookshop. Either way, she had to convince him to talk about Suzette.

CHAPTER 11

Val arrived at the wine bar ten minutes before she was due to meet Nick. She bought a glass of sauvignon blanc at the bar and sat at a tiny stainless steel table near the window. He arrived within minutes.

Judging by his clothing — a shirt and tie under a maroon pullover sweater — Nick the manager had come. But at the table with a glass of red wine in hand, he was as inquisitive as he'd been on Saturday night when dressed as a vampire.

He swirled the wine in the glass. "Where did you say you lived before you moved here?"

She hadn't said, but she didn't mind satisfying his curiosity now that they were meeting socially. Besides, she had a few questions for him too. "New York City. I worked for a publishing house and handled publicity for cookbooks."

"What brought you to this neck of the

woods?"

"After my job went sour, I needed a change. My grandfather has a big house in Bayport. I stayed in that house every summer when I was growing up. I came here for what I thought would be a few months to regroup. That was a year and a half ago. It feels like home now." Before he could get in another question, she turned the tables on him. "Where are you from originally?"

"Born and bred here on the Eastern Shore." He sipped his wine. "I live in Cambridge."

An easy commute, half an hour away from Bayport.

A server brought them snacks that Nick had ordered — small bowl of pretzels, cubed cheese, and olives.

When the server left, Val said, "What did you do before you got the job at the inn?"

"I've always been in the hospitality industry, working my way up."

"And now you're in management." Val speared a cheese cube, trying to look nonchalant. "A woman who works at your inn was killed in a hit-and-run. Suzette Cripps."

Nick ran his fingers up and down the stem of his wineglass. "Someone on the staff heard it on the radio and told the rest of us. I knew something was wrong when Suzette didn't come to work yesterday and the police asked for an emergency contact. They said she was in an accident, but they didn't tell me how seriously she was hurt." He took a large green olive from the platter. "Was she a friend of yours?"

Val shook her head. "I've only known her for six weeks. She rented a room at my grandfather's house in mid-September."

"That's when she came to work at the inn." Nick bit into the olive. "How many rooms does your grandfather rent?"

"He's not running a boarding house. Suzette was staying with us until she could find someone to share a place with. My grandfather told her the room wouldn't be available around Christmas and New Year's, when my brother's family and my parents always visit." Val reached for a pretzel. "Was Suzette friendly with anyone in particular at work?"

"Not that I noticed. The front desk people often become friendly while working together, but we've had a lot of turnover lately. The woman who worked at the desk for years left at the end of September, and the people we've tried in the job this month haven't worked out."

Had the woman quit because of something amiss at the inn? "It's hard to lose a longtime employee. Did she retire or move?"

"She got a job offer from the Inn at Perry Cabin. We couldn't compete with that."

"I understand." One of the premier properties on the Eastern Shore, Perry Cabin was the height of luxury and probably paid their staff well. Steering the conversation back to the Harbor Inn, Val said, "The staff at upscale places like that must have to cater to demanding guests. I suppose that's true for you too. Managers have to handle all kinds of problems and disputes."

"It's my job to know what's going on and prevent problems before they arise. Most of the time, I succeed."

"Was Suzette having trouble with anyone at the inn?"

Nick looked taken aback. "What kind of trouble?"

Val shrugged. "I'm not sure. I found out she left her previous job because someone was harassing her."

"We would jump on anything like that in a heartbeat."

Val got the impression that his *anything like that* meant sexual harassment. She was about to explain that she didn't mean that type of problem when Bram walked into the wine bar.

He waved and came over to the table.

"Hey, Val. I was walking by and saw you sitting in the window. We need to work out a few details about tomorrow night. Can you stop by the shop or call my mother when you have a chance?"

"Sure."

Bram turned to Nick. "Sorry to interrupt."

Val introduced the two men to each other. "Bram is the bookshop's business manager. Nick is the Harbor Inn's assistant manager. You two have something in common. You were both vampires on Saturday night at the bookshop."

Bram stared at Nick. "You look familiar. You were there for the costume contest."

Nick frowned. "I read the sign about the contest, but I didn't stay for it."

"I could swear I saw you there after it was over."

"No," Nick said. "Must have been some other vampire."

Bram raised a skeptical eyebrow. How could he be so sure that Nick had been the vampire hanging around after the costume contest? Val hadn't recognized him at the inn yesterday, though she'd talked to him for ten minutes the night before.

Val pointed to him. "On Saturday night Nick had blackened eyes and fangs. It would have been hard to tell him from any other vampire."

"Nick," Bram said, as if the name had just sunk in. "You called the bookshop so you could talk to Val about catering. Did you two work that out?"

Val was stunned at Bram's personality change. The buttoned-up businessman was acting like a nosy neighbor.

Nick glared at him. "We were interrupted before we got around to it tonight."

"I know what you mean. People constantly interrupt me too." Bram gave Val a quick smile. "Talk to you later. I wouldn't want to hold up a business meeting."

As Bram turned to go, Nick said, "How are the wedding plans going, Val?"

The question hung in the air as Val focused on Bram. She watched him go out the door and turn in the opposite direction from the bookshop, possibly on the hunt for some dinner.

She turned back to Nick. "You said something about a wedding?"

"Your friend's wedding. Did you tell her about the Harbor Inn?"

"I did." Lying had two pitfalls — forgetting what you'd said and having to keep lying. "She hasn't gotten back to me on it." She tried to think of a different conversation topic. He reached for his glass of what looked to her like blood-red wine, perfect for a vampire.

Sipping it, he watched her over the rim of his glass. "Is the guy who interrupted us a good friend of yours?"

Val would have called Bram a foe rather than a friend after her first encounter with him. Since then he'd shown her a different side of himself every time, but it was still a stretch to call him a friend. "He's a catering client." Though he'd behaved almost like a jealous boyfriend. "While we're on the subject, you were interested in my catering an event?"

Nick leaned toward her across the tiny table. "No, I was interested in you, but I didn't think the bookshop people would link us up if I said that. I hope you don't mind."

"I don't." Given that she'd had an ulterior motive in meeting him tonight, she couldn't object to his. By now she was convinced he wouldn't tell her about any tensions or trouble at the Harbor Inn. Val sipped her wine, unable to think of anything else to say to him.

"It would be hard for me to share a house with a relative who's a lot older," he said. "What's it like to live with your grandfather?"

"A challenge for both of us at first. When I moved here, Granddad still hadn't gotten over my grandmother's death. He ate badly and spent most of his time in front of the TV. But all that's changed. He has a healthier diet now, and he's tried new things, like cooking and writing a newspaper recipe column."

"That's very cool. It must have been an adjustment for you both when Suzette moved in."

Val had been wondering how to bring up Suzette again, and now Nick had done it for her. "Not much of an adjustment. She had her own entrance and staircase to her bedroom. My grandfather and I barely saw her." Val took a sip of wine. "Did Suzette get along well with the staff at the inn?"

Nick's dark brows lowered over his narrowed eyes. "She must have said something to you about working there. You keep asking about it."

"You were the one who just brought up Suzette, not me." Val decided against repeating her question about Suzette and her coworkers. He obviously didn't want to answer it. She wondered why.

He pointed to her nearly empty glass. "How about a wine refill?"

She looked at her watch. "I'd better not.

I'm supposed to meet my grandfather and a friend of his for dinner."

"Where are you going to eat?"

Even if Val knew the answer, she wouldn't have told Nick. Maybe he'd asked about her dinner plans just to make conversation or out of simple curiosity, or maybe he was hoping for an invitation to join them. He wouldn't get it. She stood up. "Granddad is going to surprise me. It was good chatting with you, Nick, and thanks for the snacks."

Her abrupt exit bordered on rude, but she had little interest in spending more time with him. His defensiveness about the inn's work environment made Val think he was hiding something. Of course, her questions about the inn probably made him think she was prying . . . which she was.

She glanced in the window of Title Wave. Dorothy looked busy with customers lined up to buy books. Val would call her later tonight or in the morning to settle whatever details remained for tomorrow's Fictionista meeting.

"Miss Val!" a woman behind her called out.

Val turned. It took her a moment to recognize the dark-haired maid. "Maria!"

"We heard at the inn that Suzette is dead. I am very sorry. She was a good person."

Maria glanced behind her. "I must tell you something. Let me go ahead. Walk a little behind, and I'll wait for you around the corner."

Val could hardly contain her curiosity. Would she finally learn why Suzette detoured rather than walk straight home from the inn? Val pretended to look in a gift shop window, waited until Maria walked half a block, and then followed her.

The maid turned the corner onto a side street and paused near a bush far from a streetlight. When Val caught up with her, Maria said, "I saw you in the window of the wine store, sitting with Nick. Stay away from him. He is a bad man."

Val had no trouble believing that. "How is he bad? What does he do?"

"He is married. He should not be with another woman."

Was Maria trying to protect Val from heartbreak or hinting that Suzette had been having an affair with her boss? "Was Nick, um, with Suzette?"

"No! She was a good girl."

But she might not have told Maria the truth about her relationship with Nick, knowing that Maria wouldn't approve. Or perhaps Suzette didn't want anything to do with Nick, but he wouldn't take no for an answer. "Is Nick interested in other women who work at the inn?"

Maria bit her lip. "I must go home now and pray for Suzette's soul. You go back." She pointed toward Main Street, turned, and hurried in the opposite direction.

Not the right time to pursue her for information. Apparently, she didn't want Nick to see her talking to Val. Something strange was going on at the inn where Suzette worked. Did it involve Nick and did it have anything to do with her death? Val was sure Maria could help answer those questions, but getting her to talk wouldn't be easy.

Val pulled out her phone, noticed it was almost out of juice, and speed-dialed her grandfather. "Hi, Granddad. I'm done. Where and when should I meet you?"

"We started on the far end of Main Street, toward the peninsula. We're working our way back to the center. We should be at the Bugeye Tavern in about fifteen minutes."

"A perfect place to grab dinner." Val was closer to the tavern and would get there even sooner than Granddad and Ned. "The Bayport Bistro is right across the street from the tavern. I'll show the staff there Suzette's photo before I meet you."

She walked along Main Street and turned

left on Locust. In warm weather the tables on the front patio of the Bayport Bistro were usually filled, but with the sun down, the nippy autumn air made the indoors more appealing. She went inside and told the hostess she was trying to find out if her friend had stopped at the bistro on Saturday night. The friend lived in Washington, had visited Bayport last weekend, and had eaten in a restaurant she enjoyed. She couldn't remember the name or the exact location, and she wanted to give the place a good online review.

Val then showed the hostess the doctored photo and pointed to Suzette's image. "Do you remember this woman being here?"

"I don't, but I greet a lot of customers. Let me show the picture to the two servers who were here Saturday night."

Neither of them recognized Suzette or the other woman in the photo. Val thanked them, turned back toward Main Street, and crossed Locust Lane. The tavern in a brick building on the corner of Main and Locust took its name — Bugeye — from the type of oyster boat used in the nineteenth century. The tavern's main room, with its wood floors and walls, hadn't changed much since hardworking watermen gathered here after a day on the bay. The much newer glass-enclosed side porch with hanging ferns gave the eatery a split personality.

Val was glad to see Keenan behind the polished wood bar. The red-haired bartender worked out at the athletic club and was a frequent customer at her café. She was a less frequent customer here.

Keenan greeted her with a smile. "Hey, Val. My turn to wait on you. What can I get you?"

Information. "Soda water with a twist of lime would be great. I'm waiting for my grandfather." When Keenan delivered her drink, she pulled out the photo she'd shown at the bistro. "Did you happen to see either of these woman here on Saturday night?"

"Solving another crime, huh?" He studied the photo. "Oh, yeah. She was here." He pointed at Suzette.

Bingo! "Did she come in alone?"

"I wish. She was with a dude."

"What did he look like?"

Keenan laughed. "I was looking at *her,* not *him.* They were sitting over there." He pointed to a small table near the window fronting on Main Street. "He was in costume, like a lot of people in the bar that night. He wore a black cape."

"Did you notice if the cape was long or short?" When Keenan shook his head, Val said, "What kind of costume was it? Grim Reaper, Count Dracula, Zorro, Phantom of the Opera?"

"Not Zorro. The guy had no mask, hat, or sword. His cape didn't have a hood like the Grim Reaper's. I guess he could have been Dracula or the Phantom without a mask."

Val had seen three men in black capes at the bookshop — Casper, Nick, and Bram. But a lot of other caped men were at the town's Spooktacular festival on Saturday. Suzette's death probably had nothing to do with what she did the night before. Still, it would be good to know who was with her.

"Did they seem to be having fun?"

"I was too busy to pay much attention, but the one time I glanced that way, they looked like they were in a serious conversation."

No surprise there. Val had rarely seen Suzette anything but serious. "How long were they here?"

"No more than half an hour." Keenan gathered the glasses of two people who'd just left the bar. "You should stop by here on Thursday. On Halloween night we usually have a fair number of people wearing costumes. Maybe that couple will come back."

He might. She wouldn't. "Are the servers

who waited on customers Saturday night here now?"

He shook his head. "Skeleton staff today. Mondays are slow. If you leave me the photo, I can ask them if they remember that couple."

"I'd appreciate that." Val passed the photo to him. She could print another one if she needed it.

"Are you going to tell me what this is about?"

"Not yet. I'm working on a hunch that may lead nowhere. When I know something for sure, I'll let you in on it. Meantime, you can tell the servers the truth — that you don't know why your friend asked about the woman in the photo." Val spotted Granddad and Ned coming into the tavern. "Here come my dates for tonight. Thank you for your help, Keenan."

"Hey, you ever want a date with someone who doesn't have gray hair or a white beard, let me know. I've got some friends you might like."

"Thanks. I may take you up on that offer."

Once Val was ensconced with Granddad and Ned in a booth, she told them that their search was over.

"You have the magic touch, Val," Ned

said. "We've stopped at a lot of places and no one had seen that girl."

"I just wish I knew who the caped man was."

Granddad's eyes lit up. "I've got an idea. If the man was in the bookshop that night, Dorothy might have a photo of him. She was taking pictures. I'll ask to see them and have her e-mail me ones with a caped man in them. Someone who works here might recognize the fella who was with Suzette."

Val opened the menu. "Good idea. Try to get a photo of Bram too. He wore a cape that night."

Granddad looked askance at her. "You think he was the man she met here?"

She shook her head, though she wouldn't rule out Bram entirely. "In a photo lineup, you need innocent men as well as suspected culprits."

The server came to take their drink orders and tell them about the daily specials, cutting off further discussion of men in capes.

Granddad said goodnight and disappeared into his room when they returned home. Val went into the study, plugged in her phone, and surveyed the room. She'd intended to clean up the mess he'd left in the study when he searched for the Patels' phone number, but she was too tired to bother. Preparing the food for the writing group's meeting would keep her busy tomorrow. Sorting through the folders and papers he'd left on the sofa and the floor would have to wait until the end of the week. Maybe he would do it before then. Wishful thinking.

She took the pages that Suzette had written upstairs, planning to reread them. She got only a third of the way through before her eyes closed. She turned off the light at ten and fell asleep.

She heard a faint sound, half groan, half squeak. Someone was on the back staircase, the one Suzette always used! Val rushed through the hall, looked down the stairs, and made out a dim figure below. Suzette stood at the landing on the first floor. She wasn't dead after all! A wave of happiness washed over Val as she waited for Suzette to join her on the second floor. Suzette remained motionless and said, "Ghosts don't climb stairs."

She disappeared, and Val woke up in the dark. Sadness weighed on her. She'd had a good dream, but it was over. Then she heard a stair creak again exactly as it had in her dream. Who was on the back staircase? Not Suzette's ghost and not Granddad. He'd have used the less steep front stairs near his room.

Val's heart thudded. Someone had broken in!

CHAPTER 12

Val held her breath and listened. If anyone was in the second-floor hallway, she'd hear the floorboards creaking. But she didn't. Whoever had been on that staircase wasn't coming closer . . . yet. She felt for her phone on the nightstand. Not there. She'd left it charging in the study.

She could hide. In the closet or under the bed. But with Granddad downstairs, she had to do more than try to save just herself. If he woke up, he'd investigate odd noises and put himself in danger. She had to prevent that.

She eased out of bed and crept toward the door. Thank goodness she'd recently oiled the hinges. She cracked it open and peered down the length of the hall. A white light shone from under the closed door to Suzette's room. What would a burglar want there?

Val slipped out of her bedroom. She took

two long strides and reached the staircase leading to the front hall. With her passion for eavesdropping as a child, she knew how to sneak down to the first floor without being heard. The wood stairs wouldn't make noise if she stayed close to the side of the tread, instead of stepping in the middle. She started down, hugging the wall.

But what should she do once she was on the first floor? Go into the study and call 911? By the time Bayport's single nighttime patrol car arrived, she and Granddad could be lying in a pool of blood.

Halfway down the stairs, a step squeaked under her weight. Darn! Would that small sound betray her to the intruder? She had no choice but to keep going down.

In the hall, dimly lit by a nightlight, she spotted a gray plastic object the size of a shoebox on the hall floor — Granddad's favorite gizmo, a motion detector, affectionately known as RoboFido. Maybe she could use it to get rid of the person who'd crept upstairs. Unlike similar devices, this one didn't turn on lights in response to motion, but it made a lot of noise.

After the ghost tour stopped at the house, Granddad had taken the gadget from the closet and pointed it toward the front door's sidelight to deter any ghost gawkers from venturing near the house that night. Now Val hoped it would scare the dickens out of the intruder. She and Granddad might never find out who'd broken in, but at least they'd be safe.

She rotated RoboFido so the sensor would detect motion in the front hall and on the staircase she'd just come down. She flipped the switch on. As she walked toward Granddad's bedroom, the sensor picked up her movement. Loud barks resounded through the house.

When Granddad peered out of his door at the end of the hall, she signaled him to go back. She followed him into the room and locked the bedroom door behind her. "I heard someone on the back staircase and saw a light coming from Suzette's room."

He pointed to the window along the side wall. "I looked outside when the barking woke me up. Someone in dark clothes and a hoodie ran by the house."

The news relieved Val. "The barks scared our intruder away. He must have gone out by the back stairs." RoboFido had stopped barking. No one was moving within range of its sensor.

Granddad grabbed her arm and whispered, "Don't jump to conclusions. One person is gone, but an accomplice could still be in the house, holed up in Suzette's room."

"If the barking starts again, we'll know someone's on the stairs or in the hall."

Granddad's face screwed up in anger. "Doggonit. My shotgun's upstairs." He looked around the room. "I need a weapon."

"I need a cell phone." Val spotted his phone on the dresser and called 911.

As they waited for the police, Val wrapped herself in Granddad's old plaid robe, and he donned the gray robe he'd worn Saturday night as Professor Dumbledore.

The doorbell rang and a man bellowed, "Police!"

When they left the bedroom, RoboFido sensed their movement and erupted in growls and barks. Val turned off the guard dog and answered the door.

A middle-aged Bayport police officer with broad shoulders and a weathered face stood on the porch. "You got trouble here again?"

Val nodded. She couldn't recall the officer's name, but she remembered his skepticism when he'd responded previously to an emergency call. This time he seemed to take her more seriously. He jotted in a small notebook as she told him what had happened.

He looked up from his notes. "What were

you doing when you heard the noises on the staircase?"

"Lying in bed."

"You were asleep before that?"

"Yes." She could read his mind. He assumed she'd dreamed those noises.

"Did you hear any noises, sir?" When Granddad shook his head, the officer turned back to Val. "How long since you heard what you thought was someone on the stairs?"

"Maybe fifteen minutes." She described what she'd done from that time until he arrived at the house.

He surveyed RoboFido. "I heard those barks. Pretty realistic. *If* you had a burglar, he'd have left by now." He closed his notebook. "You stay here. I'll take a look around to be on the safe side."

To be on the safe side, he should have called for backup before he wandered around the house and left them alone in the hall. Val had visions of the burglar slipping past him, rushing down the stairs, knocking Granddad down, and escaping into the night.

The officer strode into the sitting room, looked through the double doorway to the study, and gaped. "That room's been ransacked!"

Val caught Granddad's eye and put an index finger on her lips on the off chance that he'd own up to wrecking the room. "Oh no! I hope nothing's missing," she said.

"Computer's still there and a phone. But it looks like you were right about a burglar. I'll call another officer to help me search the rest of the house."

Officer Wade responded within minutes to the call. Val knew the rookie well. He'd tagged after the chief on last year's murder investigations.

The two officers checked the house thoroughly, including the attic to make sure the burglar wasn't hiding there, and the area around the house.

When they came back inside, the older officer said, "Looks like the lock on the door to the kitchen and back stairs was jimmied."

"Any rooms upstairs ransacked?" Granddad said.

"Not like this one." The officer pointed to the study. "Take a look in the rooms up there and on this floor. Let us know if something's been disturbed or stolen, but be careful not to touch any surfaces. A team will come over in the morning to check for fingerprints."

"A burglar worth half his salt wouldn't leave any prints," Granddad mumbled as he followed Val up the stairs.

She headed straight to the back bedroom. The top dresser drawer was open, and Suzette's computer was no longer on the table. Val groaned. The chief should have taken it after the hit-and-run. Now it was too late.

Officer Wade joined her and Granddad outside Suzette's bedroom.

She pointed to the open drawer. "That's not the way I left it."

"Anything missing?" Wade said.

"The laptop that was on the table is gone. It was old, but the burglar might have wanted it for a reason other than resale." When the officer looked perplexed, she added, "This is the hit-and-run victim's room."

Officer Wade's eyes bugged out. "I'll tell the chief first thing tomorrow. And I'll patrol this street until daylight."

Chief Yardley stopped by the Cool Down Café the next morning as Val was wiping down the eating bar. He dropped in occasionally for a decent cup of coffee, not a feature of the Bayport Police Department headquarters.

The broad-shouldered chief perched on a counter stool. "What kind of muffins you have today?"

"Apple walnut raisin and lemon blueberry." She poured his coffee.

"I'll take the one with the nuts, even though it sounds healthy. Officer Wade told me you had a break-in last night. How's your granddaddy doing?"

"He's a bit rattled. The house has never been burglarized before. Happening so soon after Suzette died makes it even worse."

"Don't jump to the conclusion that the burglary and her death are connected. We've had a rash of burglaries in this area. This is the first one in Bayport, but homes in Treadwell, Easton, and Oxford have been hit."

"So our house was a random target?" Val couldn't keep the skepticism out of her voice. "And it was just by chance that the burglar came in the door Suzette always used?"

"According to the incident report, that door was the logical point of entry. It only has a doorknob lock, easy to pick. The other doors have deadbolts or latches."

"I wonder if our burglary could have been a copycat crime rather than the latest in a string by one person or a gang. Did the burglar pick the locks the same way in those other houses?"

The chief washed down his muffin with a gulp of coffee. "Entry was via an unlocked door, an open window, or another method that left no mark."

"So last night's burglary didn't follow the same pattern as the others. Did the report on our break-in say that the burglar ransacked a room on the main level?" When the chief nodded, she continued. "That's not what happened. Granddad had turned the room upside down, looking for something. Nothing was missing or even touched in any room except Suzette's. Can you explain why a burglar would pass up the sterling silver in the dining room and go into a small bedroom?"

"I sure can. People keep jewelry in their bedrooms. Jewelry is small and light compared to a silver service. The burglar must have watched the house and seen lights in your bedroom and your grandfather's. Once all lights were out, the burglar waited a bit, broke into the house, and went to a room that hadn't been lit up."

"Yes, but then he — or she — stole an old computer. Not worth the time or effort to case the house and pick the lock."

"You woke up, turned on your dog, and spooked the burglar. He or she didn't want to leave empty-handed."

"Or the burglar really wanted that computer. Suzette, a budding author, was writing a novel." Val decided not to mention any connection between the novel and Suzette's death until the evidence of a link was stronger. "It's possible Suzette also kept a journal, which might have damaging information about someone."

"*Possible? Might have?* Pure speculation. The open dresser drawer means the burglar was after something besides a computer."

"Suzette kept bank statements, her will, and other records in the bottom drawer. The folder with those papers was still there. At least the burglar didn't get them."

The chief buttered his last piece of muffin. "Who knew which room was hers?"

"Her mother was in the room yesterday and Suzette might have told people." It hit Val that she herself had told someone. She thunked her head. "I mentioned Suzette's separate entrance and staircase to Nick Hyde, her boss at the inn." Val topped off the chief's coffee mug. "I doubt he was our burglar. Yesterday I told him Granddad and I were eating out. If Nick wanted something from Suzette's room, he'd have broken in earlier when the house was empty."

Val spotted a group of women seating themselves at the corner table. The foursome always came to the café after their yoga class. She excused herself to wait on them.

She returned to the counter to make smoothies for them. The chief had just finished his coffee. "Have you heard from the medical examiner yet, Chief?"

"The autopsy is still pending. I don't expect the medical details to tell us whether the hit-and-run was deliberate, if that's what you're really asking. The accident scene investigators might have something to say about that. I'm waiting for their report." He stood up. "You've pulled at loose threads before and managed to unravel some knotty schemes. This time I suspect you'll end up with a bunch of broken threads."

He didn't know half the threads she'd pulled. "I still want to tug every last one. Unless there's proof Suzette died by accident, I'll keep wondering if I might have prevented what happened by reaching out to her sooner. Maybe she would have told me who or what was bothering her."

"Don't beat yourself up over this. From what your granddaddy said, she didn't share her problems."

The chief left the café as more customers arrived. When business slowed down at eleven, Val called the bookshop. "Hi, Dorothy. Bram told me you had a few details to settle for tonight."

"Glad you called. Your grandfather said that all your catering has been in the homes of your clients. Do they usually set the table with the linen, dishes, and utensils?"

"Yes, but I can do that for you if you like."

"I'd appreciate it. I can't even guess which of my unopened moving boxes contains tableware. Would you also bring wine-glasses? Gillian wants wine. We don't have a license to serve alcohol on the premises, but since she's renting the room for the evening, I guess it's okay for her to bring it herself."

Fine with Val. She was glad to leave the choice of wine to her clients. "Not a problem. Some eateries without alcohol licenses advertise that customers can bring their own drinks. I'll supply the wineglasses."

"Wonderful. Your grandfather hasn't come to the bookshop since Saturday. Is he okay?"

"He's fine, just busy." And concerned that Dorothy might not want him around. "His recipe column was due yesterday, and . . ." Val hesitated, unsure how Dorothy would react to Granddad's ghost hunting. "Today he had a couple of appointments."

"I'm glad to hear he's doing well."

And Granddad would be glad to hear that Dorothy missed seeing him. Val called him as soon as she had a free moment, but he didn't answer. Nor was he in the house when she got home at two thirty.

By the time he strode into the kitchen, she'd gathered the ingredients for the appetizers, made the main course, and put the dessert in the oven.

He sniffed. "Something smells good. I hope you made a little extra for me."

"Of course. You're my official taster. The madeleines should be ready soon."

"I could use some tea with them." He filled the kettle with water. "A hot drink will take the chill out of me."

"Ghost hunting chilled you?"

"Nope. The outside temperature's dropping fast. It finally feels like fall." He turned on the burner under the kettle. "I plan to make it very warm for whoever's haunting my clients. I'm going to set a trap."

Uh-oh. Now Val was the one who was chilled. "The last time you set a trap for a criminal, you turned up the heat on yourself . . . as a murder suspect."

CHAPTER 13

Granddad opened the smallest canister in Grandma's vintage aluminum set and took out a teabag. "I'm not dealing with a murderer this time."

"That's what you thought last time." Val checked the madeleines. They were puffing up nicely and should be done in a few minutes.

"I've taken detective courses online since then. And I have a high tech tool."

"RoboFido?"

"Nope. I want to catch the culprits, not scare 'em off."

Exactly what Val had feared. "Tell me about the clients you saw today." Maybe she could talk him out of whatever he had in mind to catch their "ghosts."

"This morning I met Mr. and Mrs. King. They live just outside Bayport. Big bear of a man, hard of hearing. Little bird of a woman, a light sleeper with keen ears. One

188

night last month she woke when she heard a thump and creaking floorboards. She shook him awake. He heard nothing and told her she was imagining things. She didn't bother to wake him the next time she heard noises. By then she was convinced they had a ghost because she was missing some things but no one had broken in."

"Like your other client, Mrs. Jackson. But she didn't hear any noises, did she?"

"No. Mr. King took me aside and said his wife often misplaced things and was getting funny in the head, so I shouldn't pay attention to her." The teakettle whistled and Granddad poured the water into his cup. "When I was leaving, she walked me to the car and said she didn't want the ghost stealing any more of her mother's heirloom jewelry. Expensive stuff, like a hundred-year-old diamond ring appraised for seven thousand dollars. What do you think is going on?"

Val took the madeleines from the oven. "Her ghost might be her husband. Maybe he gave the jewelry to his mistress or hocked it to pay gambling debts."

"Or he's gaslighting his wife and wants her declared incompetent." Granddad took his tea to the kitchen table. "I changed my mind about that after I talked to my next

189

client. Mrs. Hill also heard noises in the middle of the night. I suggested she might have an animal in the attic, but she'd already had the exterminator check. No sign of wildlife up there. She wanted me to certify she had no ghosts in the house."

Val laughed. "Why?"

"She's about to put her house on the market. Her agent told her about the Maryland Real Estate Commission regulations. They require the seller to reveal all material facts, anything that might affect the decision to buy or the price offered."

"A resident ghost is not a material fact."

"According to Mrs. Hill, a survey showed that nearly half the house hunters would rule out buying a haunted place, and the folks willing to buy it want a deep discount. Mrs. Hill's agent recommended full disclosure to avoid a lawsuit after the sale. She's afraid she'll get less money for the house if she mentions the ghost. If she doesn't, the buyer might sue her for not revealing it."

"Assuming the buyer could prove the ghost exists. Does Mrs. Hill believe your certificate will protect her from a lawsuit?"

Granddad sipped his tea. "I told her it wouldn't. I also asked her if anything had disappeared from her house. She didn't think so, but she told me to wait in the kitchen while she had a look around."

Val could guess the result. "Small, expensive items were missing."

"Jewelry and her late husband's coin collection."

"Could she have moved the coins to another place in the house and forgotten where she put them?"

"The metal box was too heavy for her to move. That's why she left it where it always was — on a shelf in the coat closet."

A suspicion formed in Val's mind. "Where does she live?"

"Treadwell."

Val began to see a pattern. "You said Mrs. Jackson lives in Easton. The chief told me burglars had recently hit houses in both of those towns."

His eyebrows rose. "All the folks who contacted me about ghosts have something else in common. They use a housecleaning service. I thought it might be the same company, but it isn't." He stroked his chin. "Hmm. The same folks might clean for different companies."

Possible, since those towns were only fifteen minutes apart. "Good work, Granddad. You've found people who haven't reported the disappearance of their valuables. They live where burglars have been active. You should talk to the chief about it."

"He didn't think much of my idea that Mr. Patel might have been involved with Suzette. From now on I won't tell him anything until I have solid evidence. I've thought of a way to smoke out the burglars."

Val hoped he didn't intend to stake out the houses. "This is the trap you mentioned?"

"Yup. Mrs. Hill is going to visit a friend in Washington tomorrow and stay overnight. Her cleaning team was supposed to do her house tomorrow morning. She told them she'd be out of town from early Wednesday to late Thursday. They've postponed her cleaning until Friday morning."

She guessed what he was thinking. "You expect a burglar to visit her house tomorrow night. Did you tell her that?"

"No, but I convinced her to change her locks. I got Ned to go over there and put in new ones this afternoon. I figure the burglar has a key to her place. That key isn't going to work tomorrow night, but my motion-activated video recorder with night vision will show who's trying to break in. Ned and I are going over to Mrs. Hill's house later to set it up near the door and make sure it works."

"Where did you get that gizmo?"

"I ordered it online after talking to Mrs. Jackson on Sunday. I figured she might have a burglar. The package showed up this morning."

"Too bad it didn't arrive in time for us to test it here." Val stood up. "I have to go to the bookshop at five thirty. When you leave this evening to set up your camera, please turn on RoboFido. Our burglar might make a return visit when the house is empty."

"I'll also let Harvey know we'll both be gone. He likes looking out the windows and checking what his neighbors are doing. He'll keep an eye on the house until one of us gets back."

"I talked to Dorothy today. She asked about you and wondered why you haven't been to the bookshop since Saturday."

"She did?" He smiled. "I'll drop in tomorrow."

Bram helped Val arrange the tables and chairs in the CAT Corner for the Fictionistas' get-together. By pushing two of the small square tables together, they created a single table large enough for six in the center of the room. They stacked the spare chairs in a corner and moved the remaining tables toward the bookshelf wall. Drinks and snacks would go on those tables.

Val surveyed the Halloween decorations interspersed with books on the shelves. The pumpkins, scarecrows, and ghosts could stay, but not the skulls and skeletons. Decorative reminders of death didn't suit tonight's occasion. "I'm going to tuck a few of these items behind the counter for the evening."

Bram glanced at the shelves with a puzzled frown. "The breakable ones? You're expecting a rowdy meeting?"

"You never know. Before I leave, I'll put everything back the way it was." A ceramic black cat on the top shelf reminded Val that a real one might drop in tonight. "Can we expect Isis for dinner?"

"I'll put her upstairs. Shout if you need anything." He left for the sales floor.

Val stowed away the offending knick-knacks and got the table ready. The dried flower arrangement she'd brought as a centerpiece went well with the gold, orange, and maroon colors in the tablecloth's leaf pattern.

She'd just added the spices to the cider she was warming when Bram returned.

He held up a cordless phone. "A call came in for Gillian on the bookshop phone. A woman phoning about tonight's meeting.

194

You want to talk to her?"

She nodded and took the phone. "Hi. This is Val. Gillian's not here yet. Can I help you?"

"It's Morgan. Please tell Gillian I'll be a little late for our meeting. Fifteen minutes at most. She told me you'd be catering tonight. What kind of tea do you have?"

She turned toward Bram, who was emptying the box of dishware she'd brought, making himself useful while waiting for his phone.

"What kind of tea do I have?" Val said loudly into the phone. "Give me a second and I'll check."

Bram got the message. He opened the upper cabinet near the sink and pointed to boxes of teabags.

Val peered at them. "English Breakfast, Earl Grey, and an assortment of herb teas."

"I'll bring my own tea," Morgan said. "See you later." She hung up.

Val tried to guess what Morgan would bring. A green tea, a white tea, chai, or an exotic herbal blend?

"Did we pass the tea test?" Bram said.

"Afraid not. I suspect your chance of passing it was about the same as winning the lottery."

He smiled and slipped through the cur-

195

tains back to the shop floor.

Val looked up from stirring the cider as a tall, almost skeletal man took tentative steps into the room. Casper's elongated pasty face had only a bit more color today than when he'd covered it with the opera phantom's white mask.

"Hi, Casper. You're the first one here."

He slung his well-worn MIT jacket over the stacked chairs. Under it, he wore a shirt the color of mud. It might have been white before being washed with dark clothes. Tissue bits clung to his navy pants. Val sympathized. Anyone could forget to empty pockets before doing the laundry, but most people would brush off the evidence of the mishap before wearing the pants.

He walked over to the counter and sniffed. "What smells so good in here?"

"Spiced apple cider. Would you like some?"

He hesitated. "Never had that before, but I'll throw caution to the winds tonight."

Val suppressed a laugh, unsure if he was joking. She ladled steaming cider from the pot into a mug. "Here you go."

He took a small sip. "Not bad." He sipped again. "I'm really bummed out about what happened to Suzette. I met her six months ago at an Eastern Shore Writers Association meeting. I knew her longer than the others in our writing group."

Did he feel a sense of possession toward her because of that? "I'm sorry for your loss."

"Me too." His washed-out gray eyes glistened with tears.

Val believed his sadness and pain were genuine. The Phantom of the Opera felt those same emotions. Had Casper, like the Phantom, suffered lovesickness and burned with rage? If a costume reflected the wearer's true nature, then all the Fictionistas had a capacity for violence. Did Morgan, like her namesake, hide her vengeful nature behind a mask of goodwill? Was Ruth as ruthless and ambitious as Lady Macbeth? Had her handsome nephew become a predator like the gentleman-turned-zombie he'd portrayed? Val reminded herself to keep her inner Nancy Drew in check. Sometimes a costume is just a costume.

She lowered the heat under the cider. "What kind of work do you do, Casper?"

"Tech support at a small company, and I freelance as a bug buster."

Val had heard the term *bug buster* used for pest controllers, but she doubted Casper had gone that far afield from his primary job. "Computer bugs?"

"You got it. I fix computers in people's homes."

"Can you get into the computers of people who've forgotten their passwords?"

"I'm not a hacker, but I know a few. The key is to get users to stop panicking. Once they relax, the password comes to them or they remember where they wrote it down. Why are you asking? You have a computer you can't get into?"

"Not anymore." Would the burglar who'd taken Suzette's computer try to crack her password or simply destroy the computer?

The curtain at the entrance to the CAT Corner rustled. Gillian came in, with a small briefcase in one hand and a large tote bag in the other. The necks of wine bottles stuck out from the top of the bag. "I hoped to get here earlier and give you a hand, Val, but traffic on Route 50 was awful."

She wore a straight denim skirt and a brown corduroy jacket. As she walked, the wine bottles clinked against each other inside her tote.

Casper put down his cider mug. "You need any help with that bag?"

"Thank you. Set it down near the wineglasses." She handed him the bag and put her briefcase on the chair at one end of the large table. Then she joined him at the wine

198

table. "I'm glad you decided to come after all. It's better to grieve with other people than alone. We can give each other comfort."

And maybe, by the time the meeting was over, Gillian would have the comfort of knowing that her suspicions were unfounded and that none of the people she mentored had a reason to harm Suzette.

Gillian unpacked two bottles of red wine and two of white. If the Fictionistas drank all that wine, Val might have to chauffeur them home.

Casper brought Val one of the bottles. "Gillian cooled the white wine, but she'd like you to put this bottle in the fridge until we're ready for it." He picked up the mug he'd left on the counter. "I'll have some wine later, but first I'll finish the cider. It's very good."

He stood at the counter watching Val put goat cheese, dried cranberries, and nuts on the sweet potato rounds she'd roasted. Would this appetizer be too exotic for a man ambivalent about drinking warm spiced cider?

Wilson strutted into the room in a leather bomber jacket. "Ruth said to tell you she's running late. When I left the house, she was putting on heavy makeup. The heavy jewelry comes next." He deposited his jacket on an empty table near the bookcase and headed for the wine. "But we don't have to wait for her before we start drowning our sorrows."

He studied the labels on the wine bottles and poured red wine to the rim of a glass. "Good evening, *ladies.*" He raised his glass to Gillian at the wine table and Val behind the counter. Then he glared at Casper and downed some wine.

Casper took a step toward him, and Gillian blocked his path, positioning herself between the two men, one elegant in preppy clothes and the other clad in his laundry disasters. They'd baited each other on Saturday, but their animosity seemed greater tonight, and wine might increase their hostility.

As Ruth burst into the room, her perfume vanquished the aroma of spiced apple cider. "My dears, we must be brave. Suzette would want us to soldier on." Unaware of or ignoring the tension in the room, she unwound the black pashmina shawl that covered her shoulders and her frosted curls. Her gold bracelets clanked as she waved her arms around, exclaiming on the room's coziness and the table's charming centerpiece.

Dressed as Lady Macbeth for the costume contest, she'd spoken her lines like an

American trying to sound British. This evening she talked like a local. The accent puzzled Val. Why had she expected a Southern drawl? Then it dawned on her — she'd seen Ruth in the Treadwell Players' production of *The Glass Mendacity,* playing Big Momma in the Tennessee Williams spoof. Ruth had worn something flowered and frumpy for that play. A handsome woman in her fifties, she looked elegant in a royal blue pants outfit and a splashy silk scarf. Though the oldest member of the writing group, she was the fashionista of the Fictionistas. Her dramatic entrance was cut short by Morgan's arrival.

Though at least two decades younger than Ruth, Morgan looked much less glamorous in a long black broomstick skirt. Val wouldn't consider wearing a voluminous crinkled skirt like that, which would add bulk to her curves. What's more, the material needed special treatment. After washing it, you had to twist it around a broomstick handle to maintain the crinkles while it dried — the opposite of ironing, but no more appealing. Both the skirt and the scoop-neck black top Morgan wore had stray white hairs on them from a pet. Her straight dirty-blond hair had probably been red before its color faded. The black outfit didn't flatter Morgan's pale freckled face.

Halfway across the room, she stopped dead. She pointed at the table. "Why are there six chairs?" Her eyes lit up. "Was it mistaken identity? Is Suzette alive?"

CHAPTER 14

A tense and embarrassed silence followed Morgan's exclamation. Who would set her straight about Suzette? Not Val. She'd leave that task to someone who knew Morgan better.

Ruth took charge. "Suzette will always be alive in our hearts." She put her hand over her heart as if saying the Pledge of Allegiance.

Val gave Ruth an A for effort and a D for results as Morgan's eyes filled with tears.

Gillian put her arm around Morgan's shoulders. "The extra chair is for Val. I thought she should join us at the table because our dinner is in honor of Suzette, and they were housemates."

Morgan wiped her eyes. "Sorry. I can't get used to the idea that she's gone."

Val sympathized. She'd had a similar reaction, asking the chief if he was certain of the victim's identity.

"Come and sit down." Ruth took Morgan by the elbow, steered her toward a chair on the side of the table, and took the seat at the end next to her.

Val went over to the table. "How about something to drink, Morgan? Warm cider, wine, or tea?"

Morgan took a moment to decide. "I'll have tea later. Cider for now, please."

As Val delivered the cider, Wilson brought wine bottles to the table, poured wine for his aunt, and sat down across from Morgan.

Casper sat in the chair next to her. Val wondered if those two might become closer with the lovely Suzette out of the picture.

Gillian moved the appetizers to the table, sat down at the other end from Ruth, and took a sheaf of papers from her briefcase. "Let's start the meeting. Val will join us when the rest of the meal is ready. Later in the meeting, we'll talk about Suzette and her writing." Gillian leafed through the pages in front of her and handed a clipped set to Casper on her right. "You're up first, Casper. Please read the last three pages of your chapter aloud."

He read in a low monotone as the others at the table passed the appetizers around. Meanwhile, Val assembled the finger sandwiches, cut each into four triangles, and kept an eye on the mini quiches heating in the countertop oven. Though Val tuned out most of what Casper read and the discussion that followed, she grasped the gist of the story. His main character, a mild-mannered techie, morphed into a man of action when the woman who worked in the cubicle next to his disappeared. Val could predict the ending from the setup. Casper had created the character he wanted to be, a man who'd risk his life to rescue a beautiful colleague and win her heart. The cliché worked in Hollywood. Why shouldn't it work for Casper?

Gillian asked for comments on his chapter. Ruth made positive comments about the plot and advised Casper to give the woman who disappeared more traits than beauty. Morgan said his protagonist needed to transform sooner from dweeb to hero. Wilson suggested Casper start from scratch with a less boring character.

The Fictionistas certainly didn't mince words. Val glanced at Casper. Judging by his pinched face, he wasn't pleased, but he said nothing. Stoic silence must be the norm in the group.

Gillian then gave pointers on how to add depth to fictional characters and called on

Morgan to read next. With the dinner platters now on the table, Val sat in the empty chair between Gillian and Wilson.

Morgan began reading her excerpt. It boiled down to thirtyish females sipping tea and plotting vengeance on a man who'd harassed a woman and abused a dog. Despite all the talk, the scene ended without a workable plan.

Casper proposed a convoluted scheme for the women to exact vigilante justice. Morgan took notes. Then Gillian suggested ways for Morgan to improve the interactions between the characters. Ruth commended Morgan for subtle yet emotionally charged dialogue and advised a change of setting, any place other than a tea table. Wilson agreed that more action would increase reader interest.

The Fictionistas were less hard on her than on Casper. Morgan thanked them for their help and left the table to refill her mug with cider.

Wilson leaned toward Val and whispered, "The last time we asked Morgan for more action, she wrote a scene in which the teapot tipped over."

Val hid her smile by biting into an apple-and-brie mini quiche. Laughing at his snarky comments wouldn't win her friends at the table. She passed the quiche platter to Morgan when she returned to the table.

Ruth read her piece next. She was writing a historical saga, a Romeo-and-Juliet retread set in Gilded Age Newport. The old money Vandersnoots and the nouveau riche Wilkersons, with neighboring mansions in Newport, snubbed each other in public. Meanwhile, the Vandersnoot son and the Wilkerson daughter *canoodled,* as Ruth put it, in the bushes between the properties. In the scene Ruth read, the families were apparently using dueling décors as weapons in their feud. She described the furniture, mirrors, and paintings in the Vandersnoots' salon in excruciating detail.

Gillian interrupted her as the scene switched to the Wilkersons' home décor. "Any comments on Ruth's scene?"

Morgan spoke up immediately. "Nice details about the stuff in the house, Ruth, but get rid of the Tiffany lamps. Your book is set in the 1880s, and Tiffany didn't make those lamps until the 1890s."

Wilson turned to Val and muttered, "The walking Wikipedia strikes again."

Morgan leaned across the table. "I missed what you said, Wilson. Would you repeat it, please?"

He cleared his throat. "I said you were a

fact-checker by trade and talent. No error, however small, escapes you."

She smiled, apparently assuming he was praising her.

"You have a job as a fact-checker, Morgan?" Val said. "Nice to know someone pays money for facts. Where do you work?"

"Where? I work at home, telecommuting, most of the time. If you meant *for whom do I work,* I have contracts with trade magazines and a couple of e-zines."

Pedantic and annoying, Morgan reminded Val of someone she'd recently met, but who? It came to her in a flash. She'd met the fact-checker's clone, not in person, but on a page. The governess in Suzette's book had the same traits and mannerisms as Morgan. Did she recognize herself as the model for the governess?

Morgan turned to Ruth. "You have another historical anomaly in your chapter."

As she explained the problem, Ruth stared steely-eyed at her, reminding Val of another character in Suzette's book, the business-man's wife whose fierce looks reduced those around her to cowering. Come to think of it, the matriarch in the book used broad gestures like Ruth's. Had Suzette modeled all her characters on the Fictionistas?

Val stole a glance at Wilson in the seat next

to hers. He could have been the inspiration for the rogue son in her story. And the chauffeur, socially inept but mechanically brilliant, had traces of Casper in him.

When Morgan finished nitpicking, Gillian praised Ruth's vivid descriptions, but prodded her to focus more on character and less on setting. Casper seconded that.

Wilson found no fault in his aunt's writing. Understandable, given that she provided the roof over his head. His chapter would have been the next under discussion if he'd written one.

He fingered the edge of the table, his eyes downcast. "I'm giving up on my legal thriller. Too many scenes in offices and courts. Not enough action. Instead, I'm working on a spy thriller. I need to hammer down the plot before I begin the first chapter." He looked up. "Anybody else ready for dessert? I sure am."

Val cleared the table with help from Casper, made coffee, and boiled water for tea. Morgan reached into her large tapestry bag. She took out a tea ball and a baggie of leaf tea. She flipped the ball open and filled it with tea leaves.

Val said, "What kind of tea are you brewing?"

"Black tea, the brand that's made from

the two tender top leaves of the plant. Those leaves give you a superior tea."

Val resigned herself to drinking an inferior brew, made from a teabag filled with who-knew-which leaves of the plant. She set the madeleines and chocolate chunk cookies on the table.

When they were all seated, Gillian raised her mug of steaming coffee. "A toast to Suzette. We all wish you were here with us."

Did they? Val lifted her mug. Morgan lifted hers higher. The others raised their wine-glasses.

Gillian sipped her coffee. "I'm going to read the last few pages of Suzette's chapter aloud. Then we'll talk about her plot."

Casper frowned. "Why would we do that? She can't benefit from our comments."

Morgan sighed. "Suzette's book will never be finished." With her downturned mouth and round face, she resembled a sad smiley. "What's the point?"

Gillian took the last set of papers from her folder. "We all learn something from reading and discussing what others have written, even works in progress."

"I have a confession to make," Ruth said. "I always read everyone's chapter the after-noon before we meet, so it's fresh in my mind. I didn't read Suzette's pages today, knowing she wouldn't attend."

Wilson nodded. "Same here. We should share our memories of Suzette. That would have more meaning than talking about what she wrote."

Gillian folded her arms. "We'll have plenty of time to talk about our memories after we discuss Suzette's writing. Since half of you haven't read the chapter, would someone who *has* read it please give us a summary?"

"I can't do that," Casper said. "I read it when Suzette sent it, almost a week ago. The details are fuzzy."

Morgan rolled her eyes. "That's why you should take notes. I always do." She flipped back the pages of the legal pad in front of her. "Here it is. Most of the chapter is what the teenage niece overhears while hiding behind curtains and listening at keyholes upstairs and downstairs. The conversations are about the liaison between the business-man's son and a pert maid. His mother demands he break it off or he'll be disinherited. The governess who hoped to marry him rants about the maid. The chauffeur jilted by the maid bottles up his rage and spies on her." Morgan looked up from her notes. "That's the essence of it."

Gillian then read the last few pages of Suzette's chapter, starting with the discovery of the maid's body at the side of the road and ending with the businessman's family awaiting the arrival of the police and speculating on what had happened to the maid. The family pondered why she'd gone out of the house at night, whether she'd lost her footing or a car had run into her, causing her to fall and hit her head on a rock. The nosy niece suggested someone had bashed the maid or deliberately run her over.

Val wondered who would bring up the similarity between the victim's death in the story and Suzette's. Then she remembered that the police had not revealed that Suzette had suffered a head injury. Val had told Gillian, not realizing the police would keep that detail under wraps, but the others might not know that detail.

Gillian read the final sentence of Suzette's chapter, announcing the arrival of the police. She then took off her reading glasses. "We know Suzette was writing a murder mystery, so the maid's death will turn out to be murder. Let's try to figure out where she was going with this plot and brainstorm about how to wrap it up."

Morgan's pale blue eyes brightened. "We could vote on the best solution. Then we can finish her book, each of us writing a few chapters. We'll publish it as a tribute to her."

No one at the table rushed to second her proposal.

Ruth frowned. "You realize that Suzette wrote about a young woman who might have been hit by a car and then the same thing happened to her. What an amazing coincidence!"

Morgan piped up. "It's not a huge coincidence. Motor vehicle fatalities are a leading cause of death in young people, right behind drug overdoses. Also we don't know that the maid in the story was hit by a car. The way it's set up, it sounds more like she was bashed."

Casper had sat silent for the last few minutes, shifting his gaze from one member of the group to another. Now it rested unblinkingly on Wilson.

Val glanced at Gillian. They might not be the only ones at the table who suspected Suzette's death wasn't an accident. Gillian had hinted that a member of this group might have killed Suzette. Each of them had a counterpart in Suzette's story, a murder suspect with a motive to kill a young woman.

How would a murderer react when asked to solve a fictional crime similar to the one

213

he or she had committed?

Gillian pointed at the bottles of wine on the counter. "We have more wine, so fill your glasses and we'll get started. Who killed the maid, how, and why?"

CHAPTER 15

Val passed on the wine, but no one else in the writing group did. Would the alcohol dull their minds, release their inhibitions, or both?

"I know who the murderer will turn out to be," Ruth said with authority. "The businessman's wife. She disapproved of her son's entanglement with the maid. He must have told her he intended to marry the maid, who'd make a thoroughly unsuitable wife."

Val tried to hide her surprise. Ruth had named as a culprit the character she most resembled. Possibly, she'd looked down on Suzette for her lowly job at a hotel and viewed her as an unsuitable mate for aspiring lawyer Wilson. Based on what Gillian had said, he was more enamored of Suzette than she was of him, so Ruth had little to fear. She also struck Val as clever enough to achieve her goals without violence. Finally, if Ruth were guilty, she'd have made a case against a fictional character with a different motive than the one she herself had for getting rid of a young woman.

"But does the crime fit the character, Ruth?" Gillian said. "A pampered middle-aged woman sneaks out of her palatial home to beat up a maid."

"She could have run her over, not beaten her up," Ruth said. "But you make a good point. The businessman's wife would have paid someone to take care of the problem." Ruth looked at her tablemates as intently as if they were in a lineup. Then she rested her chin on her fist, elbow on the table, and stared at Morgan. "The governess had no such resources. The man she intended to snag fell for a more lovely and lively woman. His preference for an uneducated maid grated on the governess. She decided to clear the field of her rival rather than lose her only hope of marrying up."

Morgan removed her glasses, reached down into her handbag for a small cloth, and cleaned the lenses with it. Val watched her and thought about the parallel between the scorned woman's situation in the novel and Morgan's. According to Gillian, Casper had shown an interest in Morgan and then switched to Suzette. Wilson probably hadn't

216

even glanced at Morgan after seeing Suzette. As long as the beauty was around, Morgan couldn't compete. But were either of those men worth murdering for?

Morgan put her glasses back on. "In the Victorian era, governesses had few opportunities to advance. That's why they were obsessed with marrying. But this book is set in the 1920s. A governess could find other employment then, as a teacher or a secretary. She could get along on her own."

Gillian took a madeleine from the dessert plate. "A working woman at that time might earn enough to pay for a roof over her head, but not much more. She'd live in a dingy rooming house instead of in the comfort of a millionaire's mansion."

Morgan shrugged. "Possibly true, but there's another reason to reject both the wife and the governess as the killer. At the risk of sounding sexist, I have to say that attacking someone on a road at night is not a woman's crime. Arsenic in the tea is. Gastric distress followed by death."

Val shuddered, remembering the arsenic killer she'd encountered last year. To poison someone, you needed access to the victim's food or drink, whether at the table or in the kitchen. "How would the millionaire's wife or the governess get anywhere near the maid's tea?"

Morgan rolled her eyes. "The maid wasn't poisoned, so I don't have to work out the details. I was merely explaining why you can eliminate half of the suspects. But as long as you asked, here's a scenario that would work. The killer sneaks into the maid's quarters and leaves a heart-shaped bonbon sprinkled with powdered sugar on her night table. She assumes the man she loves has left it there, eats the chocolate and the white powder, arsenic, and is found dead the next morning."

Val couldn't resist pointing out a flaw in Morgan's plot idea. "Then the police would know that the killer is in the house. With a murder outdoors, they are more likely to chalk it up as an accident and blame a stranger." Just as Chief Yardley was predisposed to view the hit-and-run that killed Suzette as unintentional. Val reminded herself that he could be right. She noticed Morgan staring stonily at her, possibly viewing her as an outsider with no right to take part in the discussion.

Gillian folded her hands. "We've heard from the women at the table. Do the men have any idea who Suzette's murderer is?" Everyone at the table froze in shock. Gillian hastily added, "I mean, who murdered the maid in Suzette's book?"

Val doubted that was a slip of the tongue. Gillian had planted the idea that Suzette's death wasn't accidental.

"I know who the culprit is." Wilson trained a laser look on Casper. "The chauffeur. The maid tossed him over. She never cared for him, only felt sorry for him. He spied on her. His resentment festered. If he couldn't have her, then no one could." Wilson downed the wine in his glass.

While he was talking, Val watched Casper transform before her eyes. His body stiffened, his pale face turned pink, and his hands fisted.

"No way," he snarled. "The pampered son did it. The maid was infatuated with him until the housekeeper told her what happened to another maid he'd seduced. Forced to leave without a reference, she couldn't find a job and took to the streets." Casper raised his chin and looked defiantly at Wilson. "The clever maid heeded the warning. She told the creep to leave her alone. He thought he was entitled to anything he wanted and killed her in a rage."

"Why would he?" Wilson sneered. "He had his pick of women. The chauffeur couldn't attract anyone. He went after the maid like a coward, crept up behind her, and beat her head to a pulp." Wilson grabbed his empty wineglass and for a second Val thought he'd hurl it at Casper. No way he could get that worked up over the plot in the book.

Wilson put the glass down, stood up, and walked around the table. "No, that's not the way it went down." He lunged at Casper, grabbed him by the collar, and pulled him from the chair. "You watched Suzette's every move. You waited for the right moment. And then you drove your car into her."

The gangly Casper tried to push the more muscular man away, but Wilson didn't budge. Morgan cringed in her seat. Gillian froze.

Eye to eye with Casper, Wilson bellowed, "Admit it! You killed Suzette!"

"No!" Casper croaked.

Ruth stood up. "It was an accident, Wilson. Let him go!"

Casper punched Wilson in the stomach. For all the effect it had, his fist might have been a cream puff. But the other man's fist could do serious injury.

Someone had to stop him. Val jumped up, took an empty wine bottle from the table, and zoomed around the table. "Get away from him, Wilson, or I'll call the police."

Wilson ignored her. She grasped the bottle by the neck and brandished her weapon where he could see it. "I'll conk you if you don't let go of him."

Ruth came up next to her nephew. "Don't hit him." She grabbed Wilson by the shoulders and tried to pull him away from Casper.

Val pulled too.

"Stop it!" Bram crossed the CAT Corner in two strides. He shouldered himself between the two men, and pushed them apart.

Wilson backed off. He raised his hands as if someone held a gun on him. "Sorry. I lost my head."

Casper collapsed into his chair, sucking in air.

Gillian, better late than never, hovered over him. "Are you okay?" He rubbed his throat and nodded, never taking his eyes off Wilson, the hulk standing near the counter.

Bram watched the two men, his arms folded.

Val motioned him to the side, out of earshot of those at the table and counter. "Thank you. Please don't throw any of us out. We're almost finished."

"What were those guys doing? Did they act out a scene from a book and go too far?"

"Sort of."

Ruth returned to her chair. "Wilson!" She pointed to the empty chair next to her. "Here! Sit!"

Wilson followed orders.

Bram whispered to Val, "She raises dogs?"

Val coughed to hide a laugh. "I hope that pooch stays put." She wouldn't trust Wilson to behave unless Bram stayed. "Do you mind sticking around?"

"I won't leave until Wilson does. Can you get your grandfather to take my place in the shop? He came in ten minutes ago and offered to help."

"Okay." Val left the room, found Granddad near the shop's checkout counter, and asked him to take over for Bram.

She went back to the Fictionistas' table and sat down. Bram was rearranging the books on the shelves in CAT Corner — or pretending to.

"You've had quite enough wine for tonight, Wilson." Ruth confiscated Wilson's glass. "You confused the plot of Suzette's book with what happened to her. The hit-and-run was an accident, wasn't it?"

Val interpreted the pointed look Gillian was giving her as a cue to answer the question. No reason to mention the chief's opinion that it was an accident. "The police are investigating it and are awaiting the

222

results of the autopsy."

No one moved or spoke for a moment.

Gillian broke the silence. "We planned to talk about Suzette tonight, not just her book. Wilson opened the door and raised an issue I imagine we're all thinking about. What happened to her? You all saw her here Saturday night for the costume contest. Did anyone see her after she left the bookshop that night?"

Bram's head whipped around at this question. He'd abandoned the pretense of book shuffling.

Casper spoke up. "I saw Suzette. She was with *him*." He pointed at Wilson. "I don't think she planned to meet him. He was lurking around the corner. When she went by, he stood in her way and demanded to talk to her."

"I wasn't lurking and I didn't demand." Wilson banged his fist on the table. "I asked if she could spare a few minutes. Where were you, Casper the Spy? Hiding behind a bush or up a tree?"

Casper ignored him. "I wasn't close enough to hear everything they said, but I saw him grab her arm when she turned to go. Then Suzette raised her voice, and I heard her clearly. She said, *I won't live with you, I won't marry you, and I won't talk about this again. Just leave me alone."*

Ruth clamped her hand on her nephew's arm as he started to get out of his chair. "You made that all up, Casper," she said. "Wilson wouldn't have asked Suzette to marry him. But if he did, she wouldn't have turned him down."

Wilson sneered at Casper. "Suzette must have said those things to you after you dogged her. She didn't say them to me."

"I wasn't dogging her."

Morgan cleared her throat. "Casper, I saw you following Suzette along Main Street that night, a couple of blocks from here."

Casper gulped his wine. "I did that to make sure Wilson didn't bother her again, but I lost her in the crowd. Everyone was milling around in Halloween costumes." He gulped more wine. "I never got a chance to speak with her."

Ruth frowned. "Why does it matter what Suzette did on Saturday night? Didn't she go home that night? Wasn't the accident the next morning?"

Val felt six pairs of eyes on her, including Bram's. "The costume Suzette wore Saturday night was in her room, so I assume she spent the night at our house. She usually jogged early in the morning. She was jogging when she was hit by the car."

"I just remembered something," Morgan said. "When I drove Suzette to Bayport after our meeting last week, she kept turning round to check the rear window. She'd noticed a black car following her now and then. I thought she was paranoid, but after what happened to her . . . well, maybe she wasn't." Morgan turned to Casper. "You drive a black sedan, don't you?"

His pale face turned dark pink in an instant. "What's that supposed to mean? Lots of people drive black cars. I don't believe Suzette said anything about someone following her. You're lying."

Val was tempted to defend Morgan against this accusation. Suzette's routes home through backyards suggested she'd tried to shake someone following her in a car. On the other hand, Casper was right about the popularity of black cars. Val glanced at Wilson and wondered what color his car was.

Morgan held out her hands, palms up. "Why would I lie?"

"Maybe because you ran her over." Casper stared at her with narrowed eyes. "You were always jealous of Suzette. She was beautiful, and you aren't. She was a talented writer, and you aren't. You killed her, and you're trying to pin it on me."

So much for Val's idea that he and Morgan would get together. Suzette still stood between them.

Morgan's lower lip trembled. "All I said was you drive a black car, which is true. Now you're accusing me of lying and killing?"

"Stop squabbling," Ruth said. "It's terrible what happened to Suzette. She was one of us. We should be supporting each other instead of fighting." She turned to Val. "You seem to know more than we do about what happened to her. Was she in terrible pain? Did she suffer?"

Val could offer some comfort on that point. "I believe she died when she hit the ground."

"That's a blessing," Ruth said.

Morgan burst into tears. Her shoulders heaved as she sobbed uncontrollably.

"Maybe this meeting wasn't such a good idea," Gillian muttered. She went over to Morgan and tried to comfort her.

Val left the CAT Corner to give Grand-dad a mission. She found him shelving books near the rear of the shop. "Wilson, the guy who dressed like a zombie Saturday night, is wearing a bomber jacket tonight. When our meeting breaks up and he leaves the shop, can you follow him to his car? I want to know what color it is." Casper might not be the only one here tonight who drove a black car.

"Sure, but I'm not up for a long night of surveillance. If he goes barhopping, I'm peeling off."

"Let's hope he doesn't. If he has any more to drink, he'll be a hazard on the road." Val would push coffee on him and make the wine disappear even if she had to pour it down the drain.

CHAPTER 16

When Val returned to the CAT Corner, she saw that someone had put the wine out of sight. Morgan was red-eyed but calm. As Casper filled his mug with the last of the cider, Val put black coffee in front of Bram.

She joined the group at the table. Gillian suggested they talk about what made Suzette memorable to them. The responses were what you might hear at any similar gathering — nothing ill spoken of the dead. Suzette was hardworking, talented, and considerate. Any hint of unfairness or injustice bothered her. She was dogged in pursuing her dream of being a writer.

No one said she was fun to be with or had a terrific sense of humor. Val hadn't seen that side of Suzette's character either, maybe because that side didn't exist. Had she been serious by nature or had a troubled life made her somber?

Gillian adjourned the meeting and reminded the Fictionistas that she would host their final get-together at her house. Val wondered if any of them would attend.

Casper hurried out of the CAT Corner. Wilson left with his aunt holding on to his arm, and Bram followed them from the room. Morgan asked for Val's business card and drifted out. Only Gillian remained behind.

"I'll help you clean up." She collected the mugs from the table. "I thought that a discussion of Suzette's story might bring out strong feelings, but I underestimated the depth of those feelings."

"They were dealing with grief." Val washed the dishes she'd piled into the sink earlier. "If people hold back their tears, their grief can erupt as rage. I found that out when my grandmother died. My brother was angry at himself for not visiting her more often, at fate for snatching her away, and at whoever went near him. At least he didn't start a brawl like Wilson did."

"Suzette was a flash point for jealousy and rivalry before tonight. I'd hoped to convince myself that no one in our group had anything to do with what happened to her, and I wanted your take on that. Did you learn anything tonight that sheds light on Suzette's death?"

"I confirmed what I'd suspected — that Suzette was afraid of someone who was following her."

"Yes, following her in a black car. Casper's car is black, and he admitted he was stalking her on foot."

Val wouldn't have used that word to describe Casper's actions. "Stalking implies a threat. He saw himself as watching over her, making sure Wilson didn't accost her again."

"Even if that's true, protection has a dark side — hemming in the person you're protecting and infringing on her freedom to keep her from harm. The Phantom of the Opera protected the beautiful soprano and then, when he realized he couldn't possess her, he turned violent." Gillian put the mugs on the counter near the sink. "We only have Casper's word for it that Suzette told Wilson to leave her alone. Wilson denied it."

"Of course he did." His denial hadn't convinced Val. "A good-looking man who's had no trouble attracting females would be embarrassed to admit a woman spurned him. Not just embarrassed but angry, possibly enraged enough to harm Suzette. That's what Casper feared and why he felt he should keep an eye on her."

Gillian went back to the table, looking

distracted as she collected the napkins slowly.

Val spotted Granddad motioning to her from the curtain that separated the CAT Corner from the shop. "Excuse me a second, Gillian."

Val pushed the curtain aside and joined Granddad at the back of the selling floor. "Did you see what kind of car Wilson has?"

"A green BMW."

"What shade of green? Lime? Avocado?"

"Darker than that. I'd call it evergreen."

A color that might be mistaken for black, especially at night. "Was his aunt with him?"

Granddad nodded. "She stopped him from getting into his car with a warning about driving under the influence. He could be arrested, she said. He could crash his car and injure or kill someone. His life would be ruined, and her departed husband would never forgive her. She gave Wilson a choice — ride home in her car or walk with her until the alcohol got out of his system. Last I saw of 'em, they were strolling down Main Street, and she had a vise grip on his arm."

"Good for her. But how on earth did you hear all that?"

"While they were standing near his car, I browsed in the antique shop window with my back to them. They never even noticed me." Granddad tapped his ear. "I turned up the volume on my hearing aid. Luckily, there wasn't much street noise, so I caught most of what they said."

Next best thing to planting a bug on someone. "Thanks, Granddad. You get tonight's eavesdropping prize." She gave him a kiss on the cheek.

"When we get home, you'll tell me why the car color matters."

"I will. See you later."

She pulled the curtain aside to return to the CAT Corner. Isis crept behind her and paused at the threshold. She usually slipped in and out without a delay. Maybe she was picking up negative vibes from the meeting that had just taken place there. Val held the curtain open until the cat ventured into the room.

Gillian stood motionless near the table, staring into space. "I sense someone here tonight was involved in Suzette's death."

Was Gillian's sixth sense beaming messages to her?

Isis darted across the room to the back door and meowed. Val opened the door. The cat inched forward, front paws out, back paws lagging behind.

"Five seconds, Isis." Val counted down. The cat took all her allotted time and then dashed toward the cemetery. Gillian still hadn't budged. Time to bring her back to earth.

Val picked up two corners of the tablecloth. "Would you help me fold this?"

Gillian snapped out of her trance and grasped the other end of the tablecloth. "When I think about who'd have wanted to harm Suzette, Casper comes to mind first. He was fuming after our meeting a month ago when Suzette turned down a ride from him and went with Wilson." She and Val folded the cloth lengthwise. "Casper shadowed her the night before she died and might have followed her in his car before then. Do you think we should tell the police?"

Count me out. Val remembered how the chief had criticized her when she reached conclusions based on flimsy evidence. Gillian had no evidence at all, only guesses about Casper's motives and actions. "Why point a finger at Casper? Wilson behaved worse and even got violent tonight. He changed the subject from the culprit in Suzette's book to the culprit in the hit-and-run. He accused and attacked Casper. And, by the way, Wilson drives a dark car. Not that I'm saying he had anything to do with Suzette's death."

"He doesn't seem the type to obsess about a woman and follow her."

According to studies Val had read, people viewed attractive individuals as more trustworthy than unattractive ones. Gillian was no exception, giving the dishy dude the benefit of the doubt. Val had a different prejudice to overcome. Thanks to her handsome former fiancé, the cheating Tony, she had a bias *against* drop-dead gorgeous men like Wilson.

She hung the folded tablecloth over the back of a chair. "I can't reach any conclusions based on what I saw and heard here. Everyone was on edge tonight. If you give me their phone numbers, I'll contrive a reason to speak to them, one on one." And Granddad could do some research on them.

"Thank you. I'll e-mail you their contact information."

"Ruth and Morgan took my business card. They wanted to talk to me about catering. Following up with them is a good excuse to call. And if I meet Ruth at her house, Wilson might be there." Val remembered how Ruth had kept her nephew in check this evening with her canine commands. "Ruth seems to hold him on a tight leash."

"The hand that holds the leash controls the money. I got the full story when I helped her clean up after the meeting at her house." Gillian dried the mugs as Val finished washing them. "Ruth married a rich older man. They were both widowed with no children. He died three years ago. His younger brother, Wilson's father, had already passed away. Her husband's trust made her the beneficiary with Wilson inheriting after her death. She promised her husband she'd keep his nephew out of trouble."

The terms of the trust gave Wilson a reason to hasten his aunt's death, but did anyone have a reason to get rid of Suzette? "Ruth implied that Morgan was jealous of Suzette. Do you agree?"

"Not jealous, but maybe slightly envious. You saw how Morgan cried tonight. That was real grief." Gillian lined up the clean mugs. "Morgan's the last person I can imagine committing a crime. She doesn't break rules, much less laws. She holds herself and others to high standards."

"I noticed that when she nitpicked Ruth's writing." Finished with the cleanup, Val turned off the faucet. "I'm not sure how to get Casper to talk to me. I guess I can invite him for a drink."

"Meet him in a public place, and don't act as if you have a romantic interest in him." Gillian snapped her fingers. "I've got it. Tell him I mentioned his interest in cryptozoology, and you want to know more about that."

"Give me a hint what that is."

"The study of creatures like Bigfoot, the Yeti, and the Loch Ness Monster." Gillian rolled her eyes. "It's a pseudoscience."

Unlike the real science of her extrasensory perceptions? Val wiped down the counter. "Over the last few days, I've learned that Suzette's life was complicated before she moved here. Some people she used to know had more reason to harm her than any of the Fictionistas did."

"I hope you're right." Gillian picked up her briefcase. "Call me in a couple of days and let me know what you find out. I'll hold off on talking to the police until I hear from you." She left the CAT Corner.

As Val was packing the dishware in a box, she noticed Isis sitting on the sill outside the window and staring at her. She let the cat in and went back to packing. Isis brushed against Val's legs, making figure eights. "Sorry, I don't have a lap for you to curl up in, Isis."

Five minutes later, with the box, the cooler, and a shopping bag filled up, Val put on her jacket.

Bram poked his head in the doorway.

"Need a hand getting that stuff to the car?"

"Thanks, but my grandfather can help if he's still in the shop."

"He already left. You're stuck with me."

He slung the shopping bag over his arm, hefted the box of china, and followed her out the door to the side street where she'd parked.

She'd just opened the trunk when she spotted Wilson and his aunt across the street. He was helping Ruth into the driver's seat of a white SUV. He closed the car door behind her, waved as she pulled out, and headed toward Main Street. She must have cleared him for takeoff. This was Val's chance to talk to him, if she could catch him.

Val stashed the cooler in the trunk. "I need to talk to someone. Just close the trunk when you've put the other things inside. Thanks for your help."

She hurried across the street and called out to Wilson. Apparently not hearing her, he turned the corner onto Main Street, walking in the opposite direction from the bookshop. She sprinted after him and caught him when he reached for the handle on a green BMW.

"Hey, Wilson. How are you doing?"

"I've been better." He ran his hand

through his blond curls. "I'm sorry about what happened. I don't usually act like that."

"Understandable. You were broken up about Suzette. Losing her after you asked her to marry you is tough." Would he deny it and claim that Casper had lied?

"That's not exactly what I said. I wanted a serious relationship with her, not a hookup, so I suggested we move in together and try things out. I told her I wasn't in a position to settle down now. Once I was established at a law firm, if we were still getting along well, then we could marry."

Val had heard almost the same thing from her ex-fiancé, and she'd fallen for it. Suzette had either been smarter or cared less for Wilson than Val had for Tony. "So Casper was telling the truth about what he overheard Suzette say to you."

Wilson nodded. "He must have thought he'd have a chance with her after that. And when she rejected him, he went nuts."

Pure conjecture. "He wasn't the one who went nuts tonight."

Wilson looked down. "Okay, I shouldn't have grabbed him. But what I did doesn't make that turd innocent." Wilson climbed into his car and drove off with a screech of tires.

Granddad was snoozing in his lounger when Val arrived home. As she tiptoed across the sitting room, he woke up. "What was the ruckus in the CAT Corner?"

She plopped on the sofa. "It's a long story. To understand it, you need to know that Suzette modeled the characters in her book on the people in that room."

Val described the group's discussion of Suzette's story and of her death.

When she finished, Granddad said, "Let me see if I have this straight. Wilson and Casper accused each other of killing Suzette. Morgan said that Suzette noticed a black car following her and that Casper had a black car. That caused him to accuse her of killing Suzette out of jealousy."

"Exactly. And now you know why I asked you to check the color of Wilson's car."

He nodded. "It's as black as green can be."

"The evening ended with Gillian building a case against Casper. I convinced her that researching him, Morgan, and Wilson should be the next step. Are you willing to spend some time online digging up information about them?"

Granddad took off his glasses. "I can do that, but aren't you forgetting someone?"

"Ruth McWilliams? I suppose you could look her up, though she's a long shot."

"Gillian isn't a long shot. She egged the other folks on so they'd talk about Suzette's death and blame each other for it."

Val rarely agreed with him about who'd committed crimes they'd encountered in the past. This time she couldn't dismiss his theory out of hand. Gillian had set up the meeting so that the Fictionistas' suspicions of each other would come to light. If she had killed Suzette, she'd want to set up someone else as the culprit. But what motive could she have had to harm Suzette?

CHAPTER 17

Val sat forward on the sofa in the study. "Good idea, Granddad, to look into Gillian's background. But why would she have run down Suzette?"

Granddad rubbed his glasses with the bottom of his flannel shirt. "Don't know . . . yet. Why do you think she asked you to be at that meeting?"

Val thought about her first phone conversation with Gillian. "She'd researched me before returning my call. She knew I'd previously looked into a few suspicious deaths. When I told her about the hit-and-run, she said nothing about anyone wanting to harm Suzette. Then I mentioned talking to the police chief about it and hinted it might not have been an accident. Only then did she say she had misgivings too."

"She mighta thought you had pull with the police. In case they decided it wasn't an accident, she needed a fall guy — Casper."

"And she didn't intervene when Wilson attacked him." What Gillian had said and done made sense if she were guilty of running over Suzette. But Val also saw an innocent explanation. Gillian couldn't stand by and let someone get away with a crime. Maybe injustice angered her, as it had Suzette, who'd gone after a playground bully. Did the two women have more than that in common? "When you're online, see if you can dig up any connection between Gillian and Suzette before this year."

"Okay. Her cousin might tell us something we can't find online. When is she coming?"

"Not until the end of the week. In the meantime, let's not get hung up on Gillian or any of the aspiring writers as a possible killer. We have other avenues to explore before reaching a conclusion about the culprit." Val stood up and paced the room, ticking off questions that came to mind. "Who, if anyone, was following Suzette, or was she paranoid? Who was the caped man with her at the Bugeye Tavern Saturday night? Why did the maid at the inn warn me not to ask questions about Suzette? And, finally, who burgled our house and why?"

"That reminds me. Harvey saw someone slinking around our place around seven thirty last night. He opened the window and yelled *who's there?* Then he saw someone in a hoodie run off, same as I did a few hours later after the break-in."

Based on Harvey's report, Val changed her mind about Nick as a possible burglar. "I thought the hotel manager, Nick, couldn't have been the burglar because he knew we'd be out of the house at dinner time. It made no sense for him to wait until midnight to break in. Maybe he'd planned to do it when the house was empty, but Harvey stopped him, so he came back after we were asleep."

"Is he an older man? Suzette might've been involved with him."

"She wasn't, according to the maid who was her friend. Maria said Suzette would have nothing to do with a married man like Nick." Val told Granddad what else the maid had told her. "Maria is like a ghost who appears briefly to issue a warning and then disappears. Speaking of ghosts, did you make any progress on catching the thieving ghosts?"

"I set up the video camera at Mrs. Hill's house. If burglars come calling tomorrow, we'll have them on video." Granddad winced as he stood up. "I'm stiff from sitting still too long. I'm going to hit the hay. Busy day tomorrow. Make sure you write down the full names of the people you want me to research."

"I'll put the list on the desk near the computer. What's on your schedule tomorrow?"

"I'm going to go to the Patels' house with books for their children. I'll try to find out more about the harassment against Suzette, and I'll bring up Mr. Patel. If he was involved with her, his wife's reactions will give it away, unless she's a good actress."

Val would be surprised if anything came of his visit to the Patels. "Did you have a chance to see the photos Dorothy took at the bookshop party?"

"Yup, but none of them showed a caped man talking to Suzette. After the costume contest, Dorothy was ringing up sales and had no time to take pictures. She said Bram might have taken photos. Ask him the next time you see him."

When Bram strolled into the café at eight thirty Wednesday morning, Val was busy serving breakfast, too busy to look at any photos he might have or even to ask about them.

He sat down on the only vacant stool at the eating bar. He wore a dark green T-shirt and exercise shorts. "Hey, Val."

"Hi, Bram. Coffee? Something to eat?"

"Yes to coffee. I wasn't planning on eating, but what you're cutting looks good. What is it?"

"Strata. A layered casserole made with eggs and cheese. This is a sausage strata. I also have a veggie one today."

"Give me a piece of whatever you sell less of. I don't want you to run out of your best-seller."

"What sells best varies from day to day." She cut him a square of veggie casserole. "I'll bet no customers at your mother's shop ask to buy the least popular book."

"But they go to the shop to buy a book. I didn't come here mainly to eat."

"No one comes here only to eat." She poured his coffee. "They go to the club to work out. Then they stop in here to replenish the calories they've burned while exercising."

"Exercise wasn't my only reason to come here."

Val noticed the couple sitting at the bistro table looking expectantly at her. She picked up the plates on which she'd put muffins and strata. "Excuse me. I have to deliver these breakfasts."

When she returned and went around the counter, the middle-aged man at the eating bar was ready to pay. By the time she finished with him and took orders from the two women who'd just walked in, Bram had finished his coffee.

He'd also eaten most of his strata. He put the last piece of it on his fork. "I didn't come here to eat, but maybe I should. This is really good."

Val appreciated the compliment, especially because he'd doubted her cooking skills. She took it as an apology for that. As she refilled his mug, she tried to remember the last thing he'd said, something about exercising. "Where were we?"

"I was about to tell you I came here to talk to you. I planned to do that last night, but . . ."

"But I ran off." She finished his sentence. "Sorry about that. I'm sure you'd like to know more about what happened in the CAT Corner last night. The café's pretty busy now. Can we talk later somewhere else?"

"We have incompatible schedules. You work when I'm off, and vice versa. But I've found an assistant to help my mother a few evenings a week. Can we get together for dinner around seven? You pick the place."

Val was surprised . . . and pleased. She was beginning to like him. "Okay. Let's meet at the Bugeye Tavern. It's an easy walk from the bookshop and from my house." But that wasn't the only reason she'd chosen it. She doubted Bram was the caped man the bartender had seen arguing with Suzette on Saturday night, but it wouldn't hurt to confirm that.

"Super! See you there." Bram paid and left the café.

Later, in a brief lull between breakfast and lunch, Val's phone rang. She glanced at the caller ID — Morgan Roux. The spelling of Morgan's last name surprised her. She'd assumed it was *Rue* or *Rew.*

"Hi, Val. I hope I'm not catching you when you're busy."

Hard to predict when early lunch eaters would come into the café. "I have a little time to talk now."

"I'll make this quick. I'd like to set up a meeting to discuss your catering a dinner for my book club. It'll be at my house."

"Then I should meet you at your house so I can see the kitchen."

"My place is about twenty minutes from Bayport. Can we get together tonight or tomorrow night?"

"Not tonight." Val wasn't sure how long dinner with Bram would take and didn't want to cut it short to meet Morgan. "Tomorrow won't work either. It's Halloween, and I'll be at the Bayport haunted house."

"Are you haunting or being haunted?"

"I'm selling haunting baked goods. The house and the sale are fundraisers for the high school drama club." Val remembered that Morgan worked at home. "If you're going to be around this afternoon, I can stop by your house when I get off work. Would two thirty or three work for you?"

"Perfect. I always take a break for afternoon tea. You can join me. I'm surprised you get off work that early."

"I arrive at the café before seven thirty and don't get a break until I leave. What's your address?"

Morgan asked where Val was coming from, gave her turn-by-turn directions, and finally recited her address, which was all Val had needed.

When she got off the phone, she checked her e-mail and found a message from Gillian. She provided the contact numbers of the Fictionistas, putting her favorite suspect, Casper, at the top of the list.

A vision of him as the Phantom of the Opera flashed into Val's mind. Like Bram and Nick, he'd worn a black cape Saturday night, though shorter than theirs. Parading him by the bartender at the tavern might pay off.

Val took a few minutes to look up the subject Gillian had told her would lure Casper to a rendezvous. She called him, identified herself, and said, "Gillian told me you were into cryptozoology. I've just been reading about a sea monster in the Chesapeake Bay. Do you know anything about that?"

"Of course. Chessie isn't as famous as Nessie, the Loch Ness Monster, but there have been some sightings."

"I'm making cookies for tomorrow's bake sale at the haunted house. Chessie monsters would make a nice change from ghost, skeleton, and pumpkin cookies. I want to get the right shape for Chessie. I'd appreciate your expert advice. Would you be willing to meet me for a drink at the Bugeye Tavern this evening?"

"Sure. Is that the place in Bayport that's been a tavern for a hundred and fifty years?"

"Right." He apparently didn't fear being recognized at the tavern as Suzette's companion from Saturday night. "Can you make it around five or five thirty?"

"Six will work better for me."

Not for Val. Too close to the time when Bram would show up. She only hoped Casper wouldn't give her an hour's lecture on a pseudoscience. "Okay. See you later."

At two thirty Val pulled up in front of Morgan's small one-story house with an attached single garage. The weed-and-grass ground cover in the front yard could use a mowing.

Val's phone rang as she unbuckled her seat belt.

"Are you on your way home?" Granddad said.

Val detected a note of excitement in his voice. Maybe his online research had produced results. "I'm in Treadwell to talk to Morgan. I won't be home for at least forty minutes. What's going on?"

"I started to tidy up the study. You'll never guess what turned up."

Started to? That sounded as if he hadn't gotten far. "What did you find?"

"A thumb drive. When Suzette needed a hard copy of anything, she used our printer and brought her file to the study on a thumb drive. The last time she did that, she must've left it next to the printer. I put some papers on top of it without noticing it."

"Did you look at what's on the drive?"

"I skimmed it. A lot of documents and spreadsheets. I'll bet she used the drive to back up files from her computer."

Val remembered her vain efforts to guess the computer's password. Had Suzette protected the backup files with passwords? "Did you open any of the files?"

"A spreadsheet. It went back a few years. Financial stuff."

If Suzette hadn't put a password on that kind of sensitive information, she probably hadn't put one on any other files. "Are you going to give the thumb drive to the chief?"

"Not until I know for sure that her files are important. But I don't have time to go through them all. I've got to leave for the Patel house. I arranged to bring the books to the kids at three thirty, so I'll be gone before you get home. What do you want me to do with the gizmo?"

"Copy the files to my computer. Then put the thumb drive where we keep the spare house keys. I'll take a look at her files when I get home. By the way, I'm going out for a drink and then dinner tonight."

"No problem. I'll fend for myself."

"See you later, Granddad."

Val climbed out of the car. Besides talking about catering, she had questions for Morgan about Suzette, but she hoped her hostess didn't plan to linger long over tea. Val couldn't wait to get a peek at Suzette's files.

Maybe then she'd know why someone had gone to the trouble of breaking into Granddad's house to steal Suzette's computer. Could those files have anything to do with her death?

CHAPTER 18

Val rang the doorbell of Morgan's house, holding a paper plate of oatmeal raisin cookies she'd made at the café.

Morgan opened the door. She wore a green corduroy jumper that went down to her ankles. Her orange turtleneck, a good Halloween color, was a bad color for her, too intense for her pale face. She greeted Val and pointed to the cookies. "You didn't have to bring those. I already have something to eat with our tea."

"Then save these for later. I don't like to visit empty-handed." She gave the plate to Morgan.

After going inside, Val glanced toward the living area of the front room. A Persian cat was curled up on the blue velveteen sofa decorated with white cat hair, which also clung to every other seat in the room. Val expected to carry away souvenirs on her black slacks.

Morgan gestured to the dining table. "Have a seat. I'll put the water on for tea." She went through the archway to the kitchen, taking the plate of oatmeal cookies with her.

The wood dining table was set for two, with cups, saucers, and small plates in a traditional blue-and-white flowered china pattern. Val brushed off the cat hair from a tufted seat pad and sat down.

Morgan brought a crystal sugar and cream set from the kitchen. "Here's milk for English tea. Or would you prefer lemon?"

"Milk is fine." Val assumed she'd made the correct choice from Morgan's slight smile of approval. "Until your full name came up on my caller ID, I didn't know your last name was spelled with an X at the end, like the French word *roux.*"

"Meaning a fat-and-flour thickener for a soup or sauce, as I'm sure you know."

Val did know it, but Morgan couldn't resist showing off her knowledge as she had several times during last night's meeting. "Your father's French?"

"No, I married a French Canadian and kept his name after we divorced. I like having a short last name. Also, my ex wanted me to go back to my maiden name. That was reason enough not to do it."

Didn't sound like an amicable divorce. Val pointed to the dishes on the table. "I like your china. Is it a family heirloom?"

"It's my great-aunt's second-best china. My sister got the bone china. She always goes first." Morgan pursed her lips as she might after chewing grapefruit peelings. "This is porcelain based on a Chinese design, which had pomegranates on the edges. The Germany company, Meissen, redesigned it with plants more familiar in Europe. It's called the blue onion pattern. Because it was popular, other manufacturers developed their own versions."

Morgan detailed the pattern variations made by companies through the centuries. Val was grateful when the whistling teakettle interrupted her history lesson.

With Morgan responding to the kettle in the kitchen, Val stood up to study a piece of framed needlework hanging on the dining room wall. It resembled an impressionist painting of a waterfall and trees decked out in autumn leaves. The embroidery made the scene look three-dimensional. The letters MOR were stitched on the bottom right of the picture where an artist signature might be. Short for Morgan? If so, she was adept at needlework.

Morgan set a plate of store-bought shortbread cookies on the table and went back to the kitchen. Val sat down and eyed the plate. She'd much rather eat one of the oatmeal cookies she'd brought, but Morgan returned from the kitchen without them.

She carried a teapot covered in a cozy decorated with embroidered flowers. "The tea will have to steep for another two minutes." She set a small glass milk pitcher next to it.

Val noted the MOR stitched onto the cozy. She pointed to the framed autumn scene on the wall. "Did you do the embroidery on that picture and the tea cozy?"

"Yes. It's crewel work. The tea cozy was my first stab at it." When Val smiled in response to the pun, Morgan continued. "I recently finished the landscape in my Novels and Needles Club. During each meeting we talk about a book while we knit, crochet, embroider, or sew."

"Is that the book club you mentioned on the phone?"

Morgan nodded. "One member hosts the meeting each month. It's my turn next month. We usually have snacks and drinks, but we want to do something special in November because it's the club's anniversary. We were thinking of going to a restaurant, but we're afraid it'll be too noisy."

And the restaurant might not appreciate a bunch of women occupying a table to stitch and talk for hours. "How many club members do you have?"

Morgan poured tea into Val's cup. "Ten."

Eight would be a tight squeeze in this room. "You might consider doing it in the bookshop's CAT Corner."

"No! I never want to go there again." She poured herself tea. "Last night was awful. Wilson and Casper accusing each other of killing Suzette, and then Casper pointing a finger at me for no reason at all."

"When you said that his car was the same color as the one following Suzette, he took it as an accusation. Did you mean it that way?"

"Certainly not. Maybe he took it as an accusation because he has a guilty conscience." Morgan blew on her tea. "We know he followed Suzette on foot Saturday night. He could have done the same in his car."

"I wonder when she first realized someone was following her. Was it recently or a while back?"

"She didn't say, but I'm sure if it had been going on for some time, she would have told the police."

Pointless, unless they had more information than just the car's color. "If Suzette thought a car had been following her, it's odd that she didn't stop jogging and look at it when she heard a car behind her."

Morgan frowned. "How do you know she didn't look at it?"

"The police chief told me that when she was hit, she was facing forward. Maybe she did turn around and saw a car that wasn't black. So she kept jogging instead of getting off the road. I guess she assumed the driver would notice her."

"The fog could have kept her from seeing the color of the car and the driver from seeing her." Morgan abruptly clanked her cup down on the saucer. "Sorry. I can't bear to think about it." She reached for a paper on top of the sideboard. "Here's some information I prepared for catering. It's a list of the food sensitivities of the women in my club. We have a members who are vegetarians, lactose intolerant, and gluten sensitive. I hope you can come up with a menu for them."

Val didn't want to be blamed for serving the wrong food. "You can choose the dishes you want from my catering menu. It gives prices for each item and indicates which are gluten-free and vegetarian. Lactose-intolerant people usually know what they can and cannot eat, so you should check with them before making final decisions about the meal." Val stood up. "I'd like to look at the kitchen before we finalize anything."

She peered into the room. She hadn't seen a kitchen as tiny since she moved out of an efficiency apartment in Manhattan. It was what her mother would call a one-rump kitchen.

"It isn't big," Morgan said as if reading Val's mind, "but it has everything you need to make a meal."

For one person, not for ten. The kitchen had a cooktop but no oven. A microwave and a toaster oven took up most of the counter space.

"When you have a meeting in this house, where does your book club gather?"

"In the living room. I bring in dining chairs so there's a place for everyone."

"Given the size of the kitchen and your group, I recommend a buffet. I'll make the food ahead of time and set it on the dining table. People can help themselves, fill their plates, and return to the living room."

Morgan looked askance. "We'd have to eat on our laps. That's not comfortable."

"I have one other option for you. I can cater the dinner in the café at the athletic club. It's available after seven Monday through Thursday and after two on the other days when we close early. You'll have to pay a bit more to cover renting the space."

Morgan sighed. "I guess we can split the cost among the ten of us. Can you send me the prices? Then I'll let the club members decide."

Val edged toward the front door. "I'll e-mail you my catering menu with the cost of the space factored in. Thank you for tea and for contacting me about catering."

When Val arrived home, she went into the study. It looked only slightly less messy than before Granddad had tidied it today. She sat down at the computer and surveyed the list of files he'd copied from Suzette's thumb drive. She sorted them by date and opened the last file Suzette had saved, a spreadsheet called "Expenses" with tabs for the current year and the previous two years. Suzette had entered how much she'd spent on a variety of items, including tuition, food, clothing, and books. The latest date listed in the current year's expenses was Friday, the day before the costume contest, when she'd bought groceries.

Another recently updated spreadsheet was called "Log." It had four columns. The first column contained dates. The numbers in the next column looked like times of day or durations with a colon between the hour and minutes. The first date was a month ago. Then came three or four dates per week, the last one just four days before Suzette died. Each line in the third column contained a three-digit number. The entries in the last column were uppercase letters. The same ones appeared several times: A, R, E, J. They must be codes or abbreviations for something, but Val had no idea what.

She closed the spreadsheet and went back to looking at the file list. Over the past couple of years, Suzette had saved documents in a folder called "Homework." Val opened a few of them and saw what she expected — papers for college courses.

A folder labeled "Book2" contained the chapters from Suzette's work-in-progress, the historical mystery set in the 1920s, including the chapter the Fictionistas had discussed last night.

The folder's name suggested Suzette had written another book. Val skimmed the folder list and found a "Book1" folder. The documents in it were chapters one through six. She right-clicked on "Chapter 1" and viewed the file properties. Though Suzette had modified it earlier this year, she'd created it more than five years ago. That was true of the other chapters too. She must have abandoned writing her first book for a few years, gone back to revise it, and then given up again.

Was it a murder mystery like her other book? Val opened "Chapter 1." The first sentence grabbed her: *I liked him better than any of Mom's other boyfriends.*

Val felt a tingle of excitement. Could this be a memoir rather than fiction? She kept reading.

The current boyfriend treated the narrator like an adult, in contrast to her mother's earlier ones, who'd viewed the girl as a nuisance. It had been a few years since the mother's previous boyfriend took off, and now the sixteen-year-old narrator found herself the object of admiration by a grown man. When he moved into the small two-story house with her and her mother, he declared they'd be one happy family. The girl hoped he'd be the father she'd never had. The first chapter ended on a happy note. But in the second chapter, the household dynamic changed.

The boyfriend was amorous toward her mother in front of the girl and watched her reactions. Her embarrassment seemed to amuse him. When the mother took a second job working two nights a week, the girl had to fend off the boyfriend. She agonized about whether to tell her mother, her friends, or her teachers what was going on.

Val quickly moved from chapter to chapter. She seethed as she read about the girl being fondled by the man and the mother calling her a liar when the girl told her what he'd done. The girl spent as much time as she could at a friend's house, but sensed she was outstaying her welcome there. Having nowhere else to go on the nights when her mother worked, she locked herself in her room. When she wouldn't respond to the boyfriend's cajoling to open the door, he tried a variety of tools to unlock it. At the moment he succeeded, her mother returned from her job. The girl had no doubt that he'd unlock the door faster in the future, having discovered how to do it. She needed a sturdy bolt for the door, but she didn't have the money to buy one.

The next time her mother worked at night, the girl locked herself in her room again. When the boyfriend started working on the lock, she climbed out her bedroom window and lowered herself to the ground. She stayed outside even after her mother returned, wondering if anyone would come look for her. No one did. She saw the lights go on in her mother's bedroom and then go off. The girl waited another ten minutes and then crept into the house.

The next time she was alone in the house with him, he tried coaxing her to unlock her door and rattled the doorknob. When she didn't respond, he stopped. She heard nothing for a minute and assumed he'd gone to find whatever tool had worked the last time. She put on several layers of clothing because it was a cold night and opened the window, ready to climb out. Then she saw the glow from his cigarette below the window. He was blocking her escape.

Val's heart raced. What would happen next?

The girl shut the window, took off her heavy clothing, and put on a dress and makeup. She left the house by the front door, approached the man who was standing under her window, and said, "Let's go out for a drink."

There the story ended. If Suzette had written any more of it, she'd saved it somewhere other than on the thumb drive. Still tense from reading the story, Val leaned back in her chair, trying to relax. Suzette's memoir or fictionalized autobiography tugged at the heartstrings in a way that her murder mystery hadn't, and left Val emotionally drained. Yet she wanted more. She wanted to find out how the story ended.

The boyfriend's name never appeared in the chapters. Val had little doubt he was the man Wanda Cripps had talked about whose car Suzette had totaled. Maybe her cousin knew the rest of the story, but would she share it?

Val heard the front door open. Granddad. Should she show him the chapters she'd just read? No. She'd tell him about the story, maybe tone it down a little. Reading about the boyfriend and Suzette's terror would upset him. She closed the documents.

"I'm in the study," she called out to him. He came into the room, carrying a manila envelope, and sat on the sofa. She swiveled the chair to face him. "How did your visit with the Patels go?"

"Not the way I expected. When I got there, the kids were Skyping with their father. He's been visiting his sick mother in India for the last two weeks. They told me they talked with him and their grandmother every day."

Being half a world away from a hit-and-run made a good alibi. "You scratched Mr. Patel off your suspect list."

Granddad nodded. "Mrs. Patel too. She

didn't act like she was jealous of Suzette. I gave the boys the books and told them Suzette had bought them. When they went out to play, I asked their mother about the note her son found in the door. She showed it to me. It wasn't scrawled by a playground bully. It was printed on a computer."

"Kids know how to use computers. What did the note say?"

"*You will pay for what you done.* Sounds like a kid who hasn't learned grammar. I told her the Bayport police were investigating the hit-and-run, and it might have been deliberate. She gave me the note and said I could pass it on to them." Granddad patted the manila envelope. "The chief wasn't interested in what happened at the Patels', but maybe he'll change his mind."

"How did your online research go? Find any previous connection between Suzette and her writing buddies?"

"Nope. I found stuff about all of them except Morgan."

"I didn't give you the correct spelling of her last name. It's R-O-U-X. When Gillian e-mailed me contact information, she only put down first names. Speaking of Gillian, what did you find out about her?"

"She grew up on the western side of the Chesapeake, moved to the Eastern Shore when she got married, and stayed here after her divorce. I couldn't find other names she's used, but I'm pretty sure Gillian Holroyd is an alias."

"You mean a pen name?" When Granddad nodded, Val said, "What makes you think it's not her real name?"

"Gillian Holroyd is the name of a modern witch in a 1950s movie — *Bell, Book and Candle.* The first book Gillian wrote centered on a modern witch. That can't be coincidence. Using that name was probably a marketing gimmick."

A ploy geared to movie buffs like Granddad? Not a big audience. Val had another explanation besides marketing or coincidence. "Maybe her parents, the Holroyds, gave her the name Gillian because they liked the movie. What else did you find out about her?"

"She's written a lot of books, but nothing in the last five years."

Val found that hard to believe. "She's arranged to sign her new book at Title Wave, so she must have written something."

"That's a bunch of stories she wrote more than ten years ago. Some of them were published in magazines. Now she's collected them into a book."

Val swiveled the chair so she was facing

the computer again, googled Gillian Holroyd, and clicked on the Wikipedia page for Gillian. All her books were listed with the publication dates. Val scanned them. Granddad was right about the timing. "She's published fifteen novels, but none of them recently. She had one book come out each year at first. Then she wrote two a year for a while. And then nothing."

"A long dry spell." He shifted on the sofa and stood up. "I'm going to sit in my recliner and put my feet up. You get a chance to look at the files Suzette saved on that thumb drive?"

Val followed him into the sitting room and perched on the edge of the old tweed sofa. "I'll tell you about the files I found, but I have to make it quick. I'm meeting Casper for a drink in town and then Bram for dinner."

"Busy night. Ask Casper what he knows about Gillian."

"I'll add it to my list of questions for him."

Val told him what was on the thumb drive. Granddad often fell asleep within minutes of leaning back in his recliner, but her summary of the chapters in Suzette's first book kept him wide-awake.

When she finished, he said, "I don't think Suzette made up that story. She was writing

268

about what happened to her."

"I agree. Whether it's a straight memoir or she took poetic license to make it into fiction, I suspect the man in the story was based on her mother's boyfriend. Even when she was working on a historical novel, she gave her characters the personalities of people she knew." Val stood up. "Memoir or not, the chapters I read could serve as the start of an exciting novel. I'm afraid Suzette's death may have been the unhappy ending to it."

CHAPTER 19

Val changed out of her black slacks with white cat hair into dress jeans, and switched her white top for a teal sweater, a good color for her. To her surprise, when she went downstairs, Granddad wasn't asleep in his recliner. He was busy at the computer and said goodbye to her without taking his eyes off the screen.

She arrived at the Bugeye Tavern fifteen minutes before Casper was due to show up, and approached the redheaded bartender. "Hi, Keenan."

He finished filling a glass of beer from the tap, delivered it to a man at the other end of the bar, and came over to Val. "I showed the photo of your friend to the servers who were here on Saturday night. One of them remembered waiting on her and the caped man. She'll be coming in at six if you want to talk to her."

"Great. I'm going to have a drink with the

man who might have been with my friend that night. Would you and the server let me know if he's the one?"

"Okay. If you want to jog her memory, sit where your friend sat. It's the middle table by the window."

"Good. I'll grab it. Later, I'm going to have dinner with another guy who wore a cape on Saturday. If you don't recognize the first one, I'd appreciate it if you and the server let me know if the second one looks familiar."

"Your suspect lineup is good for business. How many more of them do you have?"

"I'm getting to the bottom of the barrel. Would you pour me a glass of white wine?"

"Sure thing."

Val paid for the wine and took it to the window table that looked out on Main Street.

She had a few minutes to work on her cover story for Casper. She pulled out her phone and searched online for a Loch Ness Monster cookie cutter. She was delighted to find one with a fairly simple shape.

The server, a robust middle-aged woman, stopped by the table. "I'll let you know if the guy who joins you is the one who was with your friend Saturday night."

"That would be great. Did you catch any

271

of their conversation?"

"No, but I could tell it was intense. They didn't raise their voices, but they looked furious at each other. She didn't stay long, barely touched her ginger ale."

"Did he follow her out?"

The server shook her head. "He finished his drink. Southern Comfort. Didn't seem to give him much comfort. He asked for the check. When I brought it, he reamed me out for taking so long and left a measly tip. I'll know him when I see him again. I sure hope you're not drinking with him tonight. Nasty piece of work." She left to wait on other customers.

Casper arrived, wearing his MIT jacket again, along with office-casual khakis and a collared shirt.

He greeted Val, sat down, and glanced at his watch. "Made it on time, but you wanted to meet me half an hour ago. You must have gotten off work early today."

"I start early. On weekdays I'm there by seven thirty at the latest."

He frowned. "At the bookshop?"

She shook her head. "My regular job is running the café at the Bayport Racket and Fitness Club. I cater as a sideline in the evening."

The server came to the table, stared at

272

Casper, and asked what he wanted to drink.

"Scotch on the rocks."

"What kind of scotch?"

He looked flummoxed. "Whatever you've got."

Val wondered if he'd ever drunk scotch before.

When the server brought his drink, she made eye contact with Val and shook her head. So Casper wasn't Suzette's companion here on Saturday night. Cross one caped man off the list.

She showed Casper the Loch Ness cookie cutter on her phone. "Do you think I can use this shape for my Chessie monster cookies?"

His mouth turned down. "Absolutely not. Chessie is a sea serpent, long and skinny. That has too many angles." He pointed to the image on her phone.

"Long and skinny is good. Instead of using a cookie cutter, I can roll the dough into a rope. Then I'll mold it into the serpent's head, a long neck, and one body curve. I'll assume the rest of him is underwater. Have you seen Chessie?"

"Not personally." Casper lifted his highball glass and sniffed it. "We know what Chessie looks like because the Enigma Project has evidence of encounters with it."

Though anxious to shift the conversation from Chessie to Suzette, Val gave in to her curiosity. "What's the Enigma Project?"

He swallowed some scotch, looked stunned, and appeared to choke. When he recovered, he said, "The Enigma Project is a Baltimore-based group of science and technology researchers. They investigate and document reports of unexplained phenomena — mysterious lights, UFOs, sightings of unknown animals."

Time to bring up another enigma. Val tucked her phone in her bag. "Speaking of unexplained things, several different explanations for Suzette's death came up last night. You had two of them. You blamed Wilson first and then Morgan. Which do you favor today?"

"Wilson. He thought Suzette was his for the asking. She turned him down and that enraged him."

Val wasn't impressed with Casper's argument. He hadn't added any facts to the accusation he'd leveled the night before, but maybe he could supply some about Gillian. "You told me you'd known Suzette longer than the other Fictionistas. Longer than Gillian too?"

He shook his head. "Gillian knew her before I did. Suzette took a weekend class

274

from her early this year. When she heard Gillian was offering another one in the summer, Suzette talked it up at the Eastern Shore Writers Association. She said she was signing up for it because Gillian had helped her a lot with her writing."

"Suzette took the same class twice?"

"No, our class is fiction writing. The one Suzette took earlier was memoir writing. She said she was by far the youngest person in the class."

"I'll bet." Val would stake money that Suzette had revised the chapters in her memoir during or after that class last winter. If Gillian had read those chapters, why hadn't she mentioned it? Maybe she thought sharing the details of a memoir was a violation of Suzette's privacy. "Did Gillian read what everyone wrote in the weekend class the way she does with the Fictionistas?"

"The class was too big for that. She lectured in the morning, and they had breakout meetings of five or six people in the afternoon. They each read a few pages aloud that they'd brought with them, and the small group discussed them. Gillian popped in long enough to hear what one person in each group was reading and give suggestions."

"Was it just a one-day class?"

"Two days. Suzette said they met for six hours on Saturday and Sunday."

Val calculated the odds that Gillian had listened to Suzette read her memoir. Less than fifty-fifty. But Suzette could have been among the lucky few to get personal advice from the teacher. After listening to even a few pages of Suzette's memoir, Gillian might have taken Suzette aside and requested more pages.

Casper interrupted Val's speculations by asking how she'd ended up catering in the bookshop. Eventually, the costume contest came up.

"I got a chance to see most of it," Val said, "but when it was over, I had to go back and serve snacks at the CAT Corner. Did you stick around the shop after the contest?"

"For a while."

"Did you happen to notice Suzette talking to someone dressed like a vampire?"

"There were two or three vampires." Casper rubbed his forehead as if massaging his brain. "Hmm, I think I did see Suzette talking to one of them."

Had she talked to Nick, who Bram had said had been there, or to a different vampire? As Casper brought up the subject of the Chessie monster again, Val gazed out the window. Twilight had turned to dark-

276

ness while they'd sat in the tavern. Street-lamps and the shop windows decorated for Halloween provided the only light on a cloudy night. Val glimpsed a woman across the street who resembled the elusive Maria. Maybe the Harbor Inn maid would be more talkative now than she'd been two nights ago.

Val jumped out of her seat. "Sorry, Casper, I have to run. Thanks for your information about Chessie." Leaving half a glass of wine, she grabbed her windbreaker and rushed out of the tavern.

By the time she waited for a break in the traffic and crossed the street, Maria had disappeared from view. Val walked three blocks, checking the side streets, but didn't see the maid. Heading back to the tavern, she went into all the shops still open along the way and peered around. Maria wasn't in any of them. It was nearly seven when Val went back to the tavern. Through the front windows, she saw a middle-aged couple occupying the table where she and Casper had sat. *Whew.* She was relieved that her six-o'clock date and her seven-o'clock date wouldn't come face-to-face. Awkward to say goodbye to one and hello to the other.

Her phone chimed. She fished it from her purse. Bethany was calling her, but she didn't sound like herself.

"I have a bad cold." Her voice was hoarse, her tone nasal. "Can't go to the haunted house tomorrow night. I hope you don't mind."

"Not at all. Let me know if you need anything. I make a mean chicken soup."

"Thank you," Bethany croaked. "But I stocked up on Sunday because of my soup diet. I made enough to last all week."

"Okay. Take care of yourself and get some rest."

"I will. Good-bye." Bethany coughed and hung up.

When Val went inside the tavern, Keenan beckoned to her. "Your next suspect has arrived. He wanted a quiet table. I suggested a booth." Keenan cocked his head toward a room off to the side that had been part of the original tavern.

"What makes you think he's my suspect? Did he come in dressed like a vampire?"

"No. He said he was expecting to meet a woman here. He described your hair."

Her most distinctive feature. Val finger-combed her unruly waves. "How bad is it?"

Keenan grinned. "Looks the same as usual. Anyway, he's not the guy who was here with your friend."

She was happy to hear it. "Thanks,

Keenan."

"Enjoy your dinner."

Val went into a narrow brick-walled room with six wooden booths on each side. When she moved to Bayport less than two years ago, this part of the tavern had looked as if it hadn't changed in a century, with bare wood benches, an odor of stale beer, and nautical touches like fish nets hanging on the walls and ceiling. Now, the mirrors mounted on the ceiling, Tiffany lamps over the tables, and plush red cushions on the seats gave it the look of an old-fashioned bordello.

Bram smiled as she approached the last booth in the row where he sat. He stood up and helped her off with her windbreaker. "I'm glad you made it."

Did he assume she'd be a no-show because she was five minutes late? "I'm glad you made it too." She slid into the booth and eyed the sweating glass of amber liquid in front of him. "That ale looks like the perfect drink for this tavern."

"You want one or would you rather stick with white wine?"

Val was too startled to answer. How would he know what she'd been drinking? The server came to the table, a younger woman than the one who'd waited on her and Casper earlier.

After ordering white wine, Val studied Bram as he looked at the menu. "You read my mind about the drink?"

"Deduction works better than mind reading." He brushed back a forelock of his wavy hair.

It wouldn't stay back for long, Val predicted. His hair, like hers, had an unruly streak. "Tell me your methods, Sherlock. What tipped you off about the white wine?"

"You drank it at the wine bar the night before last and here tonight when you were sitting by the window."

Had he seen her before or after Casper arrived? Maybe Bram thought she'd be a no-show because she was going to stand him up for another man.

She opened her menu. "If you like shellfish and haven't tried our local crab yet, you should do it before you go back to California. Chesapeake Bay blue crab tastes a lot different from the Dungeness crab you get on the West Coast."

"I'm not planning on going back right away."

Val was surprised. He must have decided his mother needed his help a little longer. "You might want to try the crab anyway because the season is almost over, and they do make good crab cakes here."

He took her up on the suggestion. She ordered the catch of the day, rockfish.

After the server left, Bram brought up the topic she'd expected, last night's meeting in the CAT Corner.

"When Gillian reserved the CAT Corner for her writing group, I didn't expect a fight to break out," he said. "I was even more surprised to hear a bunch of would-be writers accuse each other of killing the woman I'd found dead. Did you instigate that discussion?"

"Not me. Gillian's guilty of that. They were talking about the murder mystery Suzette had been writing. The crime scene in it resembled Suzette's accident scene. Gillian asked the others to speculate on which character in the book might turn out to be the killer."

"Your grandfather said you and he have solved a few murders that seemed like deaths by accident or natural causes. My mother was very impressed. I did some research and found out he wasn't spinning a yarn." He took a long swig of ale. "You think someone in Suzette's writing group killed her?"

"I know of people with more compelling motives to harm her than the petty jealousies that came out last night."

"You're pursuing other leads?" When she nodded, he leaned forward as if he couldn't see her clearly across the table. "Why? What motivates you to delve into someone's death?"

She squirmed. "You make me sound like a ghoul."

"I didn't intend it that way. You have an unusual hobby."

"I don't do it for pleasure. I looked into a couple of deaths because the police were investigating someone close to me. This time they aren't investigating at all. I hope they're right that Suzette died by accident, but the more I uncover about her, the more I question that." And the more Val felt a kinship with Suzette. "She didn't turn a blind eye to injustice. If she noticed any unfairness or wrongdoing, she tried to put an end to it. She deserves justice for herself."

Bram's hair had crept over his forehead again, but he didn't push it back. "Rooting out injustice can be dangerous."

"It might have been for Suzette, who went after it with a vengeance. No half measures for her. But I'm more timid. I poke around, gather bits of information, and run to the police with them." Val realized that Bram

282

could supply one nugget no one else had. "You were at the scene of the accident. I think fog dampens sound, and I wonder if it could have made it hard for her to hear a car coming. Were there any cars on the road? And could you hear them coming?"

"There was almost no traffic at that hour. No cars came up behind me while I was pedaling away from town. But a minute before I saw Suzette, a car emerged from the fog, heading toward town. I don't know if the fog muffled sound, but it certainly kept me from seeing the car until it was only yards away."

"What did you notice about it? Was it dark or light? Did it have any unusual features?"

Bram closed his eyes for a few seconds and then shook his head. "I can't remember anything special. A red or white car would have stuck in my mind. It must have been a less noticeable color. You think it was the car that ran her over?"

Val shrugged. "She was jogging away from town. The car that hit her was going in the same direction. It would have to turn around and go back."

"Unless the driver lived farther along the peninsula. I've biked through a small community there."

Val took the server's arrival with their food

as a signal to switch to a less disturbing topic than a fatal hit-and-run. She asked Bram about his work in California. He talked briefly about the tech businesses he'd started and eventually sold. Then he asked what Val had done before moving to Bayport.

She told him about her career in New York as a cookbook publicist and its abrupt end after she clashed with a celebrity chef. Prompted by questions from Bram, she described what she missed about the city, what she loved about Bayport, and how she and Granddad had adjusted to living together.

Before she knew it, her plate was clean and the table cleared. The server returned to take their order for dessert and coffee. Val passed on both. Bram ordered coffee.

She remembered what Granddad had said about photos Bram had taken at the bookshop's grand opening. "You took pictures after the costume contest Saturday night. If you have them with you, I'd like to look at them."

He fished his phone out of his shirt pocket and tapped the screen a few times. "Anything in particular you want to see?"

"A picture of Suzette." And the vampire she talked to.

"I took some shots of the crowd. You might find her in them." He passed the phone to Val.

She swiped through the photos until she found the right one — Suzette in conversation with a man in a black cape. Val enlarged the photo and zoomed in on the man. Nick.

Val showed Bram the zoomed image. "Here's Suzette with a vampire."

"That's the guy you were with at the wine bar. I told you he was at the bookshop."

"And he denied it." He must have had a reason to lie, maybe to hide the fact that he'd talked to Suzette and possibly even arranged to meet her the night before she died. Val stood up. "Could I borrow your phone for a minute?"

Not waiting for an answer, she left the room for the bar. She showed Keenan the zoomed image of Nick the vampire. "Is this the man who was here with my friend on Saturday night?"

Keenan squinted at the picture. "He might be."

Not good enough. "Can we check with the server who waited on my friend?"

Keenan called the woman over. She stared at the photo. "That's him. I'm sure of it."

Val was thrilled. One mystery person identified — the caped man in the tavern.

Two to go — the burglar and the harasser. Three, if you count the killer. Or perhaps she was looking for only one person.

CHAPTER 20

Val tamped down her excitement as she returned to the room with the booths. Talking or even arguing with Suzette on Saturday night didn't mean Nick had killed her on Sunday morning or that he'd broken in to steal her computer. But he might have.

She returned to the booth where Bram sat drinking coffee. She expected him to ask why she'd run off with his phone. That could take a while to explain. She reached for her water glass.

He leaned forward. "Are you planning to get married?"

She choked on her water. When she recovered, she said, "I hope to get married, if and when the right man comes along. I wouldn't call that planning. Would you?"

He shook his head. "No, but when I was leaving the wine bar two nights ago, I heard Nick ask you about your wedding plans."

"Not *my* plans. Nick is a manager at the

Harbor Inn, where I'd inquired about the wedding reception facilities for a sort-of friend." Val nonchalantly slid Bram's phone across the table, glad that he'd gone off on the wedding plans tangent instead of quizzing her about borrowing his phone.

"That explains it. You weren't acting like you were in a committed relationship. On Monday night you were with Nick. Last night you went charging down the street after a different guy. Tonight you were having a drink with yet another man."

Val was surprised at his interest in her social life. "I talked to those guys to find out what they knew about Suzette and to assess if they might have wanted her dead. I'm not planning another tête-à-tête with any of them."

"I get it. They're your suspects." Bram suddenly straightened up. His eyes narrowed in suspicion. "Am I one of your suspects too? Is that why you met me for dinner?"

Wow. He was less self-confident than she'd thought. "You are not one of my suspects." If she wanted to see more of him — and she did — this would be the time to give him some encouragement. "I trust you enough not just to meet you for dinner but also to go into a haunted house with you.

Are you interested in visiting the Bayport haunted house with me tomorrow evening?"

A smile lit up his face. "As long as you don't run screaming out of it."

"No fear of that. I don't scare easily. I'll be working at the bake sale table outside the haunted house until seven. I'll pick up tickets for us."

"Okay. Meet you there at seven." Bram glanced at his watch. "I hate to cut this short, but I'd like to get back to the shop before closing time in case the new assistant needs more training. I have time to give you a ride home if you'd like."

"Not necessary. It's a short walk."

Despite Val's statement that she didn't scare easily, she kept an eye peeled for anyone on foot or on wheels dogging her on the way home. As far as she could tell, no one took the slightest interest in her.

When Val walked into the house, she was surprised that Granddad wasn't watching TV in his lounge chair, his usual after-dinner activity. Instead, he was at the computer.

She glanced at her watch and joined him in the study. "Granddad! I left more than three hours ago. Have you been there all this time?"

"Nah, I took a break and walked to town for a pizza."

She sank into the sofa across from the computer. "I solved one of our mysteries. The bartender and a server at the tavern identified the man Suzette argued with there on Saturday night. Her boss, Nick, the assistant hotel manager. I wish I knew what they were talking about, but no one overheard them."

"Don't go asking him about it," Granddad said over his shoulder.

"I won't, but I'm going to try to talk to the maid who was Suzette's friend. I met her outside the inn's parking lot on Sunday at three, so I'll hang around there tomorrow at the same time. Maybe she has an idea what Suzette and her boss would disagree about. Maria might also know if Nick drives a black car." Val could tell Granddad was engrossed in the computer screen. "By the way, did you look up Morgan online after I told you how to spell her last name?"

"Yup. Her Facebook page says she graduated from Penn State and lived in Canada for a couple of years before she moved to Maryland."

"So she wasn't originally from Maryland?"

He shrugged. "It didn't say she moved *back* to Maryland. I couldn't find any con-

290

nection between her and Suzette from years ago. There's not much online about Morgan, but there's plenty about Gillian."

"Makes sense. She's a successful author."

He swiveled the desk chair around to face Val. "Her big hit was an espionage thriller, published ten years ago. The story took place in occupied France during the Second World War. The main character was a young American woman who spied on the Germans and worked with the Resistance. The book was a big hit. Then a man took her to court over it."

"Why?"

"His mother had been making notes for a memoir for years. As she was getting into her nineties, she decided to write it before she passed on. She took a class at the senior center about writing memoirs and hired the teacher, a published writer, to whip the memoir into shape. You can guess who the writer was. The old woman died before the project was done. I read her obit. Turns out she'd been an American spy in France during the war."

"How close was Gillian's book to the notes? Were the words the same?" When Granddad shook his head, Val shrugged. "So it wasn't plagiarism."

"The son claimed Gillian stole his mother's life."

Morally wrong, but was it illegal? "How did the lawsuit end? Did Gillian have to pay damages?"

"They settled. She agreed to give credit to the man's mother as the source of the story. Gillian said it was an oversight that she'd left the woman's name out of the acknowledgments and that it would appear in all future printings of the book."

Val thought about what Casper had revealed tonight. "Suzette took a weekend class on memoir writing from Gillian. It's possible she's familiar with what Suzette wrote." Would she fictionalize Suzette's memoir as she had the spy's?

Granddad's eyes grew round. "That's Gillian's motive. She wanted to steal Suzette's life story, and she couldn't do that as long as Suzette was alive to object."

Val shook her head. "Gillian based a novel on the experiences of a woman who died. That's a far cry from killing someone to steal a plot for a book."

"How do you know she didn't do that the last time?" Granddad folded his arms. "Sometimes when old folks die, people assume it's from natural causes when it isn't."

"You're saying Gillian is a serial killer?" Val had heard bizarre theories about other murders from him, but this one took the cake. "I can believe she would commit a crime with a pen, but not with a sword, so to speak."

"You said she had no motive. I found one. I'm just sayin' don't rule her out. You think that fella Nick is a better suspect? He didn't try to pin the crime on someone else like Gillian did. So what if he and Suzette had words the night before she died? That's not evidence."

Val sighed. He was right. "Neither of us has any evidence for our theories. Without it, the chief will ignore us." She stood up. "I'm going to make the cookies for tomorrow's haunted house bake sale." Mixing ingredients and shaping dough always relaxed her.

Thunder growled as Val left the house at seven fifteen on Halloween morning. In late October, the sky usually began brightening by seven, though the sun didn't rise until half an hour later. But the sun would have trouble penetrating this morning's shroud of thick clouds. Distant flashes of lightning gave the sky a momentary eerie glow. Perfect weather for the holiday.

Waiting to turn off the main road between Bayport and Treadwell, Val reached behind her for the umbrella in her seat-back pocket. All she found was an empty water bottle. She glanced at the gray sky. No rain yet, but it might be pouring when she left the café this afternoon. At least her windbreaker had a hood.

The thunder increased in volume and frequency as she neared the Bayport Racket and Fitness Club. She pulled into the club's parking lot. Lights on tall poles spaced far apart dimly illuminated the lot. It was as long as a football field but narrow, with parking spaces lining a center lane. Cars belonging to early-bird exercise addicts filled the spots near the building. Val pulled into the first free space, a third of the way down the lot.

As she hustled across the lot toward the building, lightning forked toward earth and thunder resounded. She looked around, afraid it might have hit a tree. Out of the corner of her eye, she saw the fender of a car only feet away. A car coming right at her!

CHAPTER 21

Val dove between two parked cars and stumbled on the uneven pavement. She ended up sprawled on the ground between the cars, her left arm twisted under her. Her heart raced. The thunder must have kept her from hearing the car, but why hadn't she seen its headlights? Because they weren't on. Had someone intended to run her over? If so, the driver might come after her on foot.

Thunder boomed as she tried to lever herself up with her hands. Her wrist protested the weight she put on it. The pain made her light-headed, but she didn't dare take time to recover. Using her right hand for support, she scrambled to her feet.

She crouched down to scan the lot from between the parked cars. All the spaces between her and the club building were full. No car was moving in the lot.

She spotted a woman in flowered tights

and a pink fitness jacket walking toward the parking lot from the club entrance.

Val recognized her as a regular in the early-bird aerobics class. "Hi there. Did you happen to see a car leave the lot just now?"

"As I came out of the club, a car pulled out onto the road." She pointed to the exit from the parking area. "Why?"

"It nearly ran me over. Did you notice the color or anything else about it?"

She shook her head. "All I saw was the brake lights. Are you okay?"

Val flexed her wrist. It hurt but at least it moved. "I'm fine." But disappointed that the woman could tell her nothing about the vehicle. "That car was driving without head-lights."

"My SUV has lights that turn on automatically. When I borrow my husband's car, I sometimes forget to turn on the lights manually. Maybe that's what happened, and you're hard to spot dressed in black."

Val glanced back at the dark pockets between the light poles. The woman's explanation was more plausible than the alternative — that someone had lurked in the lot and driven toward Val at the exact moment thunder drowned out the car's motor. She might have accepted the woman's theory if Suzette hadn't been killed by a hit-and-run driver four days ago. Had the driver in the lot gone for a random target or for Val specifically? She shuddered at the thought that someone had been watching her to find out her routine.

Large drops of rain burst from the clouds hovering over the parking lot. The woman in exercise clothes sprinted for her car, and Val rushed inside the club. She intended to call the chief about the close call as soon as she got a free minute, but she was inundated with customers waiting out the drenching rain. Nice to sell three times more food and coffee than on a typical Thursday morning, but not what she needed with a sore wrist.

As the weather improved, the café emptied out. Val was clearing the tables when Grand-dad came in at nine.

He sat on a stool at the eating bar. "I've got evidence the police can use. I'll show you." He pulled Val's laptop from a padded carrying case.

"Evidence of what?" Something that incriminated his latest favorite suspect, Gillian?

He set the computer on the eating bar. "Video footage of an attempted break-in at Mrs. Hill's house last night."

Val was disappointed his evidence had nothing to do with Suzette's death, but it was still a victory for him. "So your scheme worked, Granddad! Congratulations." Val glanced around the half-filled café and picked up the carafe. "I'll top off everyone's coffee. Then you can show me."

When she finished, she sat down on the stool next to his and rested her left hand and wrist on the eating bar. Maybe it would stop aching if she kept it motionless for a while.

Granddad clicked to start the video. A shadowy figure crossed in front of the camera. He slinked toward the door of a two-story house, his face mostly hidden by the hood of his jacket. In silhouette he looked to Val like a man of average height and weight. The outdoor fixture near the door gave off a weak light, but enough to see that he wore black from head to toe. His eerily pale hands suggested he was wearing latex gloves.

With one arm forward, he looked as if he was inserting a key in the door lock, though the key was hidden from the camera by his hand. He pulled his hand back and tried again.

Granddad paused the video. "I think he's using the old key. It worked for him the last time he broke in and stole stuff. But now there's a different lock. The burglar's about to give up and leave. Watch carefully, and you'll catch a glimpse of the fella's face when he turns away from the door."

Val concentrated on the small screen. The man's face appeared for a split second. Not long enough for her to recognize him, but something about him struck her as familiar. "Back it up, Granddad. Try to stop the action when he faces the camera."

After a few tries. Granddad paused the video on the correct frame.

Val saw the face clearly. "It's Nick! Hotel manager by day and burglar by night."

"He's wearing a hoodie like the guy Harvey saw casing our house and I spotted running away after RoboFido barked." Granddad pointed to the man on the screen. "Could have been him."

"Or anyone else who didn't want to be seen." Val massaged her sore wrist. "Our burglar knew how to pick a lock. Nick didn't even try to do that at Mrs. Hill's house."

Granddad frowned and then his brow unwrinkled. "I know why he didn't try. The new lock tipped him off that she suspected the house had been burgled and was beefing up her security. He didn't want to leave any evidence of a break-in. Picking the lock would be proof of a burglary."

"That's true. After our break-in, the police saw right away that the lock had been picked. Mrs. Hill has a cleaning service, like your other clients with *ghosts.* Do you remember the names of the cleaning companies?"

Granddad took a small spiral notebook from his shirt pocket and flipped some pages. "Treadwell Tidy Maids, Oxford Best Maids, Easton Green Cleaners."

Val moved the keyboard closer to her and entered the name of the Treadwell company in a search box. Her left wrist hurt as she typed, so she used only her right hand on the keys as she searched for the other two housecleaning companies.

Granddad noticed. "Why are you typing like that?"

If she told him the whole story, he'd worry about her and fret about not being able to protect her. Val decided on a half-truth. "I tripped in the parking lot and hurt my wrist." She drew his attention to the Web sites for each of the cleaning companies. "They have different company names and contact information, but the same menu items and page design. They must have used the same Web designer."

Granddad took charge of the keyboard and clicked around each site. "Look at the photos of the cleaning team. A different pose on each site but with the same women holding brooms and mops. This is a single business with multiple aliases."

A possibility. Val peered at the pictures. Amateur photography, not professional shots you could buy from a stock photo site. "It's strange to run businesses under different names. Most companies want to establish a brand name."

"Not if they have something to hide, like a sideline in theft. They don't want the police to see the common element in a bunch of burglaries. The way this fella Nick operates, he gets in by using the key the homeowners gave the cleaning team or left lying around. They don't realize anything's missing for a while. When they do, they think they've misplaced stuff. That's what happened to Mrs. Hill, the Kings, and Mrs. Jackson. If they ever call the police, they can't say exactly when the theft occurred."

Val flexed her wrist so it wouldn't stiffen up. Could Nick be a common burglar, not someone who specifically wanted Suzette's computer? Or was he both? "The video doesn't prove Nick had anything to do with Suzette's death."

"But he had a secret to hide. Maybe she found out." Granddad put the computer back in its case. "I'm showing the chief this video. I expect he'll have some questions for you about Nick." He left the club.

Later in the morning Suzette's cousin called to say she'd be at the house by three thirty to go through Suzette's things. Val's friend Chatty came into the café around noon. A massage therapist at the club, she advised Val to treat her wrist with RICE — rest, ice, compression, and elevation. She then wrapped Val's wrist in an athletic bandage. That took care of compression, but the other treatments would have to wait until Val finished work.

The sun had come out by the time Val left the club at two fifteen. While she was driving home, Chief Yardley called her. She stopped on the side of the road to talk to him.

"Your granddaddy hit the jackpot with his surveillance camera. His ghost hunting may lead to arrests for the burglaries around here."

"Arrests? Nick has accomplices?"

"At least one. His sister. She runs house-cleaning businesses under various names. She does the estimates and inspects the houses after they're cleaned."

"That gives her a chance to check out

where the valuables are," Val said. "She could probably draw a map to them for her brother."

"Almost every recent burglary reported to the police occurred in a home serviced by one of her companies. Keep this strictly confidential. We still have to build a case against her and her brother. Your granddaddy says that Nick Hyde was Suzette's boss and that you can give me information about him."

Val told the chief about her encounters with Nick — at the bookshop the night of the costume contest, at the hotel the next morning, and at the wine bar the following day. "He pumped me on how well I knew Suzette and whether she'd confided in me about her work at the inn. I think she was concerned about the work environment there and he knew that. Our house was burglarized within hours after I talked to him."

The chief said nothing for a moment. "Why would he want Suzette's computer?"

"Maybe he was afraid she'd kept incriminating information about him on her computer."

"Then he's ditched the computer by now. Would Suzette have blackmailed him if she found out about his burglaries?"

"She wasn't stupid. She'd have gone to the police about a crime like that. In the past she handled bad behavior, like bullying or leash-law violations, by confronting the wrongdoer directly. My guess is she discovered some kind of misconduct by Nick and approached him to stop it." Val rested her left hand on her head to elevate her wrist. "The night before the hit-and-run, Suzette met Nick at the Bugeye Tavern and had a far from friendly discussion with him."

After a moment of silence, the chief said, "You've been snooping."

"I won't deny it. Suzette thought someone was following her in a black car. You might want to check the color of Nick's car."

"The paint bits collected at the scene and on the victim's clothing weren't a dark color."

Whoever had been following Suzette in a black car either hadn't run her down or had used a different car, but that car might be traceable. "Isn't there a way to analyze a paint chip and match it to a car model?"

"Yes, but we don't have a chip. We've got microscopic paint fragments from the thin color coat used on newer cars. The analysis isn't as accurate. The accident reconstruction experts didn't rule out an intentional hit-and-run, but they also didn't find definitive evidence of it. Hard to believe hitting her was deliberate. If you want to kill folks on an empty road, a drive-by shooting works better than bumping them with a car."

"Maybe bumping her was supposed to be a warning or a threat." Val wondered if the driver in the parking lot had intended to warn or threaten her. "Don't mention this to Granddad, Chief, but someone nearly ran me over this morning."

"What?" The chief's voice was so loud that Val held the phone away from her ear. "Tell me what happened," he said more quietly.

She described the incident, and he peppered her with questions. Had she observed anything out of the ordinary in the parking lot when she drove in? Only the darkness because of the storm. Did she generally arrive at work around the same time? Yes. Did she notice the color, type, size, or anything at all about the car?

"Based on the height of the fender, I think it was small to medium size, not an SUV. The headlights weren't on." Tired of elevating her wrist, Val rested her hand on her lap. "I keep asking myself why anyone would want to go after me. Maybe I've dug up incriminating information, but I have no idea what it is."

"You can quit digging right now, and leave this to us. The Treadwell police will haul in Nick Hyde for questioning."

"I hope they question him about where he was on Sunday morning when Suzette was run over. In case Nick has a solid alibi, there's another person whose whereabouts that morning you should check — Lloyd Leerman, Suzette's mother's ex-boyfriend. Suzette wrote what sounded like a memoir about her experience with Lloyd, who demanded sexual favors when her mother wasn't around."

"Your granddaddy told me about it. He brought me the USB drive with Suzette's files on it. We made copies of those. I sent an officer to search her room, hoping to find a key to a storage unit or a safety deposit box. No luck."

At last! The chief was at least rethinking his assumption that the hit-and-run was an accident. "She might have left things with her cousin, who's coming this afternoon to pick up personal items from Suzette's room. Do you want to talk to her while she's in Bayport?"

"Yes. Ask her to call me."

When he hung up, Val pulled back onto the road, convinced for the first time that the truth about Suzette's death would come out before long. Amazing that Granddad's ghost hunting had led to progress on the case.

Granddad was napping in his lounge chair when Val got home. She unwrapped her wrist and put an ice pack on it for ten minutes. Then she wrapped it again, woke him up to tell him that Suzette's cousin would be there around three thirty, and drove to the Harbor Inn. Usually, she would have walked to the inn, but she was pressed for time. She didn't want to miss Maria leaving work.

CHAPTER 22

Val lingered outside the four-foot-high brick wall surrounding the Harbor Inn parking lot. To make herself less recognizable, she'd tucked her distinctive curly hair under a baseball cap and turned her back to the inn. She held her phone against her ear to suggest she'd stopped to take a call.

When she spotted Maria coming out of the parking area alone, Val was elated. She stepped away from the wall. "Hello, Maria."

The maid looked startled and then smiled. "My prayers were answered. I hoped to see you."

Really? She hadn't skittered away this time, so maybe it was true. "Let's walk along River Road. It's quiet there." And no one from the hotel would see them together.

Maria fell into step next to Val. "The police came and took Nick Hyde away. Do you know why?"

Val studied her. Maria didn't look worried

about Nick, just curious. "They think he committed crimes."

Maria's brown eyes grew wide. "Because Suzette told them?"

That convinced Val that Suzette — and probably Maria — knew exactly what Nick had been up to, and maybe it wasn't just burgling houses. "Suzette didn't have a chance to speak to the police before she died. But she and Nick talked on Saturday night, not in a friendly way."

"*Madre de Dios!* Maybe he killed her so she cannot talk to the police." Maria hugged herself, as if shivering under her gray sweat jacket. "I wish I said nothing to her about it."

About what? Val took a stab at the subject Maria and Suzette had discussed. "You wish you didn't talk to her about the maids?"

Maria nodded. "She told you too? She was angry and wanted to help them. She said she would keep records, dates, and times."

Dates and times. Val thought about the spreadsheet Suzette had saved on her thumb drive. Each row had a date, a time, a three-digit number, and a letter. Maybe those three digits — all starting with a two, three, or four — were room numbers in the four-story inn. The remaining column in the spreadsheet must relate to the maids. "Who

309

were the maids Suzette was concerned about?"

Maria stopped walking. "No names."

Val didn't need names. She just wanted to know if the last column in the spreadsheet could possibly refer to the maids. She tried to remember which letters appeared in that column. Two vowels, an E and an A, as well as a J and another consonant. The J rang a bell. The first maid she'd questioned on Sunday had worn a name tag. Juana. What about the other letters? "I know you don't want to give me anyone's name, Maria. But could you tell me if one of the maids Suzette tried to help has a name starting with A?"

Maria nodded.

"Does the name of another one start with E?"

Maria's jaw dropped. "How do you know this?"

"I've found the records Suzette was keeping. She didn't have any names in them, but she used the first letter of each maid's name. Please help me understand why Suzette was keeping records. I can tell the police what Nick was doing without giving them any names."

Maria looked out at the river behind the houses on the street. "Is Nick coming back to work?"

"I don't know. He's in serious hot water." Noting Maria's puzzled look, Val rephrased her statement. "He is in a lot of trouble that has nothing to do with his job at the inn. Once the police find out he also did something wrong at the inn, he will never, ever work there again."

"Okay. I'll tell you. He follows the young girls into the rooms when they are doing housekeeping. He kisses them and touches them where he shouldn't. He says they will lose their job if they tell anyone." Maria turned from the water and made eye contact with Val. "They need to make money. They have papers. They are legal, but some have family who are not legal, and they don't want problems. I told them they could trust her."

Suzette's reaction to a playground bully suggested she would stand up to Nick. "Did Suzette ask the girls to tell her where and when he bothered them?"

Maria nodded. "She said that when she had enough records, she would speak with Nick, and he would have to stop. The girls were very worried about her when she didn't come to work. And now she is dead. It's terrible." Maria glanced nervously up the street. "You must be careful, and I must go. My children will be home from school soon."

"Thank you, Maria, for helping me understand." And maybe helping to get justice for Suzette.

"Remember. No names." Maria crossed the street and went around the next corner.

Val walked to her car. The spreadsheet now made sense to her. But what good would that data do? If Suzette told Nick she knew what he'd done, he could simply deny he'd molested the maids and fire her and the maids. Suzette must have had a way to prove he'd been in the rooms when the maids said he was.

Val conjured an image of the hallways she'd walked through on Sunday at the inn. Of course. The halls had surveillance cameras. They would record Nick entering a room with a cleaning cart parked outside. Suzette could tell the security team and Nick's boss the exact dates and times when he'd gone into rooms to take advantage of the maids, and the footage would prove it. A manager might have a reason to go into a guest room now and then, but the pattern of Nick's room visits would make it clear they were not work-related. Probably no one even looked at the footage unless a crime had taken place.

Val wasn't sure how long surveillance footage would be kept. Maybe Suzette knew or feared that the older footage would be erased soon. So she'd confronted Nick before that could happen.

Val climbed into her car for the short trip home. Suzette knew of a crime, but wouldn't report it. The maids might not back her up for fear of losing their jobs, and she didn't want to put the maids or their families under police scrutiny. With her habit of attacking problems head-on, she would have dealt with Nick directly. Val imagined what Suzette might have said to him: *I can prove you've been messing with the maids. Try it again, and I'll turn over my records of your assaults to the police. I'll do the same if you fire me or any of the maids.*

Hard to believe Nick would kill her so he could continue groping women, but maybe he didn't believe she'd stay quiet about what she knew. If he'd killed her, he'd acted quickly, staking out the place where she lived, tailing her the next morning when she went jogging, and waiting until no other cars were in sight before he struck. Knowing that Suzette had specifics about his assaults gave him a reason to break in and try to steal any evidence she might have.

He had a motive for getting rid of the

woman who threatened him. He didn't have a reason to run down Val in the parking lot. He'd pumped her to find out if Suzette had confided in her, but that was three days ago. Val hadn't spoken with him since then. What could have led him, or anyone else, to go after her this morning?

Val pulled into the driveway at home, itching to tell the chief what she'd learned about Nick. She might have even more to tell him once she talked to Suzette's cousin. The unfamiliar car parked behind Granddad's on the street suggested that Sandy Sechrest had arrived.

Val went in the side door and sniffed the delicious aroma of butter, sugar, and vanilla. She followed her nose to the kitchen. "What are you baking, Granddad?"

"Some more of those Chessie monster cookies. I ate a few, so you needed another batch for the sale. I didn't think you'd want to roll dough with your sore wrist."

Val hadn't given a thought to her wrist for the last half hour, but now that Granddad had brought it up, she became aware of the discomfort. "Thank you. Where's Sandy?"

Granddad pointed at the ceiling. "In Suzette's room."

"Did you give her the will and other papers we put aside?"

314

"Not yet. The police made copies. The originals are on the desk in the study."

Val took the papers upstairs and paused in the doorway of the small bedroom.

A woman sat at the table by the window, staring at the yard, her back to the door. Her long, thick hair was the same color as Suzette's, and when she turned, Val saw a family resemblance, though Sandy's features were smaller and her eyes lighter. They were also red-rimmed from crying.

Val introduced herself, gave Sandy the folder with Suzette's papers, and expressed her condolences.

"Thank you," Sandy said. "I'm five years older than Suzette and thought of her as a little sister, though we didn't live near each other when we were growing up." She sighed. "I should get to work, looking through her things, but it's hard."

"Take your time. Would you like anything to eat or drink?"

She shook her head. "Your grandfather gave me some cookies and milk. I want to thank you for giving Suzette a place to stay. She told me you both were so welcoming and good to her. That meant a lot to her. She didn't have a great home life."

Val sat on the edge of the bed. "She didn't tell us much about her life before she came here. I know she was sexually harassed by her mother's ex-boyfriend Lloyd, and her mother didn't believe it. Mrs. Cripps told us that Suzette had crashed his car."

"The accident wasn't her fault."

"She didn't give me the details. What happened?"

"Suzette went out for a drink with Lloyd to avoid being home alone with him. He drove her to a bar outside Cumberland, probably so she couldn't make her own way home. He drank so much that he could barely see straight. People in the bar helped her get Lloyd into the passenger seat of his car. On the way back to town, he got a second wind and began groping her. She was distracted, went through a stop sign, and plowed into a car."

Val hadn't realized another vehicle was involved. "I hope no one was seriously injured."

"A family who'd come to Maryland for a funeral went to the hospital, all of them with contusions, and one had broken bones. Suzette was bruised, but had no major injuries. Lloyd hit the windshield because he'd taken off his seat belt to paw at her. He was pretty banged up and hospitalized."

"Mrs. Cripps blamed her daughter for the accident."

"The police didn't, once they checked Lloyd's alcohol level and heard Suzette's story. They charged Lloyd, but Aunt Wanda made Suzette's life miserable." Sandy stood up, went over to the dresser, and opened the top drawer. "I was worried Lloyd would come back. Six months after the accident, I graduated from college, got a job in Frederick, Maryland, and asked Suzette to move in with me. That put her ninety minutes from her mother. Suzette finished high school in Frederick and worked to save money for college. A couple of years later, she took a job as a live-in nanny."

"With the Patels?" When Sandy nodded, Val said, "Did Lloyd ever try to contact her while she was living with you?"

"Possibly. To intimidate her." Sandy slammed the drawer shut and turned to face Val. "Before she moved out of my place, she got malicious mail, not e-mail but typed letters that came through the post office. They said things like *I'm watching you* and *You owe me.* Lloyd was mean enough to do that."

Val jumped up as if a spring had propelled her off the mattress. Suzette had been harassed even before she moved to the Eastern Shore, before she met Nick, Gillian, or any of the Fictionistas. "How did

317

Suzette react to those letters?"

"Mildly upset at first. Then other nasty things happened. We found a dead bird on the doorstep, and my tires were slashed. That's when Suzette decided she had to leave. I was sorry about why she left, but by then I had a boyfriend and having her in the apartment wasn't ideal. She was careful not to leave a forwarding address with anyone but me."

"Whoever was pulling those tricks eventually tracked her to the Patels' house and started up again," Val said. "When the threats against her became a problem for the family, she moved out and came here. We don't know of anyone harassing her here, but she was concerned that someone might be following her. And the police are considering the possibility that someone ran her down on purpose."

Looking dazed, Sandy stumbled back to the chair by the window. "Do they know about Lloyd?"

"I passed on his name and what little I knew about him. Your information about how long Suzette was harassed will focus attention on him. The Bayport police chief is anxious to talk to you. I'll try to set up an appointment for you today if you can speak with him before you leave."

318

"I'll definitely do that." Sandy glanced at the dresser and the closet. "I don't want to spend any more time than necessary in this room. I just want to pick out a few things to remind me of Suzette. I'll pack up the rest for donation."

Val remembered how hard it had been for her mother to go through Grandma's things after the funeral. "Leave whatever you don't want, and I'll donate it."

"Thank you. That would take a burden off me."

Before calling the chief, Val had a few more questions for Sandy. "I'd like to tell you the names of people Suzette had come to know here and find out if you've ever heard of them." And especially if Suzette had mentioned them years ago when the harassment began. "Did she ever talk about Nick Hyde?"

Sandy shook her head. "Who is he?"

"Her boss at the inn. I'm surprised she never brought him up."

"She and I spoke on the phone a few times since she moved to Bayport. I'd go on and on about my job, but she never got into specifics about hers. She only talked about her college classes and what she was reading."

"Did Suzette ever mention Gillian Holroyd?"

"The writer. Suzette was excited about taking a class with her and talked about her a couple of times."

"When did she first talk about Gillian?"

Sandy frowned in concentration. "Late winter. And last month she told me Gillian was meeting her and a few others to give them feedback on their writing."

Val then gave Sandy the Fictionistas' names. Sandy hadn't heard of Casper, Wilson, Ruth, or Morgan. Apparently none of them had impinged on Suzette enough that she brought them up in conversation with her cousin. "Do you remember the name of the family in the car that got smashed in the accident?" After Sandy shook her head, Val went on to her next question. "When did the accident happen?"

"Between Thanksgiving and Christmas eight years ago. I can't get any more specific than that. I was away at college with exams on my mind."

Val now had enough details to research the incident. She stepped toward the door. "I'll call the chief of police while you finish what you have to do here. Let me know if you need more bags or boxes to pack things in."

She went downstairs, elated at the progress she'd made this afternoon. The information from Maria and Sandy had cemented the front-runners among the suspects. Lloyd Leerman was the most obvious person who could have harassed Suzette for years, but that didn't necessarily mean he'd killed her. Anyone who sent poison-pen notes and engaged in dirty tricks for such a long time obviously enjoyed that activity. What was the point of killing the prey you loved to torture?

Nick remained high on Val's list, though he almost certainly hadn't been the person who'd harassed Suzette for years. But the harassment and the hit-and-run didn't necessarily have anything to do with each other.

Val called the chief and recounted her conversations with Maria and Sandy. He said Sandy was welcome to drop in and talk to him anytime. He'd be in his office until seven. After giving Sandy directions to the police station, Val sat down at the computer in the study.

She had no luck finding any mention of either Suzette or Lloyd in an accident near Cumberland. She left the names out of her next search and restricted it to the time period Sandy had given her. Scrolling through the results, she found a short article in the *Cumberland Times-News,* which included details about the location and time of the accident.

The article reported that a car driven by a minor had hit another vehicle. The driver had escaped serious injury but the car owner, an adult male sitting in the passenger seat, had been taken to the hospital. The driver and three passengers of the vehicle that was struck, members of the O'Shaughnessy family from Pittsburgh, Pennsylvania, had been hospitalized, one of them in serious but stable condition. An investigation was pending.

Val found no follow-up articles about the investigation, leaving her in the dark about the consequences Lloyd suffered. Had he been jailed, fined, or otherwise punished so that he'd carried a grudge against Suzette for years?

Val got up from the computer and glanced at her watch. She had just enough time to grab a bite to eat before heading to the haunted house. She looked forward to laughing at mock horrors rather than puzzling over real evils.

CHAPTER 23

The Bayport haunted house was a misnomer in all ways — not in Bayport, not a house, and not haunted by the dead who used to occupy it. It was commercial space currently without a tenant in a strip mall outside town.

The bake sale table was set up in the arcade that ran along the storefronts. Val found a spot for the Chessie monster cookies between the tombstone brownies and a chocolate cake topped with a spider web of white icing.

With ten minutes to go before her shift at the bake sale table started, Val went over to the ticket table outside the haunted house entrance. Ruth McWilliams was collecting money and handing out tickets. Instead of the Lady Macbeth costume she'd worn Saturday night, Ruth had opted for a glamorous witch outfit. Sequins covered her pointed hat. She wore a black beaded evening jacket, a long velvet skirt, and red claw-like fingernails.

"I've been meaning to call you about catering," Ruth said. "It's for the New Year's Day brunch I hold for my neighbors."

"That day's available. Let's talk soon." Val glanced around. "I'm surprised there isn't a line snaking around the mall to get into the haunted house."

"Tickets sales have been brisk," Ruth said. "Our orderly system avoids lines. People buy tickets to enter at a certain time. They can walk around the shops until their time slot. While they're waiting, a lot of them buy snacks from the bake sale."

"A smart strategy." It would increase the money collected for the high school drama club. "I'd like two tickets for seven o'clock."

"Sold out. You can go in at a quarter past seven." Ruth watched Val fish money from her shoulder bag. "Why is your wrist wrapped in an elastic bandage? Nothing serious, I hope."

"I tripped on my way to work this morning. I think it's a mild sprain."

"Ice it and, if the pain doesn't go away in the next day or two, have a doctor look at it."

"Thank you for the advice." Which Val had also heard from several café customers. She gave Ruth the money and took the tickets.

"There's Wilson." Ruth pointed to a dark green sports car going into a parking space. "You know, I wouldn't have minded if he and Suzette got together. She was such a hard worker and would have had a good influence on him. He was quite torn up when she died."

"I noticed that." Val also noticed that Ruth was now signaling that neither she nor Wilson had a reason to harm Suzette.

"Wilson needed cheering up, so I contacted his ex-girlfriend from law school and invited her to visit."

He and a young woman with long blond hair got out of the car. Val watched them cross the parking lot, talking and laughing. Apparently, Wilson was recovering from Suzette's death. "Are they visiting the haunted house?"

"Later. First, they're going to that escape room place that just opened." Ruth pointed toward a storefront at the other end of the strip. "Have you been there?"

"No, and I'll never go. I avoid small locked rooms."

"Claustrophobic?" When Val nodded, Ruth looked sympathetic. "Me too. I hope Wilson's ex isn't. Maybe they'll rekindle the spark if they're enclosed in a tiny room.

She's already passed the bar exam and offered to help him study for it. Her family has the right connections."

Unlike Suzette's. Val went back to the bake sale table. She waited on enough customers to keep from being bored during her stint at the table. Bram arrived while she was passing the baton to the next volunteer. He asked about her wrist, and she gave the same evasive answer she'd given everyone except Chief Yardley.

At a quarter after seven, Val and Bram handed in their tickets and met their guide, a young man dressed like the Grim Reaper in a hooded black robe. He held the door open for the six people in the group — Val and Bram, two teenage girls, and a middle-aged couple. They stood in a dimly lit room the size of a vestibule. Fog swirled around a gate across from the door. Ominous music played, the kind that announces something bad is about to happen in a horror movie.

The Grim Reaper spoke in a somber voice, "Hello, Boils and Ghouls. Welcome to the Bayport Halloween haunted house. Please silence your cell phones so as not to disturb the spirits." He gave them a minute to do that and then said, "To get into the house, we must first pass through the burial ground and by the family crypt. Don't make any loud noises in the graveyard, or you'll wake the dead."

The teenagers giggled.

He waited until they quieted down. "On Halloween night, ghosts and demons are especially active in the graveyard. I'll follow you and try to keep the spirits from grabbing you from behind. Don't be nervous, ladies. Remember, demons are a ghoul's best friend."

Val and Bram groaned, while the girls went into fits of laughter.

One of them moved toward the gate. "Can we go first?"

"Only one of you can go first. The path through the graveyard is narrow. Single file, please."

The gate creaked open, as if pushed by an unseen hand. Val followed the girls through the gate and stepped into a cold, damp fog, Bram right behind her. The Grim Reaper pulled the gate shut once the middle-aged couple came in. It clanged with the finality of a prison-cell door. For a moment they were in total darkness.

He switched on a flashlight that faintly illuminated the foggy space.

The "path through the graveyard" was a three-foot-wide hallway with crypts painted on the side walls and moldy tombstones, probably plastic, sticking up from the fog-shrouded floor. Val was reminded of the fog on the peninsula road the morning Suzette was killed.

Menacing sounds came through the flimsy wall on her right — jungle noises punctuated by screams of the visitors who'd made it through the graveyard and now faced more terrors inside the house. With her mild claustrophobia, Val began to get nervous. Once she made it through this tunnel-like antechamber, though, she could handle anything.

The girls in front of her squealed, a sign that something creepy was about to happen. Val tensed up. Bats swooped down on her. She jumped back with a cry.

Bram steadied her, his hands on her shoulders. "You promised me you wouldn't scream."

"That wasn't a scream. It was an *eek*."

His grip on her grew firmer. "You're trembling. Are you okay?"

"It's chilly in here. I'm shivering." Then she blurted out the truth, "I'm also a bit claustrophobic."

"Please continue," the Grim Reaper said. "You're holding things up."

The sooner Val got out of this passage, the better. As she moved forward, the floor seemed to tilt upward. She couldn't see it because of the low-lying haze, but it felt as if she was on a ramp. The fog dissipated as she went higher and the ramp leveled off. She could clearly see the teenage girls a few feet in front of her.

They screamed and ran forward, shaking the wood ramp.

Val stopped and steeled herself for spiders, snakes, or slimy creatures to descend on her. She took three cautious steps. Below her, under broken floorboards, was a decomposing body with bugs crawling all over it. Yipes! She edged around the hole in the floor, assuring herself it couldn't be a real hole or it would be a safety hazard. It must be plexiglass. She rushed down the ramp and huddled with the teenagers near the end of the passageway. Good to know that a rotting corpse being eaten by bugs could make her forget her claustrophobia.

Where was Bram? She peered behind her and saw him dimly outlined. He was on his hands and knees peering down at the corpse. He scrambled up and came down the ramp toward her.

"What were you doing there?" she said.

"Checking out the insects. That was a pretty good illusion. They're mostly plastic bugs, but with live crickets moving around them, the activity makes you believe they're all real. Little dishes of water down there keep the crickets alive longer."

"Someone caught all those crickets?"

"Someone bought them at a pet store. Food for reptile and amphibian pets."

Was he going to dissect every illusion at the haunted house?

The guide followed the middle-aged couple down the ramp and said, "Now we'll go into the house. You must not enter any room unless I tell you, and you must never touch anything. If you don't follow those rules, one of two things will happen. You will immediately die of fright, or you will be led out by security guards. Either way, your ticket is not refundable."

He led them through a door in the wall behind which they'd heard squeals and screams. They entered a hall, not as narrow as the path through the graveyard, and short enough that Val could see an opening at the end. She'd gotten through the worst of the experience.

The Grim Reaper said, "I'll send you down this hall and the next one in pairs so you can appreciate the works of art on the walls. They have come down from the cursed family who lived here until the last one died. Some of them were murderers, others were murder victims." He paused. "None rest easy."

Val and Bram stopped at a portrait of a bearded man in Renaissance garb. His image faded to reveal a hideous ghoul.

Ugly, but way better than that pit full of crawlies, Val decided. She angled right to go down another hall, passing a painting.

Bram said, "Hold on. We're supposed to look at all the art."

Val went back to study the distorted still life with dead animals hung above a table of food. A hairy hand reached out to grab them. They both jumped back, and the hand disappeared.

As they followed the teenagers around another corner, the guide moved forward and used his flashlight to illuminate a dark hallway. "Take a peek at the room on your right, the butler's pantry. It's best not to disturb the butler. He always loses his head when visitors come to the house."

A wire spider web prevented visitors from entering the dark room. As the group peered through the web, a dim light went on. A headless man in a white shirt and suit stood in front of a window. He held a tray of glasses in one hand and his severed head in the other hand. He stood so still that Val assumed he was a dummy. Then the butler stepped toward them, the teenagers cried out, and the room went black.

Val was sorry to move on. "If I saw him in the light again, I might figure out where his head really was. It must have been inside his suit."

Bram slowed down to widen the gap between them and the teenagers. He whispered, "The thing that looked like a window behind the butler is really just a piece of black fabric with a frame around it. The butler wears a hood made of the same fabric. With the proper lighting, you can't see the hood against the background."

"How do you know that?" She expected him to say he'd studied optics or stagecraft.

"I had ambitions to be a magician as a kid. I practiced my tricks and illusions a lot, but sadly, I wasn't good enough to make a living at magic."

Val was surprised and intrigued. She loved magic shows. "You're the first magician I've known. I hope you'll show me some of your tricks. But why are you whispering?"

"The magician code of ethics forbids telling the public the methods used in any illusion."

"You broke a rule." Possibly to impress her? "I won't reveal your secret to anyone."

The Grim Reaper directed them to gather

in an empty room off the hallway. When they were inside, he closed the door behind them. The dim lights in the room went out. The teenagers giggled nervously.

Val tamped down her growing anxiety. The room had space for all of them, and the walls were nowhere near as close as those in the tunnel-like graveyard.

The distant hum of an engine came from outside the building. The noise increased, suggesting an approaching vehicle. It got louder and louder.

Val's heart thudded. Hearing something come closer and not seeing it was terrifying. If she were outside, she'd be looking for the source of the noise and diving for cover. Why hadn't Suzette jumped out of the way of an approaching car?

The motor roared louder.

One of the teenagers shouted over the noise, "I'm getting out, feeling my way to the door. I've got the knob. It won't turn. We're locked in!"

She pounded on the door.

CHAPTER 24

The motor noise became deafening. Val covered her ears. A second later, the side wall lit up with the headlights of a huge truck coming straight for them.

She cringed. Bram wrapped an arm around her.

The girl at the door screamed.

The room went black, the truck disappeared, and the Grim Reaper opened the door. "How did you like that?"

"You shouldn't have locked us in," the middle-aged woman grumbled.

"The door wasn't locked, ma'am. That's against fire regulations. But it fits tight in the frame. Pulling harder would have opened it."

Val took deep breaths to calm herself. "Why did I think this would be fun? I was scared, even knowing it was a trick."

Bram nodded. "That was pretty intense."

The Grim Reaper directed them around

another corner. The partitions had turned the space into a maze. Val felt as if she was now doubling back to where they'd started.

The Reaper passed them and stood before a closed door at the end of a short hall. "You'll have to go through these doors and the next corridor in pairs. On your way to the next turn, you'll pass by the nursery. Be very quiet, or you'll wake the baby. Let sleeping babies lie."

A discordant version of "Rock-a-Bye Baby" came from a speaker in the hall. He opened the door for the teenagers and closed it behind them. Half a minute later, the girls' squawks were audible in the hall.

Then it was Val and Bram's turn to proceed through the hall. Within a few steps, they came to a large hole in the wall. Chicken wire was stretched across the opening and beyond it was only blackness. The sound of whimpering came from the other side of the wire. Val backed away from the hole. "I'm not up for carnage in a nursery or anything disgusting coming at me through the chicken wire."

The baby wailed lustily as if protesting Val's indifference. The crying reminded her of Morgan's breakdown when the Fictionistas met in the CAT Corner. After holding her grief in check during most of the meeting, it had burst out when Ruth asked about Suzette's injuries.

Val watched the black hole in the wall from a few feet away. The baby's howling verged on hysteria. Bram peered through the chicken wire. The crying stopped.

Then a huge gruesome face slammed into the wire and a banshee shriek rang out.

Bram sprang away from the distorted face. The teenagers watching from the far end of the hall laughed.

Val was relieved when the Grim Reaper announced their tour of the haunted house was almost over. He shepherded them toward a ten-foot-wide opening in the wall with drapes across it. "This is our final treat for the night. You have standing-room tickets for the theater, and the curtain will soon rise."

A voice came from behind the curtain. "It was a foggy, cloudy morning," a man with a British accent narrated. "The dull weather and the melancholy business upon which we were engaged depressed my spirits."

Ominous organ music played as the curtain opened and a spotlight illuminated a dingy yellow wall with peeling wallpaper. The rest of the room remained dark. The unseen narrator spoke up again. "It was a large square room, looking all the larger from the absence of all furniture. A vulgar flaring paper adorned the walls, but it was blotched in places with mildew, and here and there great strips had become detached and hung down, exposing the yellow plaster beneath."

The description matched what little Val could see in the dark room. A second spotlight focused on the fireplace. The disembodied voice said, "Opposite the door was a showy fireplace, surmounted by a mantelpiece of imitation white marble. On one corner of this was stuck the stump of a red wax candle."

"The candle doesn't look red," the Grim Reaper said loudly.

It immediately turned red. Writing appeared on the yellow wall for a split second, long enough to grab Val's attention, but not for her to read it. Then the wall went dark as the light went off.

The disembodied voice spoke again, "My attention centered upon the single grim motionless figure which lay stretched upon the boards."

A spotlight trained on the floor illuminated a black-bearded man in a horrible contorted position. His eyes were open but vacant. Val and the teenagers gasped. The man's hands were clenched and his legs twisted like a pretzel. His face was a mask of horror.

"I have seen death in many forms," the British narrator said, "but never has it appeared to me in a more fearsome aspect. A murder had been done. A word written on the wall drew our notice, written in blood."

As he spoke the last sentence, the light changed in the room and the red letters Val had glimpsed on the wall earlier appeared again. RACHE.

"Rachel?" Val muttered. Had the victim used his own blood to write his killer's name and then died before finishing it? That would make sense if he had a bloody wound on him, but he didn't.

After a brief silence, the narrator said, "What did the word on the wall mean? The police assumed the killer had intended to write Rachel. Sherlock Holmes disagreed. *Rache* is the German word for revenge, he said. The blood belonged to the murderer, not the victim."

With a clash of cymbals, the curtain closed.

The Grim Reaper stepped forward. "I hate to leave you in suspense, but that's the end of the show. You can find out who the murderer is by reading a story called . . ."

He waited for someone to finish his sentence.

"*A Study in Scarlet,*" Bram and the middle-aged woman said simultaneously.

She nodded. "The speaker mostly used the exact words from the original story."

"Bravo!" The Grim Reaper handed her and Bram a coupon for a free cookie at the bake sale. "I told you this would be a treat."

Once outside, Val breathed in the night air, thankful to escape the oppressive atmosphere of the haunted house.

Bram surveyed his options at the bake sale table. "I want to use my coupon for the dessert you made, Val. Which is yours?"

Val scanned the table. "Looks like my Chessie monster cookies sold out."

While he pondered which of the remaining treats to choose, Val took out her phone. Granddad had left her a voice mail. Not sure how late she'd return home, he wanted her to know that Sandy would be staying overnight at the house. She'd found out Suzette's body would be released tomorrow and offered to handle the arrangements for Suzette's mother, who'd readily agreed. Granddad had then invited Sandy to stay in a larger spare bedroom upstairs for as long as she needed to deal with the formalities.

Val tucked the phone back into her shoulder bag.

Bram ended up with an assortment of sweets. He'd used his coupon for the most expensive item, an iced jack-o-lantern cookie. He also bought a chocolate witch hat, a rum-ball eyeball, and a pumpkin-chip cookie.

They sat on a wood bench outside a gift shop. Bram munched on the jack-o-lantern.

Val took a bite of the witch hat, a dark chocolate cookie with a flat part as the hat brim and a chocolate kiss for the peak of the hat. "Tell me about *A Study in Scarlet.* Was revenge the motive for the murder?"

He nodded. "Revenge for a crime decades before. The killer stalked his prey from Utah, where the crime occurred, to Ohio, and eventually to London. He devoted his life to vengeance. Shortly after he took his revenge, he died . . . and with a smile his face."

Within a more compressed time period, Suzette's tormenter had followed her across the state from Frederick, where Sandy lived, and then to the Eastern Shore. Val knew of only two people who could have pursued Suzette that long — her mother and her mother's ex-boyfriend. Hard to believe that Wanda, for all her faults, would run over her daughter, but the man in Suzette's memoir wouldn't think twice about hurting a young woman. Still, a parallel between Suzette's situation and a Sherlock Holmes plot did not make Lloyd guilty.

Val warned herself against letting what she'd seen in the haunted house influence her too much, but her mind kept going down that path. "So many things in that house reminded me of Suzette. The misty graveyard made me think about the fog the morning she was killed."

"I was trying to figure out where the fog machines were hidden in the house." Bram brushed cookie crumbs from his lap. "On Sunday morning the Chesapeake Bay created the fog. It burned off quickly when the sun came up, like a machine running out of fog juice."

Val had never heard of fog juice. She'd have asked how it worked if she weren't so preoccupied with the haunted house. "The room with the engine noise frightened me the most. If Suzette had heard that sound, she'd have jumped into the bay to save herself. I certainly would have."

"Are you sorry you went into the haunted house?"

"Definitely not. My wrist didn't ache at all while I was scared silly." But it bothered

Val now. She flexed it. Time to apply ice again.

"You must have liked something there. No, don't tell me. Think hard about your favorite spot, and I'll try to read your mind."

She pressed her fingers to her temples, waited two seconds, and said, "I'm ready."

He leaned toward her and gazed deeply into her eyes. He looked more like he was going to kiss her than read her mind. Her heart sped up.

He sat back. "A murder victim is on your mind. The last room appealed to you most."

"You used deduction again, not telepathy. The first time you saw me, I was dressed like Nancy Drew. My costume told you who I was. Yours was a ruse. You're not anything like Dracula." Whereas the other vampire, Nick, had revealed his character with his costume.

He took advantage of women desperate for jobs and burgled the homes of seniors, both crimes of opportunity with little risk. He had only a slim chance of being caught and severely punished. Killing someone was another matter. Val wondered why she was now less convinced of Nick's guilt than she'd been an hour ago, before going into the haunted house.

Bram watched her intently. "I can see the

wheels turning in your mind."

"I wish you'd tell me where they're going."

"I'm not sure, but you and I could go for a drink somewhere." When she didn't respond immediately, he said, "On second thought, let's do it another time. You look tired, your wrist hurts, and you want to go home."

"You read my mind. Thank you."

When Val returned home, she put an ice pack on her wrist and then joined Granddad and Sandy in the sitting room. Granddad wanted to hear about the haunted house. Val described the highlights, starting with the bugs crawling on the corpse. By the time she got to the final room, Granddad's eyes had closed. She told Sandy about the scene from *A Study in Scarlet* and the word on the wall that signaled the killer's motive — revenge.

"I remember that story," Sandy said. "The desire for revenge took over the killer's life. Maybe that happened to Lloyd."

"Can you think of anyone besides him who had had a long-standing grudge against Suzette?"

"Not aside from Wanda, but I don't believe she'd hurt Suzette physically."

Val had other candidates. "Did Suzette ever talk to or about the people in the car she hit?"

"No. Ambulances took them and Lloyd to the hospital while she was still in shock. She asked about them the next day. My mother told her they'd been treated and released."

That didn't square with what Val had read online about the accident victims. Either the family member who'd been in serious but stable condition had made a miraculous recovery or else Sandy's mother had lied, possibly to ease Suzette's guilt about the accident. "Do you remember what type of injuries they had?"

"I knew nothing about them. I was away at college. Your police chief could probably find out, if it's important."

"I'm sure he could." But in the past Val had gotten a better response when she gave the chief information than when she asked *him* to dig it up. Chief Yardley had made it clear to her that the police weren't a detective agency at her disposal.

She removed the ice pack from her wrist and said good-night.

Granddad opened his eyes. "I almost forgot to tell you. You don't have to get up early tomorrow. I called Irene and told her you hurt your wrist. She's going to manage

344

the café tomorrow."

Val and Irene alternated Fridays, when the café closed at two. "That was good of her. Thanks, Granddad. I'm looking forward to sleeping in."

Though anticipating a restless night, Val slept peacefully, possibly thanks to the painkiller she'd taken. She woke up to sun streaming into her room. A nice change. It was usually dark when she got out of bed. She'd expected nightmares after her haunted house visit, but she could remember only one dream, and it was puzzling rather than scary. People shouted *Read the writing on the wall.* She turned to look at the wall, but before she could read what was on it, she woke up.

Lying in bed, she thought about how important writing had been to Suzette — her own writing, her writing group, her writing teacher, and the anonymous note-writer. Then there was the writing on the wall in the haunted house, where nothing was what it first seemed. With the haunted house's illusions at the back of her mind, Val reviewed what the Fictionistas had said the night of the costume contest, at the get-together when they'd discussed their writing, and during her one-on-one talks with them. Details stuck out that she hadn't realized were important until now.

Every room in the haunted house had given her a clue to the culprit. The more she thought about those clues, the surer she became that she was right about who'd killed Suzette and why. Though Val could gather facts that fit her theory, proving it would be another matter. Maybe she could coax a confession from the killer with the help of an illusion. But would Chief Yardley go along with it?

CHAPTER 25

Chief Yardley looked up from his desk as Val came into his office. "You have to cross off one of your suspects. Lloyd Leerman couldn't have been the hit-and-run driver. He's behind bars, serving a prison sentence. Been there for a couple of years."

Val sat down in the metal visitor's chair. "That's what I'd call an iron-clad alibi."

"I thought you'd be disappointed to hear about Lloyd. Instead, you made a pun."

"He'd already fallen from the top of my list." Before Val told the chief who had taken Lloyd's place as the number-one suspect, she wanted to make sure the other main suspect hadn't confessed to the hit-and-run. "Where do things stand with Nick?"

"When we started questioning him about Suzette's death, he copped to the burglaries. He said his sister roped him into it. According to her, it was the other way around. I think the sister's the brains of the opera-

tion. She was the quality controller checking the houses after the cleaning teams
finished, supposedly for missed cobwebs,
but really for valuables."

"What did Nick say about Suzette?"

"He admitted she confronted him Friday
night. He was furious over what he took as
her blackmail attempts. But he swore he
didn't kill her. He even offered to take a lie
detector test."

"Does he have an alibi for Sunday morning?"

"He was at the inn early, helping the night
manager deal with a leak in a guest bathroom. Nick's alibi isn't watertight." When
Val smiled, the chief said, "One bad pun
deserves another. The staff at the inn backed
up Nick's story. He might have managed to
slip away long enough to drive to the
peninsula road for the hit-and-run, but I
doubt it."

"Me too, Chief."

She told him who she was convinced had
killed Suzette and what the motive was.

The chief jotted notes and, when she
finished talking, studied them. "Your theory
explains the most puzzling aspect of this
case — the weapon. But the motive you've
come up with rests on an assumption. Let's

see if it's valid. When did that accident happen?"

"November or December eight years ago. That's as close as I can get."

The chief picked up his phone, told the person at the other end what to check, and then hung up. "Even if we confirm your guess about who was in that car, there's not enough for a search warrant, much less an arrest."

"I have a plan that will get you the evidence you need, straight from the horse's mouth."

The chief rolled his eyes. "If your last plan to expose a murderer hadn't worked, I wouldn't even listen to this one. But I owe you that."

As she outlined her scheme, several phone calls came in for him. By the time she finished, half an hour had gone by, enough time for an officer to confirm her guess about who'd been in the car Suzette had hit.

"It will surprise me if your ploy works," the chief said. "But it can't hurt to try. To get the evidence, you have to do this in a public area where there's no expectation of privacy. We need a location where the suspect can be watched, heard, and cornered if necessary."

"The Cool Down Café would be perfect."

Within an hour Val had arranged for her assistant manager to prepare the food for this afternoon's encounter and for Suzette's cousin and Granddad to play key parts in the ruse.

By three o'clock Val and Granddad had created the illusion that the café was something other than a sleek eatery in a fitness club. With tablecloths and mini-vases of flowers on the bistro tables and a lace-edged runner on the granite eating bar, the room looked as if it belonged in a Victorian bed-and-breakfast.

Granddad sat at a table with no cloth or flowers on it. Hunched over a chessboard, he wore a stars-and-stripes bandanna headband, gray sweats, scuffed athletic shoes, and tinted glasses instead of his bifocals. No one who'd seen him briefly once or twice before would recognize him. The chief sat on the other side of the chessboard, dressed for a gym workout in a T-shirt and shorts, the brim of his baseball cap low on his forehead. The actors were in place, and the stage was set.

A tiered tray held the dainty sandwiches and sweet morsels Val's assistant manager had prepared. Irene had owned a teashop in

Bayport for years and relished the chance to prepare food for a high tea. Val put the tray on the table near the café entrance and within earshot of the chess players. Though set for two with vintage china and cloth napkins, the table had only a single chair at it. For Val's scheme to work, her guest had to face the club's reception area and therefore could not have a choice of seats.

Val set a pot of tea on the bistro table. Too bad she couldn't spike the tea with truth serum, but she hoped to get to the truth anyway by unnerving her guest, using a combination of fact and illusion. She looked toward the café entrance.

A woman crossed the club reception area and paused at the sign on a stand. It said that the café was closed for a private event. She wore a cardigan over a beige turtleneck. Her slinky brown knit skirt skimmed her ankles. Not the usual attire at an athletic club. Val was relieved that Morgan's clothes hugged her body. She couldn't have a weapon on her or it would create a bulge. Her shapeless tapestry handbag, though, could hold a small arsenal. Val would do her best to separate Morgan from her handbag.

Morgan smiled as she came into the café alcove. "I didn't expect this place to be so homey."

"It looks rather basic, but it only takes a few touches to change that for special events. We hold children's birthday parties here, but I'd also like to attract civic and women's clubs with a different menu and ambiance." Now Val would appeal to Morgan's vanity. "I thought high tea would be perfect, and I was hoping you'd give me the benefit of your expertise and sample some of the food. Maybe you'll decide that high tea here is what you'd like for your next Novels and Needles Club meeting."

Morgan glanced at the chess players. "Are they going to sample food too?"

Val shook her head and said in a low voice, "They sat down just before I closed the café. I figured their game would be over by now, but I can't ask them to leave in the middle of it. They're regular customers. Sorry."

"No problem." Morgan pointed to the tiered plate on the table. "It all looks scrumptious. I love high tea."

"Take a seat here, and I'll grab another chair."

If Morgan thought it was weird that only one chair was at the table set for two, she didn't show it. She sat down, put her handbag on the floor near her feet, and adjusted her glasses.

Val positioned her chair across the table, but at an angle so she didn't block Morgan's view of the area outside the café. She poured tea for herself and Morgan, tea brewed with leaves instead of teabags.

Morgan sampled the savory items. She approved of the ham on a mini corn muffin and the chicken salad with watercress on white toast. But she didn't care for Val's cucumber sandwiches.

"The hummus overwhelms the cucumber," Morgan said. "The only thing you spread on the bread should be butter so the flavor of the cucumber comes out."

Val tapped her temple. "I'll make a note of that." She bit into a cucumber sandwich with hummus.

After devouring more of the ham and chicken salad, Morgan put each type of sweet on her plate. "I hope these taste as good as —" She broke off, her attention on the reception area. Her jaw dropped. She took off her glasses and held them up to the light as if inspecting them for smudges.

With Morgan's attention diverted, Val leaned down and slid the tapestry purse closer to herself. Unlikely that Morgan had a weapon in it, but with her bag out of reach, she'd have trouble making a quick getaway. "Is anything wrong, Morgan? You look flustered."

Morgan put her glasses on. "I thought I saw someone I knew. Couldn't have been." She went back to sipping tea and sampling food.

She pronounced the strawberries and cream cheese on date nut bread passable, the lime tartlets in phyllo pastry quite good, and the scones heavenly. "The clotted cream is less than perfect."

"I'll tell my assistant manager, Irene, that you liked the scones. Those are her specialty." Val would keep silent about the rest. Irene wouldn't appreciate the slur on her clotted cream.

Morgan took another scone. "I haven't seen any news about the hit-and-run investigation. Have you?"

As Val had hoped, the killer couldn't help but return to the scene of the crime, at least over a tea table. "The police haven't made any new public statements, but I've learned a lot about Suzette's life before she moved here."

Morgan's barely visible eyebrows rose. "Really? She never talked to me about it. What did you find out?"

"The family she worked for as a nanny said she was driven away by a campaign of harassment, ugly pranks, and at least one nasty note. No one knows who's responsible."

Morgan grimaced. "That's terrible. Do you know what the nasty note said?"

"The exact words were *You will pay for what you done.*"

"Bad grammar." Morgan looked pained. "An uneducated person wrote it."

"Or that's what the educated person who wrote it wanted everyone to assume." Val toyed with a scone. "The police have the note now, so they'll be able to get DNA, if not fingerprints, from it."

Morgan's eyes widened. She looked past Val. Her face turned the color of bleached flour, making her freckles more pronounced.

Her reaction elated Val. The ruse was working. "Are you okay? You look like you've seen a ghost."

"I — I feel light-headed." Morgan lifted her teacup with a shaking hand and took a few sips. When the color returned to her face, she said, "Whoever left that malicious note must have traced Suzette to Bayport after she changed jobs."

Val hadn't said the note had been *left.* Most people would have said *sent the note,* but not the person who'd hand delivered it. "Suzette tried hard not to be traced."

"Her nemesis found her anyway. No wonder she was worried about the black car following her."

A black car that only Morgan had mentioned. "But it wasn't a black car that hit her. My grandfather's friend, the chief of police, said the paint evidence at the accident scene suggested a light-color car was involved." Right now in the club parking lot, a police officer who'd waited for Morgan to drive in was checking her car.

She flicked her wrist. "You can always borrow a car or rent one."

"Good point." Val wondered if Morgan had done that. "Going back to the malicious note, it wasn't the first one Suzette had received. Someone hounded her for more than five years."

Morgan picked up her cup. "That's awful. Why would anyone do that?"

"A member of her family believes it had something to do with a car accident Suzette had as a teenager." Val enjoyed watching Morgan's eyes bug out. Was she starting to suspect an ulterior motive for this tea party? "The accident that sent you to the hospital."

Morgan choked on her tea. "What are you talking about? This has nothing to do with me."

"You told me you kept your married name

because it was short, which means you must have had a much longer maiden name. I remembered that when I found out the people injured in that accident were named O'Shaughnessy. An Irish name, three times longer than Roux, and you do look Irish. The needlework hanging on your wall is signed MOR. At first I mistook that as the start of your name." The same mistake Val had made with RACHE. "Later I realized those were your initials. Morgan O'Shaughnessy Roux."

Morgan appeared distracted. She stared straight ahead, her face a mask of fear. Her lips trembled. "Who *is* that woman? She keeps going back and forth slowly, like a sleepwalker."

Or a ghost. Val glanced behind her. "I don't see any woman. What did she look like?" Val knew the answer. Sandy Sechrest looked remarkably similar to her cousin, especially when averting her face and wearing Suzette's clothes.

Morgan raked her hair. "She's gone now. She's haunting me!"

Val sensed that Morgan was close to breaking and let her stew for a moment. "Other poisoned-pen notes might turn up in papers Suzette had in storage." Not that Val knew of any storage. "The police will have plenty of evidence to identify the sender and a strong incentive to go after that person if the hit-and-run was deliberate."

Morgan looked haunted, her eyes wide, her face rigid. "Okay, okay, I wrote the notes. Do you know what Suzette did to me? Compound fractures two months before my wedding. I had to limp up the aisle on crutches. What bride dreams of that?"

Why not postpone the wedding? Val didn't ask the obvious question. "I'm sorry. You must have been in a lot of pain."

"For more than a year. I had multiple surgeries. My husband couldn't handle the burden of my pain. My marriage ended in divorce because of her." Morgan spat out the last syllable. "After that, I lived to make her miserable. I tracked her down and forced her to move to get away from me. I didn't want her dead. I wanted her in pain. She escaped me by dying."

"I know you didn't want her dead." The way Suzette was hit made sense if Morgan intended injury rather than death. "That's why you didn't ram her at high speed. You only wanted to break her legs so she'd feel what you felt."

Morgan hissed, "You can't prove that."

"I can't, but the police can. Forensics

evidence, the paint at the accident scene, will tie you to the hit-and-run." Val glanced at the chief, who was on his cell phone. "If you confess, you'll have a chance at a much lighter sentence."

"I'll hire a good lawyer. When I tell my story to the jury, they'll sympathize with me."

"Maybe, but they'll still find you guilty, and you'll spend a long time behind bars."

"I don't have to listen to this any longer." Morgan reached down under the table.

Val beat her to the tapestry bag. "I've got your handbag."

"Give it to me!"

Val tightened her grip on the bag. "I will, but first I'll tell you something you don't know about that accident. Suzette lost control of the car because her mother's boyfriend, a sexual predator, was molesting her while she was driving. It wasn't her fault. You should have hounded him, not her."

Morgan's face crumpled, and tears rolled down her cheeks. She sobbed as she had at the end of the writers' group meeting, her shoulders heaving. Val flashed back to that moment and realized what had touched off Morgan's crying jag — the news that Suzette had died instantly and felt no pain.

But what explained Morgan's breakdown now? Remorse for having killed Suzette or frustration at not having broken Lloyd's legs?

Granddad and Chief Yardley stood up and approached Morgan.

She seemed not to notice them or the officer who joined them. She glared at Val across the table. "Do you know why I always wear long dresses?"

Was she unhinged, talking about clothes after being accused of killing someone? "I have no idea," Val said.

"My legs are scarred. They're hideous. They were wrapped in bandages and casts for months. Since then I can't bear having anything encasing them. No pants. No tights. No pajamas. If it weren't for her, I could wear normal clothes."

A prison jumpsuit would be Morgan's new normal unless she had a darn good lawyer.

Chief Yardley showed her his badge. "I'd like to talk to you. Please come with me."

He and the uniformed officer led her out of the café.

Val watched them leave and added a thank-you call to her to-do list. If Gillian Holroyd, namesake of a modern witch, hadn't sensed a killer among the Fictionis-

360

tas and stirred the pot, Suzette's death
might have remained a mystery.

CHAPTER 26

On Saturday night Granddad made dinner for Dorothy and Bram with a little help from Val, who was still nursing a sore wrist.

As they filled their plates with lemon garlic shrimp and pasta, she announced what the chief had confirmed that afternoon — Granddad had supplied the evidence that led to the capture of burglars.

Dorothy turned to him. "Tell us about it, Don."

Granddad beamed. "It all started when I teased the folks who were on a haunted house tour that stopped here." By the time he ended his tale with Nick's arrest, the others had half-empty plates. "Suzette's killer was also arrested. Val's the one who got the goods on her."

"Her?" Bram said. "A woman killed Suzette?"

Val nodded. "Morgan Roux. Her car is the color of the paint found at the accident scene, and it has a small dent consistent with sideswiping Suzette."

Granddad twirled spaghetti on his fork. "The police wouldn't have checked that car if Val hadn't convinced them that Morgan was guilty."

"Why did she kill that girl?" Dorothy said.

"She didn't intend to." Val explained Morgan's motive for ramming Suzette.

Bram caught Val's eye across the table. "What tipped you off that Morgan did it?"

"Our visit to the haunted house. It focused my attention on what I'd overlooked. The fake fog there reminded me of a comment Morgan had made. She'd said the fog could explain why Suzette didn't notice a car approaching her. But the police hadn't mentioned the fog in their statement about the accident and neither had the media."

Bram nodded. "Only someone who was on the peninsula road would know about it. The fog came off the bay there, but it wasn't along the riverbank in Bayport."

"Morgan lives even farther from the bay in Treadwell." Val sipped her wine. "The headless butler in the haunted house gave me a new perspective on the hit-and-run."

Bram chimed in, explaining the illusion and the trick behind it. "I'm not sure how the butler helped you solve the crime."

"His black hood made his real head invisible, so we looked at the dummy head he was holding," Val said. "Morgan distracted me from what was important by inventing a black car that supposedly followed Suzette. With that lie, she shifted attention away from what really mattered about the car — not its color but its sound, or rather, the lack of it. Which brings us to the engine room in the haunted house."

Bram described the dark room in which the sound of a vehicle coming closer and closer made everyone want to get out of the way.

Val picked up her fork. "Suzette didn't react that way. As I puzzled about that, I remembered something Morgan said the night of the costume party. She told Casper he should replace his old car with one that polluted less. He replied that not everyone likes to get off the road to recharge."

Dorothy's eyes lit up. "Morgan drives an electric car?"

Val nodded. "Casper knew that, but I didn't. I never saw her car. Like Suzette, I also didn't hear a car coming at me when Morgan tried to run me down in the club parking lot."

"Why did she go after you?" Granddad said. "You didn't do anything to her."

"She must have realized she'd slipped up by mentioning the fog. I think she tried to hit me so I'd be engrossed in my pain and forget what she'd said."

Dorothy frowned. "She took a chance. You might have seen the car and been able to identify it."

"She took the same chance when she ran down Suzette, not a big chance, because it was dark on the peninsula road and in the parking lot. Her car was barely visible. I couldn't have described it, read the license plate, or seen who was driving." Val turned to Bram. "Tell them about the last room of the haunted house. You know the story behind it better than I do."

Val finished her dinner as he described the stage setting and summarized the plot of *A Study in Scarlet.*

When he finished, his mother said, "Morgan had the same motive as the killer in the story — revenge."

Granddad's face screwed up in disgust. "That Sherlock Holmes story doesn't make sense. The killer wouldn't write that word on the wall. In his mind he was getting justice, not revenge."

Val agreed. "Morgan thinks the same way. Unfortunately, her code of justice is an eye for an eye."

They were all silent for a moment. Then Granddad surveyed the table. "Does anyone want seconds? There's more of everything." He looked disappointed when no one spoke up.

He had finally become what he'd pretended to be for the last year — a proficient cook. Val had to give him credit for that. "It was delicious, Granddad, and very filling."

Dorothy nodded. "That was the best shrimp I've had in a long time, but I can't eat another bite right now." She pointed toward the shelves in the sitting room. "I'd love to browse your video collection, Don. I really enjoy classic movies, and you've got hundreds at your fingertips."

Granddad and Dorothy went into the sitting room while Bram cleared the table and Val loaded the dishwasher, a task she could do with one hand.

Bram brought in the last plates from the table. "My mother's really impressed with your grandfather."

Granddad would be thrilled to hear it. "Because of the burglars he caught?"

Bram grinned. "Because of the dinner he made. She's not fond of cooking."

"The last time Granddad made dinner to impress a woman, I was the ghost cook, like a ghost writer. This time, he did it all

366

himself. He's come a long way." Val remembered how deeply she'd resented it when that woman had sat in Grandma's chair at the table. Tonight Dorothy hadn't sat there, but if she had, Val wouldn't have reacted as negatively. Maybe she'd come a long way too. She closed the dishwasher. "You know what I liked best about visiting the haunted house?"

"Picking up clues that led you to the killer?"

"That, and finding out you were a magician and a Sherlock Holmes fan. You should have dressed as a magician or Holmes for Halloween."

"I see myself as Watson, the family man, not the aloof genius." Bram locked eyes with her. "But I'll dress as Sherlock next Halloween, if you come as Irene Adler. You know who she is?"

"I vaguely remember." She was the object of Holmes's admiration, the only woman who touched a nerve with him. Was a literary parallel how a bookshop owner's son flirted? Val hoped so. "So you're planning to visit Bayport next Halloween?"

"Definitely not." He grinned. "I'll be living here. For the Title Wave to succeed, Mom will need more than foot traffic. I have ideas for expanding the customer base online."

The news elated Val. "I need to read up on Irene Adler to see if the role suits me."

"If it doesn't, we can go as Watson and Holmes. Watson has a mustache, and it'll be easier for me to grow one than you. You can be Sherlock."

Holmes and Watson. Less romantic than Sherlock and Irene. Still, they were a compatible pair. Good enough for now.

Granddad poked his head in the room, looking pleased. "Dorothy and I are gonna watch *The Trouble with Harry*. She's a big Hitchcock fan."

Granddad had met a soul mate.

"Is that a Hitchcock movie?" Bram said.

"Yup. Not one of his greats, but it's good for a few laughs. Come join us if you're finished in here."

Val nodded. "I could use some laughs after this week."

As Bram followed Granddad out of the room, she lingered in the kitchen, where she often sensed Grandma's presence. Val felt her here again tonight, assuring her that Dorothy would be good for Granddad. And, just maybe, that Bram would be good for Val.

ACKNOWLEDGMENTS

I'd like to thank those who helped me as I researched and wrote this book. For details about vehicular homicide and the forensic investigation of accident scenes, I relied on D. P. Lyle, MD, who generously shares his expertise with crime writers. Thank you, Dr. Lyle. The haunted house in *Crypt Suzette* came alive thanks to *Haunted House Halloween Handbook* by Jerry Chavez. The book covers all aspects of creating such an attraction and helped me understand how various illusions work. I derived the rotting corpse insect pit, the scary artwork, and the headless butler's room from the Chavez book. Other spaces in the Bayport haunted house were my own inventions to further the plot. In writing this Halloween book, I liberally borrowed character names from authors of famous creepy tales.

I'm again grateful to my critique partners, mystery writers Carolyn Mulford and Helen

Schwartz, who have helped me with each of the Five-Ingredient Mysteries. They read this book, the sixth one, chapter by chapter and gave me suggestions for its improvement at each stage. They are far kinder and more helpful than the Fictionistas in *Crypt Suzette.* Carolyn also edited the final draft of the book. Many thanks to Mike Corrigan, Cathy Ondis Solberg, and Elliot Wicks for reading and commenting on the book's first draft, to Paul Corrigan for sharing his crêpe-making expertise, and to Susan Fay for testing the recipes.

I'd also like to thank my agent, John Talbot, and my editor, John Scognamiglio, as well as the production, marketing, and sales teams at Kensington Books who helped bring *Crypt Suzette* to readers.

As always, I'm grateful to readers who enjoy mysteries. Thank you for your support.

THE CODGER COOK'S RECIPES

CRÊPES

You can't make crêpes Suzette with just five ingredients, but you can use two recipes with five ingredients each. The first step is to make the crêpes. You can serve them as is with sweet or savory fillings or toppings, or you can proceed to the next recipe to make the orange sauce for crêpes Suzette.

2 eggs
1 cup flour
1 1/2 cups milk
1/4 teaspoon salt
1 teaspoon oil for the pan plus additional
   oil as needed

Whisk the eggs, milk, and salt until well mixed. Slowly whisk in the flour.

Note: You can cook the crêpes immediately, but refrigerating the batter for 20 minutes will smooth out any lumps or bubbles. Letting the batter rest makes it less likely the crêpe will tear in the pan. The batter can keep for a day or two.

Heat a 10-inch skillet or crêpe pan at a medium setting. To keep crêpes from sticking, do not put the oil or batter in until a few drops of water sizzle in the pan and disappear in 2 seconds.

Add enough oil to cover the bottom of the heated pan. Pour a scant 1/4 cup of batter into the pan and tilt it so the batter spreads into a thin circle coating the bottom. Cook at medium heat until the edges turn light brown and the center of the crêpe has hardened past a liquid stage. Gently loosen the crêpe with a spatula and flip it. Cook for another minute and transfer it to a large plate or platter, where the crêpe can lie flat.

Repeat the preceding step, stacking the cooked crêpes on the plate, until the batter is gone. Add a small amount of additional oil after every other crêpe to keep the batter from sticking.

Yield: 10–12 eight-inch crêpes

Orange Butter Sauce for Crêpes Suzette

10–12 crêpes
4 tablespoons unsalted butter
1/4 cup sugar
1 orange for 1 tablespoon grated orange
  zest and 1/3 cup orange juice
1/4 cup Grand Marnier, Cointreau, or
  other orange liqueur [optional]

Melt the butter in a large skillet over medium heat until it foams. Stir in the sugar, orange juice, and liqueur. Simmer on low heat until the sauce thickens a little and looks syrupy. Remove the skillet from the heat.

With tongs, add a crêpe to the pan, coat both sides in the syrup, and fold it into quarters or roll it into a flattened cylinder. Put it on a warm plate.

Repeat the previous step for each crêpe.

Serve crêpes as is or with ice cream for dessert.

Yield: 10–12 eight-inch crêpes

SWEET POTATO ROUNDS WITH GOAT CHEESE, CRANBERRIES, AND NUTS

This makes a good autumn appetizer or side dish. It's easy to make and healthy to eat.

An elongated unpeeled sweet potato, scrubbed and cut into 1/4-inch rounds, about 2 inches in diameter or smaller
1 tablespoon olive oil
1/2 cup dried cranberries, chopped
4 ounces goat cheese at room temperature
1/2 cup chopped walnuts or pecans

Preheat the oven to 425 degrees.

Spread the olive oil on a rimmed baking sheet. Lay the rounds on the sheet in a single layer, and then flip them so both sides are oiled.

Put the pan on the middle rack in the oven and bake for 8 minutes. Flip the rounds and bake for another 5 minutes or until the potatoes are soft.

Remove the rounds from the oven, top them with goat cheese, and sprinkle them with a mixture of chopped cranberries and nuts.

Serve warm or at room temperature.

Yield: Serves 4 (may vary depending on the size of the sweet potato)

PARSNIPITY PORK

Orange marmalade gives this recipe for bone-less pork a tangy flavor. The parsnips add a bit more sweetness.

1 1/4 pounds of pork tenderloin, cut crosswise into 1-inch thick slices. For faster cooking, pound the slices with a meat mallet until they are half as thick.
1/2 cup chopped onion
2 cups of cubed parsnip pieces about 1/2 inch on a side
1/2 cup orange marmalade, made with sugar, not artificial sweetener
1 teaspoon dried thyme
Olive oil to coat the skillet

Heat a teaspoon of oil in a 10-inch skillet at medium heat. Sauté the onions until they turn translucent. Add the parsnips and cook until slightly softened. Set aside the onions and parsnips.

Wipe out the skillet and heat 1/2 teaspoon oil in it. When the skillet is hot, but before the oil starts smoking, add the pork slices, and sear them for 1 to 2 minutes a side (until they brown).

Combine the marmalade and thyme. Add

it and the onions and parsnips to the skillet. Simmer for 3 to 5 minutes until the pork is tender.

Serve with wild or white rice.

Yield: Serves 4

MADELEINES

A madeleine is a small shell-shaped cake often treated like a cookie because of its tiny size. Crunchy on the edges and firm on the inside, it's perfect to eat with tea or coffee. To bake madeleines, you need a special pan with shell molds.

2 eggs

1 lemon for 1/2 teaspoon of freshly squeezed juice and 1/2 teaspoon lemon zest

1 cup confectioners' sugar (more if you want to dust the madeleines with sugar when they're done)

3/4 cup sifted cake flour/self-rising flour. (If you have all-purpose flour, add 1/4 teaspoon of baking powder to it before sifting.)

1/2 cup butter, melted but no longer hot

Preheat the oven to 375 degrees.

Before mixing the ingredients:
- Grease and flour 24 madeleine molds
- Zest the lemon
- Melt the butter, setting it aside to cool

Beat the eggs, lemon juice, and zest at high speed with an electric mixer for 3 minutes. Add the sugar gradually while beating the mixture for an additional 4 minutes. Fold in the sifted flour little by little. Then fold in the butter, stirring until it's blended with the batter.

Spoon the batter into the shell molds, so they're 3/4 full. Don't smooth out the batter. It will fill the shell evenly as it bakes.

Bake for 10 minutes or until the edges are brown. The tops should be golden yellow and spring back. Add another minute or two in the oven if needed.

Cool the pan for 1 minute, then loosen the madeleines around the edges with a knife. If they don't come out easily, you may need to tap the bottom of the pan. Cool them on a rack.

You can serve madeleines plain or dress them up by sprinkling them with confectioners' sugar, dipping one end in melted chocolate, or glazing them with a mixture of lemon and confectioners' sugar thinned with water to a spreading consistency.

Yield: 24 madeleines

ABOUT THE AUTHOR

Maya Corrigan lives near Washington, D.C., within easy driving distance of Maryland's Eastern Shore, the setting for this series. She has taught courses in writing, detective fiction, and American literature at Georgetown University and NOVA community college. A winner of the Daphne du Maurier Award for Excellence in Mystery and Suspense, she has published essays on drama and short stories under her full name of Mary Ann Corrigan. Visit her at maya corrigan.com.

The employees of Thorndike Press hope you have enjoyed this Large Print book. All our Thorndike, Wheeler, and Kennebec Large Print titles are designed for easy reading, and all our books are made to last. Other Thorndike Press Large Print books are available at your library, through selected bookstores, or directly from us.

For information about titles, please call:
(800) 223-1244

or visit our website at:
gale.com/thorndike

To share your comments, please write:

Publisher
Thorndike Press
10 Water St., Suite 310
Waterville, ME 04901